"Are you going to show me how you prepare the new trees, or are you going to stand there staring at me?"

"I wasn't st—" Yes, he probably had been. He couldn't take his eyes off her lately. "Fine. I was. You've got some flour on your face." He brushed her cheek to remove the powdery white streak, and she shuddered.

An aching hollowness filled his chest. After all this time, Becky was still repulsed by his touch. No matter what he did, he couldn't seem to break through her defenses. Well, she'd just have to endure being close to him, because it was nearly impossible to teach someone how to graft without making contact. She'd need help making the cuts and fitting the two pieces of wood together correctly.

She picked up a grafted whip and studied it, her back to him. "So is this what a baby tree looks like when you finish."

Her reluctance to look at him was understandable, but the catch in her voice was puzzling.

Award-winning author **Keli Gwyn**, a native Californian, transports readers to the early days of the Golden State. She and her husband live in the heart of California's Gold Country. Her favorite places to visit are her fictional worlds, historical museums and other Gold Rush–era towns. Keli loves hearing from readers and invites you to visit her Victorian-style cyberhome at keligwyn.com, where you'll find her contact information.

Books by Keli Gwyn

Love Inspired Historical

Family of Her Dreams
A Home of Her Own

KELI GWYN

A Home of Her Own

HARLEQUIN® LOVE INSPIRED® HISTORICAL

Recycling programs
for this product may
not exist in your area.

TM LOVE INSPIRED BOOKS

ISBN-13: 978-0-373-28353-8

A Home of Her Own

www.Harlequin.com

Printed in U.S.A.

Therefore if any man be in Christ,
he is a new creature:
old things are passed away;
behold, all things are become new.
—*2 Corinthians* 5:17

In memory of my beloved mother-in-law,
Mary Lu Gwyn, a victim of breast cancer.
Her faith inspired me.
Her strength amazed me.
Her love blessed me beyond measure.

Chapter One

April 1871

Becky Martin had escaped one bad situation only to find herself in the middle of another.

With her heart as heavy as a blacksmith's anvil, she trudged along the planked walkway after her newfound friends in search of a café where they could eat their midday meal. The rough makeshift handle of her faded carpetbag cut into her palm, the stinging sensation reminding her of the many tongue lashings her brother had given her when she hadn't done his bidding fast enough. Then he'd gone too far. She'd stood her ground, and the drunken lout had raised his hand to strike her.

No. She wouldn't dwell on the ugly scene that had sent her fleeing to California. She must keep her mind on the task ahead. Despite her present state, she had no choice but to convince James O'Brien she was capable of caring for his mother.

You helped me get away from Dillon, Lord, so I trust You to help me muster my courage once again.

"Don't be dragging your feet, Becky. There's not much

time left before you're to meet Mr. O'Brien, and you can't do so on an empty stomach."

Leave it to matter-of-fact Jessie to state the obvious. "I'm coming."

"Of course you are." Cheerful Callie looked over her shoulder and offered an encouraging smile. "Even so, I can't help but notice that you've grown pensive."

Becky struggled to remember what the word *pensive* meant, but the definition eluded her, no doubt due to the bone-deep weariness following their week's travel. Perhaps if she said nothing, Callie would continue, giving a clue to the meaning.

Both Callie Hunt and Jessie Sinclair had no trouble talking. That must be nice. As far back as Becky could remember, she'd been more reserved than her new friends. Being quiet gave her time to form the most articulate response possible before speaking.

This time she had no choice. She would have to say something to Mr. O'Brien, even if her words weren't polished. If not, her silence could cost her the job.

She needed work desperately. After paying for her meals during their travels, her reticule held a grand total of fifty cents, just enough for a simple dinner. Her dreams of standing on her own two feet would have to wait until she got them back under her—and figured out what an uneducated woman like her could do. Surely the Lord would guide her, as He always had.

Callie drew alongside Becky. "Judging by that faraway look on your face, you're thinking mighty hard about something. Why don't you tell us what's on your mind?"

Jessie stopped, forcing Callie and Becky to do the same. "Yes. Tell us. We're friends now, and friends help one another."

There'd been little time for socializing in Chicago,

but Becky had formed a fast bond with these two confident young women. Like her, they'd come to California eager to leave their pasts behind and start anew. They'd confided in her, so they deserved to know the rest of her sad tale. Well, most of it anyhow. She couldn't tell anyone the real reason she'd had to leave.

She glanced up and down Placerville's bustling main street, assuring herself no one was close enough to overhear, and blurted her confession. "I told you I was coming here to nurse Mr. O'Brien's mother, but what I didn't tell you is that he provided the money for my train ticket. No matter what kind of man he is, I have no choice but to work for him until I've paid him back. What if he turns out to be as cruel as my brother…or worse?"

Jessie nodded. "I understand your concern. You know next to nothing about him."

That was true. The only things Becky had learned in the telegram from Dr. Wright to his former minister in Chicago was that James O'Brien, a railroad engineer-turned-orchardist, had given the doctor permission to send for a woman who would serve as his mother's nurse. If the doctor hadn't vouched for Mr. O'Brien's character and said he was a God-fearing gentleman willing to pay her way to the West, she wouldn't be here now.

Callie patted Becky's shoulder. "I'm sure everything will work out. You had good reasons for leaving, didn't you?"

She did, but she'd acted in haste, taking the first offer that had come along. "After our father's heart gave out last month, my brother changed. Things kept getting worse. And then came that horrid evening." She shuddered at the memory of Dillon standing before her, reeking of alcohol. She'd challenged his ludicrous accusations, and he'd let loose with a string of curse words that stung her ears. The blows had followed.

"My choices were to stay in Chicago and live in fear of Dillon finding me or embrace the opportunity that came my way and disappear. With less than ten dollars in my reticule, I couldn't go far. I stuffed my things in my carpetbag and ran all the way to the church. The request the doctor sent on behalf of Mr. O'Brien came at just the right time. Reverend and Mrs. Hastings said it was a godsend."

The offer had seemed providential. Dr. Wright's telegram had arrived minutes before she'd sought refuge. It had taken her all of thirty seconds to decide to head to California. Reverend Hastings had sent a reply soon after she'd shown up at the parsonage—out of breath and out of options. He'd told the doctor that if he would wire the funds from Mr. O'Brien, she would be on the next westbound train. His wife had introduced Becky to Jessie and Callie, who were also headed to Placerville, and had agreed to be her traveling companions. Jessie was eager to embark on a career as a draftswoman out West, and Callie had set out to find her brother, who had come to California earlier.

Although Becky had been in a hurry to get away from Chicago, the knots in her shoulders had grown tighter with each mile of track the chugging locomotive devoured. That stiffness was the least of her concerns, though. After Dillon had shown her what he thought of her refusal to take the blame for his heinous act by slapping her and shoving her into the sideboard, simply drawing a deep breath had made her want to double over. Her midsection didn't hurt as much now, as long as she didn't cough. If all went well, her sore ribs would heal quickly.

At least her face didn't look as bad as it had when she'd embarked on her journey. She'd forced herself to peek in the looking glass when she'd visited the women's lounge at the Shingle Springs rail station before they'd boarded the stagecoach bound for Placerville that morning.

A shop door opened, and someone stepped into Becky's path. She came within a hairbreadth of crashing into the broad chest of a tall man wearing a brown tweed frock coat. She winced, moved back and rested a hand on her aching middle.

Looking up, her gaze passed over his puff tie and landed on a jagged scar. It began below the clean-shaven man's right ear, curved around the side of his face and stopped just shy of his mouth. His lips were pursed, and his hazel eyes glinted green. She'd seen that heated look before—in Dillon's dark eyes when he'd yelled at her, as he so often did.

Despite the warm spring day, a chill swept over her. "I'm sorry. I didn't realize you were coming out."

"That's evident." He dismissed her with a sneer that puckered his crescent-shaped scar and turned to offer his arm to a small woman with a gray braid peeking from beneath the edge of her bonnet. A rather sloppy braid. He leaned over and spoke to her in a surprisingly gentle tone. "I know you don't want to go, but we have no choice. No matter what he says, I'll be there for you."

The frail older woman wrapped one hand around his elbow and patted his arm with the other. "*Ja.* I know. You are a good boy." She must be German, as Becky's mother had been. A wave of sadness washed over her. How she missed her *Mutter.*

A wagon sped up the street, the harness jangling. A scraggly dog darted into the street—and into the horses' path.

Fear surged through Becky, and she took off running. "Look out!"

She'd made it halfway across the wide rutted road

when two strong arms grasped her from behind, bringing her to an abrupt stop.

Her carpetbag flew from her fingers, landing in front of the briskly moving wagon. She watched in horror as a wheel lifted the bag and spun it around, showering the dusty street with her few possessions. The dog loped off.

She swatted at the hands clasped in front of her. "Let me go. I need to get my things."

"I'll do it." The scarred man she'd nearly run into moments before released her, grabbed her carpetbag and scooped up her belongings. He stuffed her unmentionables and nightgown inside so quickly that the gawkers gathered around couldn't possibly have gotten a good look at them. His thoughtfulness in choosing to go after the intimate items first surprised her. She'd half expected him to hold up her undergarments and let loose with a derisive laugh the way her scoundrel of a brother would have, but the stranger had behaved like a true gentleman.

The puzzling man set her carpetbag at his feet and folded her spare cotton work dress, treating the worn black bombazine with the care one would give a fine silk.

Becky realized she was staring, shook herself and immediately regretted it. Due to the man's firm hold moments before, her injured ribs were screaming in protest. Even so, she had to get her books before another wagon passed by.

With halting steps, she covered the few feet to where one of them lay. She wrapped an arm around her belly and, as carefully as possible, squatted and picked up her well-worn Bible. She rose and found herself facing her self-appointed helper. Seen from his uninjured left side, he wasn't frightening at all. Quite the contrary. He wasn't merely handsome. He was downright striking. With his wavy caramel-colored hair, perfectly formed nose and strong jaw, he could be a model for the drawings in one of those fashion magazines Callie favored.

What captivated Becky were his expressive eyes, which held a mixture of concern and something else. Pity, no doubt. She was plain on her best days. With the sickly looking bruises, she was downright pathetic.

He set her bag at her feet, dusted off her dictionary and handed it to her. "Here you go, miss."

She took her treasured book—the first thing she'd grabbed before making her escape—and hugged the dilapidated volume to her. If anything had happened to it, Becky would have wept then and there. She could get a new Bible, but she could never replace her mother's dictionary. "Thank you, sir."

"You shouldn't go chasing after a mongrel like that. You put yourself in danger."

Although he'd chided her, the warmth now lighting his captivating eyes eased the sting.

"Good day." He tipped his hat and returned to the older woman waiting for him on the walkway.

The dog. Becky had forgotten about him.

Callie rushed up to her. "Are you all right?"

"I'm fine, I think." She stared at the back of the man who'd come to her aid. "Did you see what happened?"

"Oh, yes. It was quite romantic, the way he raced across the street to save you. And then he collected your things in an impressive show of chivalry."

Romantic wasn't the word she'd choose. *Embarrassing*, perhaps. Even a little scary, albeit deliciously so. Her roguish-looking rescuer evidently had a softer side. "Not that. What happened to the dog?"

Callie shook her head and smiled. "You're such a caring person, Becky. You would risk your life for a mutt."

Mongrel. Mutt. The words rankled. Every creature

was special, even the lowliest of them. "I don't like seeing an animal get hurt."

"Well, you can relax. The dog dodged the wagon wheels and ran off unharmed."

Callie took Becky's arm and led her to the wooden walkway where Jessie waited, her forehead creased with concern. "Are you all right? I saw you wince, and you're moving slowly."

"I'll be fine." She would be, once she figured out how to overcome any objections Mr. O'Brien might have—and what to do if he proved to be impossible to work for.

Dr. Wright perched on the corner of the large desk in his private office, his left leg swinging like a pendulum. The steady swipe of his heel brushing the oak panel as he stared into space made James O'Brien want to cry out in protest. In his experience, when a doctor took his time searching for the right words, the news wasn't good. "Just tell me. How bad is it?"

The compassion in the young doctor's eyes when he focused on James gave him his answer. "My examination today confirmed the suspicions I had when you were in last week."

"So it's spread. Is there nothing that can be done to stop it?"

Dr. Wright ceased his motion. "I'm sorry, James. Cancer's an ugly disease, but we'll do everything we can to make your mother as comfortable as possible. Thankfully, we have morphine these days."

"How long—" James's voice cracked. "How long does she have?"

"I can't say for sure. My best estimate is six months, more or less."

"I see." If *Mutti* put up a good fight, she might be

around for another harvest. He couldn't imagine one without her. She enjoyed preparing the meals for the extra workers they hired every September. Not that she'd be up to cooking this year, even if she hung on that long. He'd have to find someone else to feed the hired hands.

The thought of another woman in *Mutti*'s kitchen jerked James back to the present. "I've done some thinking since that visit, and I've changed my mind."

Dr. Wright quirked an eyebrow. "About?"

"About your idea of finding a young woman from the East to care for *Mutti*. I know I gave you the funds for the ticket, but I've decided to find a nurse myself and reduce my cash outlay. Since you couldn't think of anyone available around here, I'm going to expand my search. I'll go to San Francisco, if necessary."

Kate wouldn't leave her comfortable life in the famed city. Not that he could blame her, since she had a young daughter. But his sister, with her many society connections, might know about a matronly woman with nursing experience. An elderly widow would do nicely. He wanted nothing to do with having a young unmarried woman living in his house.

The doctor's forehead furrowed. "I understand your hesitation, but when you left my office last week I was certain you'd given me consent to seek someone for you."

"I did, but that's only because I was taken by surprise when you told me how rapidly the disease is progressing. When *Mutti* brightened at your offer to locate a young lady to help her, I couldn't say no. But I've realized how hasty I was and have come up with a more prudent plan."

James gave a single nod, firm and forceful. He'd put a stop to things, and now he could proceed with his plan to locate a nurse himself.

Dr. Wright stood, leaned against a tall bookcase filled

with medical books and raked a hand through his hair. "It seems we have a problem."

His serious tone didn't bode well. "What do you mean?"

"As a physician, I'm used to taking immediate action. Before you'd even reached Diamond Springs that day, I'd stopped in at the Wells Fargo office. I sent a telegram to the minister of my church back in Chicago, asking if he knew of a young woman willing to come West and received a reply within the hour. A positive one. I've been looking forward to surprising you with the good news. I knew you could use some."

Apprehension swirled in James's gut. He would do anything for *Mutti*, but he couldn't allow a young lady to live in his home. No good could come of such an arrangement. Not that she'd even agree to stay if she did come. She'd probably take one look at him and change her mind. He wouldn't blame her if she did.

After the accident, he'd come to his senses. He'd planned to ask for Sophie Wannamaker's hand, but he'd realized that a lowly man like him didn't deserve a woman of society like her.

He could still hear the shouts of those asking who'd tumbled down the snow-covered bank following the explosion—along with the clipped response. *That Irishman, O'Brien.*

No one had mentioned the fact that he was an engineer. He was just seen as another immigrant, even though he'd been born in the States and spoke with no hint of the musical lilt his dearly departed father had.

While James might have been able to overcome the handicap of his heritage, he could do nothing to conceal the ugly scar that frightened small children and caused adults to avert their gazes. It would come as no surprise if this woman were similarly affected. Not that he would have to worry about that, since she wouldn't be coming anyhow.

He stood. "You're not saying he has someone in mind already, are you? Because if that's the case, you'll have to tell him the need no longer exists."

"I would relay your message if I could, but Reverend Hastings and his wife put the young woman on the train the next day." Dr. Wright flipped open his pocket watch and nodded. "Barring any delays en route, she should be in my waiting area with your mother."

Shock surged through James. "She's *here*?"

Chapter Two

Ten minutes in Dr. Wright's waiting room with Mariela O'Brien was all it had taken to strengthen Becky's resolve. She wasn't sure what to make of Mr. O'Brien, but she was eager to care for this courageous woman. Although Mrs. O'Brien's days were numbered, she possessed the same inspiring faith Becky's mother had.

Before she could secure the nursing position, Becky had to figure out how to dodge the obstacle in her path. Mr. O'Brien had seen how gingerly she moved when she'd stooped to pick up her Bible and was sure to have concerns about her ability to do the job. Although Mrs. O'Brien insisted he was a kind, loving man, Becky had her doubts.

Mr. O'Brien might have come to her aid and treated her with respect, but she couldn't forget the fierce look in his eyes when she'd first encountered him or the way he'd sneered at her. A man like that couldn't be trusted. Her brother could appear charming in public, but she'd seen how quickly Dillon could change into someone entirely different when no one else was around.

Eager to learn more about her present situation, Becky shoved the past aside and focused on the friendly woman seated beside her on the elegant settee. It hadn't taken long to figure out that she was James O'Brien's mother and that she was German, as Becky had suspected.

Mrs. O'Brien continued, speaking in German as they'd done since she learned it was Becky's second language. "I had a weak moment earlier this morning and wanted to put off seeing Dr. Wright, but my dear boy calmed my fears."

The stouthearted woman couldn't be blamed for being hesitant to hear how bad things were. Such news could be difficult to accept, even for a brave soul like her.

"The good doctor examined me a few minutes ago. He tried not to show any emotion, but I knew from the look on his face he'd found another tumor. I forced him to tell me when to expect the end. He did his best to sound optimistic, but the truth is I'll be meeting my Maker sometime in the next six months." A smile spread across her softly wrinkled face. "I can only imagine what it will be like to look into His eyes and thank Him for all He's done for me."

As had been the case with Becky's mother, Mrs. O'Brien didn't sound scared to be facing the end of her life. "I sense you're at peace."

"When it comes to myself, yes. I'm eager to see my beloved William again, but I long to see my son end his feud with his heavenly Father before I go." She heaved a wistful sigh. "James isn't one to be forced into something. I pray for him regularly."

Perhaps the doctor had overstated Mr. O'Brien's relationship with the Lord in his telegram or didn't realize that his mother saw things differently. "I like to think God takes a special interest in the prayers of a parent, since He's one Himself. My mother was convinced He heard hers. She certainly lifted plenty of them for my brother and me in her last days."

"Did your mother have cancer, too?"

"Consumption. Both are such terrible diseases." She ached to think of what Mrs. O'Brien would have to endure in the months to come.

"When the doctor told James it was time to hire a nurse, I was excited at first. I'd had a tiring day, you see, and welcomed the idea of a helper. But then that night in the quiet of my own room, I balked a bit. The Lord and I did some talking, though, and that helped. I trusted Him to provide someone special, and He has."

Becky rested her hand on the older woman's arm. "I'll do all I can to help, Frau O'Brien. I was at my mother's bedside day and night until the Lord took her home. I know it was only a mother's love talking, but she said I was the best nurse she could have asked for."

Mrs. O'Brien patted Becky's hand with work-roughened fingers. "My dear girl, since you're going to help me with my most intimate needs, we can dispense with the formality. You may call me *Mutti* as James does."

"I couldn't possibly!"

"I insist. And no more *Sie*, either. We'll be spending a lot of time together the next few months, and I want us to be good friends, so please use *du*."

Becky was at a loss for words. Once she'd turned twelve, her own mother had no longer allowed her to use the informal word for *you* in their conversations, and yet Mrs. O'Brien had invited her to do so after a brief conversation. The honor sent Becky's spirits soaring.

She would stand up to Mr. O'Brien, come what may, because she was going to care for his mother. And she wasn't going to let any concerns he might have about her qualifications or abilities get in the way.

As though she considered the matter settled, Mrs. O'Brien—*Mutti*—changed the subject. "The warm days of spring are lovely, aren't they? When I was a girl in the Old Country, our window boxes were full of flowers like those in the half barrels out front. Seeing them brings back such good memories. Do you know what they're called in English?"

Becky glanced at the big red blooms with their bright green leaves. "It's spelled the same, but it sounds a bit different." She said the word using the English pronunciation. "*Geranium.*"

The door leading from the waiting area to the rooms beyond opened. Becky caught a whiff of a strong, fruity scent that wrinkled her nose. She'd never been to a doctor's office before, and the odor surprised her.

Mutti leaned over and whispered, "It's ether. Dr. Wright said he'd used some earlier when he had to anesthetize a patient. Potent, isn't it?"

"Indeed." Her mother's doctor used to show up at their house smelling of onions and cigar smoke and looking as if he'd slept in his clothes. The dignified blond man in the doorway was the picture of professionalism.

He saw her and smiled. "Good afternoon. I'm Dr. Wright, and you must be Miss Becky Martin. Welcome. I trust your journey went well."

"Thank you, sir. It did." She still hadn't gotten used to people calling her by her new name. She'd gone by Rebecca Donnelly all her life, but when she was forced to flee she'd chosen to use the nickname Becky along with her middle name, Martin, which had been her mother's maiden name.

Mr. O'Brien stepped from behind the doctor and frowned. "It's *you.*"

Dr. Wright's eyebrows rose. "You two have met?"

Lord, please give me courage.

She stood, lifted her chin and looked into Mr. O'Brien's eyes without flinching. "We haven't been properly introduced, but he did assist me earlier."

"Assisted you? I saved you. If it weren't for me, you could have been crushed by that wagon wheel." He shook his head and addressed the doctor. "This impetuous young woman took off running after a flea-bitten stray. If I hadn't been there, she could be in on your examination table with a broken leg—or worse."

She wasn't familiar with the word *impetuous*, but his disapproving tone indicated he wasn't paying her a compliment. If he didn't have her at a disadvantage, she would choose a fitting word to sling back at him and show him what she thought of his high-handed manner.

His mother rose and linked arms with Becky. "Do not talk to her that way, *mein Sohn*." *Mutti* spoke English now, but she had a marked German accent, with her *w*'s sounding like *v*'s and her *t-h*'s like *z*'s. "This lovely young woman only wanted to help the dog. There is nothing wrong with that. It proves she has a kind heart."

Mutti's approval renewed Becky's determination to be strong. This was her opportunity to show Mr. O'Brien she expected to be treated with respect. The Lord was with her, and she could trust Him to look out for her, as He had when Dillon had come after her. "Thank you, *Mutti*. Now, I think it's time for your son and me to have a talk."

Mr. O'Brien's mouth fell open. "What did you call her?"

His mother gave Becky's arm a reassuring squeeze. "She called me *Mutti* because I asked her to. And she is right. You two have much to talk about. Go." She fluttered a hand toward the front door.

Dr. Wright extended his arm. "You may use my office, if you'd prefer, since I'm sure you'd like some privacy. It's the first door on the right."

Becky didn't wait for Mr. O'Brien to respond. "That's kind of you. We will." She ignored the pain in her midriff, marched through the doorway and didn't stop until she reached the paneled room. Two burgundy chairs faced a desk with beautiful scrollwork. She perched on the armless chair, leaving the wingback armchair for Mr. O'Brien.

He sat and angled his right side away from her. Interesting. His scar must bother him. She could understand, having spent the past week with her face to the floor so people wouldn't see her unsightly bruises.

She smoothed the skirt of her best dress. The faded fabric had seen many washings. The black crepe mourning gown was sorely in need of another after her week on the train. And she was in need of this job.

A good thirty seconds went by with the ticking of the desk clock the only sound. Although it was a man's place to initiate a conversation, she could take no more. She drew in a deep breath and launched into her carefully crafted speech.

"Your mother and I had a good conversation. She's accepted the fact that she needs help, and I'm just the woman for the job. I spent years nursing my own dear mother before she lost her battle with consumption back in '69, and kept house for my father and brother after she was gone. I've become a fair cook, and I can clean and sew, too. I know it cost a lot for you to bring me out here, so I'm willing to work for nothing more than room and board until I've earned enough to repay the money you had Dr. Wright wire for my train ticket. When would you like me to start?"

There. She'd stood firm and taken charge of the situation. Jessie would be proud of her. Now to find out if Mr. O'Brien would accept her offer.

He stared at the patterned rug for the longest time, his eyes clouded with sadness.

The impending loss was going to be hard on him. In her experience, men were at a disadvantage when dealing with such devastating news, especially strong men like him, who were used to being in control. They felt the need to shoulder their burdens in silence. At least he had the Lord to lean on, provided he would turn to Him.

"Dr. Wright said you're qualified, but I believe in being honest. I was seeking an older woman, not a young one like you."

"I'm not that young. I'm twenty-one. I was only sixteen when my mother took to her bed and I began caring for her. I was up for the task then, so I don't think my age will be a problem. It's clear your mother likes me."

"I can't argue with that." He smiled, crinkling his scar the same way he had when she'd come close to colliding with him. Perhaps he hadn't been sneering before, after all. He really should smile more often because he looked quite dashing when he did, reminding her of a rogue from one of the stories she'd read.

"It seems to me you'd be eager to give me the position. How else could you be sure I'd have the money to pay you back?"

He braced his right elbow in his left hand and covered the scarred side of his face with his palm. "You've made your point. The position is yours."

She couldn't believe how easy it had been to get him to agree.

"I do have one condition."

Oh, no. "Yes?"

"I want Dr. Wright to examine you."

Mr. O'Brien was full of surprises. "That's not necessary."

"It's obvious you're in pain. The job will entail a fair amount of lifting. I want to make sure you're able to handle it."

"I'm fine. I don't need to see the doctor. I c-can't." She'd intended to sound forceful, not fearful. If only her voice hadn't betrayed her.

"You can, and you will—if you want to work for me."

His clipped words and sharp tone riled her. Dashing rogues were one thing. Rude, unyielding men were another. "As I told you, I can't see him. I don't have the money for an examination. Besides, I'm sure I'll be better in a few days."

"Who did this to you?"

His rapid change of subject took her aback. "What?"

He leaned forward and peered at her beneath the wide brim of her simple muslin bonnet. "Who struck you, Miss Martin?"

Shame surged through her, so bitter she could almost taste it. It had been hard enough telling her new friends that her own brother had slapped her. She couldn't tell this stern-faced stranger. "That's not important. I'll never see him again." At least she hoped not.

Mr. O'Brien narrowed his eyes. "It's important to me. I don't want an angry suitor showing up at my door seeking to get you back. I won't put *Mutti* in danger."

She blinked several times. "I can assure you it wasn't a suitor. I've never had one."

Now, why had she said that? Her romantic life—or lack thereof—was none of his business.

"How do I know you're telling the truth? A woman in your situation could go to great lengths to get away from her attacker. She might even...lie."

"I'm not like that. I'm a follower of Christ and would never deceive you."

The words had scarcely left her lips when guilt soured her stomach. She hadn't lied, but she hadn't exactly told him the truth, either. She'd misled him, just like she'd misled everyone else since she'd embarked on her journey.

Although she felt like a fraud every time someone called her Becky or Miss Martin, her pastor and his wife had agreed that altering her name was necessary in order to keep Dillon from locating her. If her brother found her, there was no telling what he would do to her. A man who would set fire to a factory and accuse his own sister of having committed the crime was capable of almost anything.

He nodded. "I'm glad to hear that. I put great stock in honesty."

She couldn't be entirely truthful, but if her admission could help ease his misgivings about hiring her, perhaps she should be forthcoming about this particular issue. "If you must know, my brother did it."

"I see." Mr. O'Brien studied her. She resisted the urge to look away. Since she was going to be working for him, there would be no hiding beneath her bonnet. She might as well let him satisfy his curiosity. Lifting her head, she focused on his thick hair, admiring the lovely wave over his right eye.

"He must have used a good deal of force to leave bruises that haven't faded yet. Did he make a habit of this?"

She couldn't let him think she'd tolerated such behavior. "That was the first time. The only time. We'd just lost our father, and Dillon didn't take it well." Her understatement had taken on epic proportions. If she told

Mr. O'Brien what she really thought about her brother and how many times she'd had to ask the Lord's forgiveness for her dark mutterings the past few days, he might question her faith.

"That's no excuse." His voice was low but firm. "Nothing gives a man a reason to lash out at a woman. The scoundrel had better never show his face around here, or he'll have me to deal with. You'll be safe at my place."

"I appreciate that, but I don't expect to see him again." She wasn't in danger since Dillon had no idea where she'd gone, but Mr. O'Brien's protectiveness warmed her all the same. He wasn't a rogue. How she knew, she couldn't say, but something told her he was an honorable man, the kind a woman could trust.

"That's good. Now, let me get Dr. Wright to examine you."

The warmth that had enveloped her fled, replaced by a quickly spreading case of gooseflesh. If the doctor told Mr. O'Brien how much pain she was in, he'd find out she hadn't been truthful. She'd seen his temper, and the possibility of it flaring up again gave her pause.

"Before you call him, there's something you should know."

James stood at the window in Dr. Wright's waiting area. An inebriated miner staggered out of the Arch Saloon across the street and weaved his way up the walkway, clutching each of the posts supporting the balcony at the Cary House hotel as he passed.

Turning from the disturbing sight, James crossed the room and sat beside *Mutti*.

Miss Martin had suffered at the hands of her own brother, and yet she'd made excuses for him. It made no sense. Judging by the sickly yellowish-gray on her cheeks and her cautious movements, he'd obviously hit her repeatedly and hard. Well, she wouldn't have to worry now. If the brute was to show up, he'd be sorry. James would make sure of that.

Mutti placed a hand on his bouncing leg. "Everything will be fine, *Sohn*."

"I know you're taken with her, but I'm not sure she's up to the task of caring for you."

"She will heal soon. You will see." A radiant smile lit *Mutti*'s face. "The Lord sent this dear girl to us, I am sure. She is the answer to my prayers."

He didn't put much stock in prayer these days. God didn't seem to care what happened to him. He just kept taking things away. His father. His future. Now *Mutti*'s days were numbered.

Before he could think of a tactful way to reroute the conversation, Miss Martin returned to the waiting area, followed by Dr. Wright. James shot to his feet. "How is she, Doctor?"

Miss Martin answered. "Nothing's broken, so I'll be better soon." Her reassurance rang truer than before.

James grasped the back of the settee. "You need time to heal. Housework is out of the question. I'll find someone else to take over for *Mutti*."

"I don't think that's necessary." Dr. Wright addressed Miss Martin. "If you'll get plenty of rest and avoid doing any heavy lifting during the next three weeks while your bruised ribs heal, you should be able to complete the household chores."

Relief squeezed a sigh from James. He wouldn't need to go in search of a nurse, after all. Since Miss Martin had generously offered to forgo payment in order to repay him for her train ticket, he wouldn't have to increase his monthly expenses, either. Things were working out after all.

Mutti stood. "Then we can all go home now. I am eager for you to see the place, Becky. I am sure you will like it." She paused and turned to James, her eyes wide. "Where will she stay? We cannot have a young woman living in the house with you there."

Miss Martin's audible intake of breath drew his attention. She pressed a hand to the frayed collar of her dingy black dress and smiled. But that wasn't just any smile. It began with a wobble and grew until her lips parted and her eyes shone with unmistakable gratitude. Despite her discolored cheeks, she looked almost pretty with her face alight like that. "Your concern for my reputation means a great deal to me, but I won't be a guest. I'll be a hired worker. Besides, you'll be there, so everything will be proper."

"That will be good for the days, but I am thinking of the nights." *Mutti* gently patted the young woman's mottled cheeks. "I want you to care for me, but I do not want to make you the talk of the town's gossips. An unmarried lady needs a chaperone." She turned toward James.

Miss Martin faced him, too. A pink tinge added welcome color to her bruised face. He hadn't noticed before, but the fair-skinned woman had a sprinkling of freckles across her nose. She'd said she was twenty-one, but she looked all of sixteen with the blush on her cheeks and expectancy in her eyes. "What can we do?"

Clearly, she meant what she'd said about wanting to care for *Mutti*. While he hadn't wanted a young woman as a nurse, he had his answer. Miss Martin *was* the right person for the job. He'd have to come up with a solution. "I'll think of something."

Dr. Wright cleared his throat. "If I might make a suggestion. Would it be possible for you to move an extra bed into your mother's room, James?"

He relaxed his tense shoulders and nodded. The ever-practical doctor had come up with the perfect solution. The propriety issue had been dealt with, and *Mutti* would have help close at hand. "I could put my sister's old bed in there. I'll see to that right away."

They bid the doctor farewell. James helped his mother onto the wagon's bench seat while Miss Martin waited. Something brushed his leg, and he jumped.

That pesky dog was back. "What are you doing here?" He held up his hands to keep the bedraggled animal at bay. "Shoo."

Miss Martin patted her side and made a kissing sound. "Here, boy."

The dog dashed over to her, and she stroked its matted coat. "You poor thing. Someone needs to give you a bath. I'm sure underneath all that mud you're a fine-looking fellow."

James had his doubts. The dog was so dirty it was impossible to tell what color fur it had. "Perhaps, but we need to be going." The dog plopped down at James's feet and peered at him with enormous brown eyes.

"I think he likes you. It appears he's a stray. If you don't have a dog, maybe you could—"

"I've got horses, a milk cow and chickens to tend. The last thing I need is a mutt like that." He snapped his fingers at the filthy animal and pointed down the street. "Go on now."

The mud-encrusted cur stood with his tail wagging as enthusiastically as ever. The dog needed someplace to call home, but the orchard wasn't it.

Miss Martin cast a wistful look at the friendly animal. "I'm sorry, boy, but I'm afraid I can't do anything for you. You'll have to go." The dog trotted off.

James fought the urge to give in just to see her smile again, but what he'd said was true. Having a dog would add to his workload. He held out a hand to help Miss Martin into the wagon.

A shout rang out from down the street, followed by the pounding of horses' hooves on the hard-packed earth. "Mr. O'Brien!"

His neighbor's ten-year-old son rode up to the wagon, leading his father's saddled gelding behind him.

James patted the neck of the boy's winded mare. "What is it, Bobby?"

The breathless boy forced the words out in snatches. "You gotta come. Quick. Me 'n' Davy need your help."

Chapter Three

Worry dug its claws into Becky. She looked up at *Mutti* on the wagon seat above her. "What do you think is wrong?"

Mutti's gaze was riveted on her son, who was talking with the troubled boy, but she didn't seem overly concerned. "It might not be too serious. Since Bobby's father is out of town, the young fellow probably panicked."

Mr. O'Brien straightened, spun around and marched to the wagon with a frown on his angular face. "There's a problem at the Strattons' place. I need to get there right away."

Becky's fear intensified. "Is someone hurt?"

"No. Bobby's younger brother broke the valve I installed up at the ditch, and there's water gushing everywhere. It'll cost their father and me a fortune if I don't stop it. I need to get *Mutti* home. Can you drive a wagon?"

She couldn't, but she didn't dare tell him that. He already doubted her ability to handle the job. "I'll do whatever you need me to."

He yanked off his derby, swiped an arm across his brow and jammed the hat back on. "You didn't answer my question. Can you, or can't you?"

"I'm sure I can." She'd seen Dillon and their father do it many times.

"Yes, you can." *Mutti* reached down and rested a hand on Becky's shoulder. "Do not worry, *Sohn*. I will help her."

"You haven't driven in years."

"That is true, but I have not forgotten how. You can go. We will be fine."

Mr. O'Brien scraped a hand over his scar. "The road to Diamond Springs is full of twists and turns, but it seems I don't have any choice."

Becky drew herself to her full height but only came to his chin. She did her best to sound confident. "You needn't worry. We'll take it nice and slow."

He studied her a moment and shrugged. "I expect the repair to take a while, so don't wait supper for me." He strode to where Bobby waited and swung into the saddle on the larger horse in one graceful movement.

She climbed onto the driver's seat, clutched the reins and watched as Mr. O'Brien and the red-haired boy took off with a flurry of dust. "What was he saying about a ditch?"

"It's what they call a canal here. It delivers water to the gold mines, but farmers and orchardists use the ditches for irrigation. They pay a daily fee whenever they tap into one. If they use more water than the slow, steady stream they've contracted for—what's known as a miner's inch—the cost goes up." She'd switched to German, as she had before when it was just the two of them.

Becky did the same. "No wonder he's in such a hurry. Shall we head out, then?"

Weariness had bowed *Mutti*'s shoulders. Becky was eager to get the dear woman home.

"Let me show you how to hold the reins." *Mutti* demonstrated. "Now switch them from your right hand to your left, release the brake and reposition them."

She did, moving slowly so as not to hurt her ribs.

"Next you give the team their command. James uses 'walk on.'"

As soon as the horses heard the words, they started up. When the wagon reached a road taking off to the south, *Mutti* placed her hands over Becky's and showed her how to navigate the turn.

"Well done, my dear. It's three miles to Diamond Springs. As James said, the road is curvy. We're in no hurry, so we'll let the horses walk and give you time to get used to driving."

Thanks to *Mutti*'s gentle coaching, it didn't take Becky long to feel comfortable. She kept a watchful eye on the road ahead.

The California countryside with its abundant trees and wildlife was much different than Chicago. She flinched when a bright blue bird *Mutti* said was a Steller's jay let out a scratchy, scolding call and chuckled when a squirrel frolicked in the crowns of nearby oaks.

A flash of something brown caught Becky's eye. The dog she'd befriended earlier bounded toward the wagon. His gleeful bark startled a flock of wild turkeys. The ungainly birds bolted from the underbrush, zigzagging their way across the clearing and into the road, screeching loudly.

The horses reared and took off running. Becky's heart galloped along with them. She gripped the reins so tightly her knuckles turned white. "Hold on!"

Mutti clutched the edge of the seat as they went around a hairpin turn and gasped as the wagon rose up on two wheels.

Becky's mouth went dry. The wagon wheels returned

to the earth with a jarring thud. Bracing her boots against the footboard, she held the reins taut and prayed the team would slow before the next turn.

Gradually, the startled animals returned to a walk. *Thank you, Lord.* She spun to face *Mutti.* "Are you all right?"

"Yes. Just a bit shaken up, but I'll be fine."

"Good. For a minute there I wasn't sure how things were going to turn out. I'd better see to the team." She pulled to a stop, handed the reins to *Mutti* and climbed down. Using slow, soothing strokes, she patted the horses' broad faces.

Once she was convinced they were over the worst of their fright and that there was no apparent damage to the wagon, she looked for the dog, but he was nowhere in sight. She couldn't fault him for upsetting the horses. From her place on the wagon seat, it had been clear he was chasing after her and not the flighty flock.

She returned to the wagon, and they set out again.

Mutti patted her arm. "You handled that well. I'll tell James you make a fine driver."

The rest of the drive to Diamond Springs went smoothly. At *Mutti*'s request, Becky stopped at the butcher shop. She'd been wedged between Jessie and Callie when they'd passed through the town on their way to Placerville and hadn't seen much from the stagecoach.

A handful of shops lined both sides of the wide, rutted road. She recognized Harris's general store, where the coach had stopped to pick up a passenger on their way through town. Tantalizing scents wafted from the restaurant at the Washington House hotel nearby. "So this is Diamond Springs. There's not much to it, is there?"

"It might be small, but it has the basic necessities. The people are friendly. My William and I liked it here.

That's why we stayed. James liked it, too, but Katharina couldn't wait to grow up and move to the city. My girl lives in a fancy house in San Francisco with her lawyer husband, Artie, and their five-year-old daughter, Lottie. We don't see much of them."

Mutti gazed into the distance with a faraway expression on her face. "James went away, too, but he came back after the terrible accident that nearly took him from us. He was with me when William died two years ago and has been here ever since. I don't know what I'd have done without him. I couldn't manage the orchard on my own."

As much as Becky wanted to ask what kind of accident and if it had caused Mr. O'Brien's scar, it wasn't her place to pry. "Was the town always so small?"

"It's always been pretty much a one-street town, but when we arrived in '54 it was busier. A lot more mining was going on then. There are only nine hundred or so in Diamond Springs Township now."

What would it have been like to grow up in a place like this? To look into the distance and see nothing but rolling hills and the distant Sierras beyond instead of buildings? To breathe fresh air instead of inhaling the smoke belching from the ever-increasing number of factories in Chicago, like the small one where she and Dillon had worked?

A newcomer would stand out here, though. She'd have to be mindful of that. The less people knew about her, the better. If Dillon was to show up, she wouldn't want to make it easy for him to find her. Not that he would, but she couldn't shake the fear that made her want to look over her shoulder whenever she heard a man with an Irish accent. She was mighty glad Mr. O'Brien didn't have one.

"I should pick up your order. I'll just be a minute."

Becky returned from the butcher shop a short time

later, stowed the meaty-smelling package in a crate behind the seat and climbed aboard.

Mutti directed her to a road heading south. "It's only half a mile or so, and it's flat from here. I can't wait until you see the orchard in bloom. It's a sight to behold."

"What kind of trees are they?"

"Apple. There are five different varieties, and James plans to add another next year." Sadness clouded *Mutti*'s blue eyes, as though she realized she wouldn't live to see that day. She brightened quickly. "My boy isn't content to leave things as they are. He's always seeking ways to improve the orchard and make tasks easier. He figured out a way to give me running water in the kitchen."

"Running water? I can't imagine having such a thing."

"I know he can seem a bit gruff at times, but he really is a fine man. You'll see."

Since Becky didn't know how to respond, having only her initial impression to go on, she kept quiet.

Before long they approached rows of trees crowned with pink and white blossoms. "How beautiful!"

Mutti patted her arm. "I knew you'd like them."

"*This* is your orchard? It's wonderful. The bees like it, too. I can hear them buzzing from here. And the fragrance…" She inhaled deeply. "It's delightful."

Pride shone in *Mutti*'s eyes. "William started the orchard when we first arrived. James helped until he left for college, but my boy's the boss now. He hired Quon and Chung Lee to help him. He met the brothers while he worked on the railroad."

"They're Chinese?" She'd never met anyone from China before, although she'd walked past two Chinese men working at a laundry in Placerville. They wore unusual clothing—loose-fitting, hip-length tunics, flowing trousers and pointed wicker hats. What she'd found most interesting were their long black braids and lovely singsong way of speaking.

"They are. They're hard workers just like James and are fiercely loyal to him. He thinks the world of them."

"Will I be cooking for them, too?"

"No. They live in one of the two cabins beyond the barn and get their own meals. Get ready for another turn." *Mutti* pointed to a wooden sign bearing the name O'Brien Orchard. "That road ahead is ours."

Becky led the team down a narrow lane to their left, with the O'Brien's property on the north and an oak-studded field on the south. Before long there was a break in the apple trees. A house came into view, a darling place with white clapboard siding and a redbrick chimney. Green shutters with hearts cut out of the centers hung at every window.

She parked in front of the house, looped the reins over the porch railing and helped *Mutti* from the wagon. A whiff of peppermint from an herb garden on either side of the two steps gave Becky a sudden longing for a cup of tea and a nap. She might be able to enjoy the first, but the second was wishful thinking. The next few hours she'd be busy getting settled in and doing her best to convince Mr. O'Brien she could handle the job.

Mutti propped open the door and invited Becky inside. "Welcome to your new home. I would show you around, but the trip tired me out. I think I'll lie down for a few minutes. If you'll get your carpetbag, I'll show you where you'll be sleeping."

Excitement swirled in Becky's chest. For the first time in years, she wouldn't have to worry about waking in the night when her brother stumbled in drunk.

It didn't take her long to stow her few items in *Mutti*'s bedroom, the far one of the three that occupied the western half of the house. She took a quick peek out the window. A huge wooden tank supported by a sturdy base towered over one end of the backyard—the source of the running water, no doubt. A clothesline had been strung across the other end. Beyond the yard were trees, trees and more trees. She couldn't begin to imagine how many apples they would produce. "Would you like me to close the curtains, *Mutti*?"

"Yes, please. And then feel free to get acquainted with your new home."

"I'll see to the horses first." Although Dillon had never let her drive, he'd left her to see to the team many times.

"One of the Lee brothers should be around and would be happy to take care of that for you. Now, you must promise you won't let me sleep too long. I want to help with supper."

"By all means." Becky closed the bedroom door and smiled at the cheery scene that greeted her. A breeze fluttered the red-and-white gingham curtains at each of the three windows. Sunlight bathed the spacious room, and the sweet scent of apple blossoms filled the air. Four chairs formed a half circle in front of the impressive rock-faced fireplace that took up a large portion of the back wall, giving the room a homey feel.

The most well-appointed kitchen she'd ever seen occupied the other end of the room. A modern stove with a hot-water reservoir sat in the corner, with varnished counters stretching several feet from it in either direction. Shelves and hooks above the counters held a seemingly endless supply of pots, pans and utensils. There was even a pie safe. She put the meat inside, where the cooler air from below would rise up through the mesh shelves and keep it fresh.

She opened the floor-to-ceiling cupboard just inside

the front door and stared in disbelief. She'd never seen so much food in one pantry before. No more racking her brain to come up with decent meals from next to nothing. Working in a kitchen as pretty and well stocked as this one would be a real treat. "Thank you, Lord."

The horses whickered, reminding her they were waiting. She went in search of the workmen. Wooden barrels were stacked under the eaves of a massive barn to the east. Hens clucked and pecked at the ground in a fenced area in front of a sturdy chicken coop. Smoke curled from a soot-black chimney pipe at one of two cottages beyond the huge building.

A short man wearing a plaid shirt, trousers and slouch hat wielded a hoe in a good-sized plot between the barn and the orchard. If it wasn't for the long black braid hanging down his back, she wouldn't have known he was Chinese. She made her way to him. "Good afternoon."

He jumped.

"I'm sorry I startled you. Are you Quon?"

He shook his head. "I Chung. Who you?"

"I'm the new nurse Mr. O'Brien sent for—Becky." She wouldn't provide her last name unless necessary. The fewer people who knew it, the better. Not that Dillon would be asking for Becky Martin, but just in case… "His mother said I could ask you to help me with the horses."

"Yes, miss. I go." The short man dropped the hoe and sprinted toward the wagon. *Mutti* had said the Lee brothers were helpful, but Chung's quick response went beyond that. No wonder Mr. O'Brien thought so highly of his hired hands.

She should go inside and get to work, but the apple trees whispered her name, begging her to pay them a visit. After her days cooped up on the train, she could use a walk. *Mutti* wouldn't need her for a while, and Mr. O'Brien wasn't around, so she could do a little exploring.

Becky strolled beneath trees bursting with pale pink blossoms. A single flower floated from a branch overhead, the soft petals brushing her cheek as it passed. She caught the beautiful bloom in midair, buried her nose in it and inhaled nature's perfume.

Several rows in, she spotted trees frosted with white flowers. She started toward them, but a movement in the distance caught her eye. Squinting, she tried to make out what it was. An animal. Not too large, but quick. It flew toward her, a streak of grayish-brown with a gleeful bark. She smiled. "Oh, it's you. Come here, boy."

She dropped to her knees, opened her arms and welcomed the friendly dog she'd seen earlier. He gave her a sloppy kiss. "Aren't you a charmer? I wish you could stay, but…"

Mr. O'Brien didn't want the dog, but the least she could do was give the poor fellow a bath. Maybe if he was clean, someone would take him in.

She found the supplies she needed in the barn, filled a pail with water and set to work behind the empty cabin, where she couldn't be seen from the house. She scrubbed the dog until all traces of mud were gone. He gave himself a good shake, splattering her with water droplets.

"I knew it. You are a handsome fellow. Look at your shiny red coat. If Mr. O'Brien could see you now, he might change his mind. I need this job, though, so you'll have to go."

The dog nuzzled her and looked up with such trust in his eyes that she couldn't send him away. She petted the friendly animal. "I could get in trouble for this, but I'm going to do what I can for you while I try to find you a home. I'll slip you some table scraps later. In the meantime, you'd be wise to keep out of sight." As though the handsome fellow understood her, he bounded off toward the rolling hills at the eastern edge of the property.

She put away the items she'd borrowed and hurried inside to change and start supper. If all went well, no one would find out that she was feeding the stray.

Chapter Four

"You come back late, boss."

James started at Quon's words, and the wrench he was cleaning clattered on his workbench. He'd been so preoccupied he hadn't heard the elder of the two Lee brothers enter the barn. "It took a while to make the repairs."

If only Ralph Stratton had shown his young son how to operate the release valve James had installed. Instead, Davy had gotten frustrated and whacked the spigot with a shovel, breaking it off, when all he'd needed to do was twist the handle. Water had gushed from the pipeline James had installed that led to both his orchard and Stratton's farm, creating a small lake in no time.

Quon sat on an apple barrel, his heels drumming a steady beat as they struck the empty container. "You very dirty. Need to take bath before you go in house. Must look good for new lady."

"New lady? Oh, you mean Miss Martin."

"Is she your special friend?"

"No!" James lowered his voice. "She's *Mutti*'s nurse. She'll be taking over her chores, too."

Quon stilled his feet. "Good your mother have helper. Not good she need one."

"I wanted an older woman. Miss Martin is seven years younger than I am."

"You talk with mad voice. Why? She pretty? Make your head move?" He swiveled his in an exaggerated imitation of a man watching an attractive woman walk past, with his eyebrows doing a ridiculous dance.

James chose not to encourage Quon. "Did everything go all right while I was gone?"

"No trouble here."

He wiped the mud off the last of the tools he'd sent Bobby to get and suspended the pipe cutter between two nails on the board over his workbench. "I see you and Chung finished plowing the garden plot this afternoon. Good work."

"Miss Martin will plant soon?"

"I suppose so, but I'll have to show her how. Since she's lived in the city her whole life, I doubt she knows one end of a rake from the other."

Quon thumped his chest. "I will teach her. I good teacher."

"I know, but..."

"What? She not like Chinese people?"

"I don't think she's ever met any before." James wasn't sure how she'd react. Many people maligned the Chinese. Some went so far as to threaten them—or worse. He wouldn't subject Quon and Chung to any mistreatment.

"She seem nice."

"You've met her?"

"She look out kitchen window, see me and... I not know how to say it." Quon waved.

James supplied the word. "I'll talk with her about the gardening and let you know."

Quon jumped to the ground. "I think Miss Martin have supper ready for you soon. It smell good. I go."

James entered the lean-to at the back of the house minutes later and yanked off his muddy boots. The large washtub they used for bathing sat on the floor with steam rising from the surface of the water.

The door from the great room opened, and Miss Martin stepped inside, lugging a large pail. She sent hot water splashing into the tub. "Did you get everything fixed?"

"I did."

"That's good. I figured repairing a water line would be a dirty job and you'd want to bathe. I put clean clothes up there." She tilted her head toward the shelf over the coat pegs. "I'll have supper on the table shortly." She left and closed the door.

She'd anticipated his every need.

"Thanks. I won't be long." The mouthwatering scents in the air had set his stomach to growling. He was eager to sample her cooking.

Minutes later he entered the kitchen. Miss Martin bustled about with confidence. A thick brown braid hung down her back, swinging from side to side as she moved, a captivating sight. He forced himself to stop staring.

She must have helped *Mutti* with her hair because the braid coiled atop his mother's head was neat and tidy. Such tasks had grown increasingly difficult for her, although she had a hard time admitting it.

His mother sat at the table stirring a creamy concoction. He appreciated the young woman's consideration. By including her, *Mutti* would feel as if she were making a valuable contribution.

Miss Martin turned from the stove and smiled. "You look a whole lot better, but…"

"But what?"

She tapped a finger to her head. "You might want to brush your hair."

"Yes. I'll do that." He hadn't meant his words to have such an edge. It wasn't as though he cared what she thought of him, but he didn't like that hint of amusement in her eyes.

"Be quick, *Sohn*. It is past suppertime."

"I told you not to wait."

Miss Martin set a pitcher of milk on the table. "We didn't want you to have to eat alone."

He completed the task as quickly as he could and took his place on the end of one of the two benches flanking the rectangular dining table, opposite *Mutti*. Miss Martin set the dishes before him. *Jägerschnitzel* and *Spätzle* with gravy—a good German meal.

She sat beside *Mutti*, her hands in her lap and her head down. *Mutti* bowed hers, too. "Would you please give thanks, *Sohn*?"

James bit back a sigh. *Mutti* knew he had difficulty praying, but she asked him to say grace every night. She couldn't seem to accept the fact that he wasn't on speaking terms with God. But as he had before every other meal, he would do his duty.

"Thank You, Father, for the food we're about to eat. Please give *Mutti* a restful night and help Miss Martin's ribs heal quickly. Amen."

He heaped generous portions on his plate. The *Jägerschnitzel* tasted every bit as good as *Mutti*'s. The veal cutlets were tender, the small dumplings served with them were cooked to perfection and the mushroom gravy he'd ladled over everything was as rich and smooth as buttermilk. Miss Martin smiled when he helped himself to seconds.

"Becky is a good cook, *ja*?"

"Almost as good as you are."

Mutti chuckled. "You do not have to humor me, *Sohn*,

but I love you for it. You will soon see that she is the better baker."

When everyone had finished eating, Miss Martin cleared the supper dishes, opened the oven door and flooded the room with the tantalizing aroma of peaches and cinnamon. She topped each slice of peach pie with a dollop of the whipping cream *Mutti* had made. He wasn't going to have any complaints about his food with Miss Martin in the kitchen.

A short time later he shoveled in the last bite of the fruity dessert and tossed his napkin on the table. "*Mutti*'s right, Miss Martin. The pie was delicious."

She focused on her plate, but a hint of a smile lifted her lips. "I'm glad you like it, Mr. O'Brien."

Mutti's brow creased. "I am glad you two are talking, but I do not like the stiffness. You both call me *Mutti*, so I think you should call each other James and Becky."

Miss Martin's fork froze in midair.

Leave it to *Mutti* to interfere. She meant well, but he couldn't let her take charge. "She has a good point. Quon and Chung are my employees, and I use their first names. If you don't object, I'll use yours, and you may use mine."

Calling a young woman by her first name seemed odd. He'd escorted the highly regarded Miss Sophronia Wannamaker to parties in Sacramento City for over a year before she'd given him permission to call her by her Christian name. That was often the case with a cultured lady of society such as Sophie, but Becky was different. This battered young woman with the warm brown eyes would become part of their family for a time, whether he liked it or not.

Becky set her fork down. "You may call me that if you'd like."

Mutti patted Becky's hand. "This is better. *Ja?* Now,

I must go to bed. For some reason I cannot get enough sleep today."

James jumped up. "I'll get Kate's bed moved."

It took him no time to accomplish the task. He scooted the bed into the corner of *Mutti*'s room opposite hers and spied Becky's books on the bureau between them. She'd placed a piece of ribbon in her dictionary. Curiosity compelled him to flip to the page she'd marked. A quick scan showed she must have been looking up *impetuous*. As he'd suspected by her furrowed forehead when he'd used the word earlier, she didn't know the meaning. Quon, ever the teacher, would appreciate her eagerness to learn.

"*Mutti* wondered if—" Becky balanced a pile of bedding in her arms. She stared at the book in his hands, opened her mouth as though she intended to say something but clamped it shut.

His chest tightened, and he set the dictionary down.

Her words came out clipped. "If you're done in here, I'd like to get the bed made up so I can help *Mutti* get settled for the night."

"Of course." He paused in the doorway and assumed an authoritative tone. "Come out when you're finished, and we'll talk."

James gave *Mutti* a good-night kiss on the cheek, and she disappeared into her room. He knelt on the hearth and added a log to the fire. Settling into his wing-back armchair, he watched as the blaze crackled and popped, sending sparks flying. He'd seen another kind of spark in Becky's eyes when she'd caught him snooping. You would think he'd been pocketing priceless jewels instead of looking in a dictionary that was falling to pieces. Perhaps since she had so little, she held tightly to what she did have.

He'd often wondered what possessed a woman to leave

everything and everyone she knew and head West. Becky had escaped her abusive brother, which took courage. Her quiet strength would serve her well as she cared for *Mutti*. She could be somewhat obstinate at times. He'd doubted Becky's abilities when he'd first met her, but it seemed she would make a good nurse, after all.

He tried to imagine Sophie in the role. The picture of her nursing *Mutti* was so inconceivable he nearly laughed out loud. How vastly different the two women were. Unlike unassuming Becky, Sophie oozed sophistication. No one could carry on a conversation or make people laugh the way she could. She was stunning, too, with her black hair and artistic features. He'd never felt more like a man than when she'd graced his arm at social functions. But he'd severed ties with her after the accident, sparing her the unpleasantness of further acquaintance. A woman of her social standing deserved a man others admired, not the disfigured son of struggling small-town immigrants.

Becky returned and leaned against his father's large leather armchair, looking bone-weary. "You wanted to talk?"

"Please take a seat. I'll be brief."

She glanced longingly at *Mutti*'s rocker beside James but perched on Kate's fancy purple chair on the far side of it, instead.

His conscience held him in its clutches. "I want to apologize for invading your privacy. It won't happen again."

Incredulity danced in her clear blue eyes, followed by appreciation. "I know the dictionary's seen better days, but it's important to me. Now please, tell me about my duties."

Strong and forthright, too. A promising combination.

"In addition to caring for *Mutti*, I'd hoped you could take over her chores—cooking, cleaning, laundry and so forth. She's helped with the milking, chickens and gardening, too. I know that's a lot, but…"

Becky nodded. "I can do everything inside, but I don't know how to do the things outdoors. We didn't have a garden or animals, other than the horses, of course."

"Quon's offered to teach you how to tend the garden, and I'll show you how to do the rest. The milking is done early, so I'll knock on your door in the morning if you're not up. Any questions?"

"Will I have any free time?"

He hadn't given that any thought. "I suppose so, when your work's done, but you'll need to be available to *Mutti*."

"Of course. But would you mind if I read when she's sleeping?" She glanced longingly at the books on his side table.

He loved to read, so he could understand her desire. "Not at all. Feel free to borrow any book in the house."

"Thank you." A smile lit her face, drawing attention to her round cheeks. He'd been so focused on the bruises marring them earlier that he hadn't noticed the matching set of dimples. "Did you have anything else for me? If not, I have a full day ahead of me tomorrow and would like to get some rest."

"That's all."

"Then good night, sir."

"You may call me James."

"I understand." She rose and headed straight to *Mutti*'s room with her head held high.

He stared at the closed door. Becky's show of independence surprised him. Having the spirited woman around could be interesting—and distracting.

* * *

Bacon sizzled in the skillet, and the invigorating scent of brewing coffee filled the kitchen. Becky sliced two thick slabs of bread for toasting.

A bedroom door opened promptly at five, and James appeared. "You're up early."

"Yes." She'd always been an early riser, but her internal clock must still be adjusting to California time, because she'd awakened at four. Not that she minded. She'd had time to read her Bible, pray and sneak some leftovers out to the dog. The friendly fellow had been waiting for her behind the cabin where she'd bathed him. "How do you like your eggs?"

"Over medium."

She set James's breakfast before him in short order. He dove into the meal, not even stopping to say a blessing, and finished it in silence while she began preparations for dinner.

The moment he set his fork down, she reached for his empty plate. "Would you like more?"

"I'm fine. Thanks." He stood and grabbed his hat. "Come with me, please. I want to show you how to do the milking before *Mutti* wakes."

"I'll be right there." She put the dirty dishes in the tub of soapy water to soak and met him at the door.

He waited with his hand on the latch and held out a cloak. "This was Kate's. You'll need it. The temperature fell overnight."

She was tempted to forgo the oversize woolen garment since it hadn't felt cold when she'd visited the dog earlier, but it wouldn't do to challenge James about something like this. She'd have to choose her battles wisely, because she was certain there would be some.

A short time later Becky sat on a small three-legged stool in the barn beside a large cow.

James stood behind her. "It's quite simple, really. Grasp the back teat from the two on the left and the front one from those on the right, clamp them between your thumbs and first fingers and squeeze down, alternating the pressure between the two."

The teats felt a lot different than she'd expected. Firmer and stiffer. She gave one of them a squeeze, but nothing happened. Adding a little pressure, she tried the other, but once again there was no stream of milk.

"Don't be so timid. Give them a good squeeze. You won't hurt her."

After three more unsuccessful attempts, she sighed. It couldn't be that hard, could it?

"Let me show you."

She stood.

"No. Stay there."

She sat. He reached around her and covered her hands with his own. A chill raced down her spine, and although she did her best not to, she shivered. She'd never been in a man's arms before, and yet here she was with James's brushing her sides and his breath warming her ear.

"Do it like this." He squeezed her hands—hard—sending streams of milk pinging against the sides of the metal pail. He kept at it for what felt like an eternity.

She leaned forward and forced herself to ignore him, which wasn't easy. When she could take no more of his closeness, she glanced at him. The uninjured side of his face was mere inches from hers.

My, but he was handsome. She swallowed in an attempt to moisten her throat, which had become as dry as stale bread. "You can move. I've got the idea."

He shot to his feet, took several steps backward and

leaned against the pen with his arms folded over his broad chest. "Let me see you do it, then."

His high-handed manner rankled. Taking the teats in her hands, she squeezed one and then the other, shooting milk into the pail. She kept at it and silently rejoiced as the amount of frothy white liquid grew. Just as she turned to smirk at him, the cow's tail smacked her across the face.

James chuckled. "You have to watch out for that. Buttercup likes to flick her tail when you least expect it. And be sure to keep your knees around the bucket, or she could kick it over."

She huffed. "You don't have to laugh at me. I'm doing my best."

He held up his hands in mock surrender. "Whoa! There's no need to get a polecat in your petticoats. It was funny. That's all."

"I doubt you'd be laughing if you'd just gotten a mouthful of tail."

"You're right, but I know to watch out for it."

She lifted her chin. "I'll learn."

"You can finish up and leave the pail outside the pen. I'll carry it in when I finish with the horses." He sauntered off toward their stalls with his shoulders shaking.

Fine. She'd show him. She would get the milking done quickly and beat him to the house.

She'd barely resumed the milking when James returned. He stood at the back end of the cow, but Buttercup didn't seem to care. She kept munching her breakfast. He patted her hindquarters. "There. She won't get you again."

He'd tied a piece of twine to the cow's tail and secured it to the top rung of the pen. His thoughtfulness touched her. "Thank you, sir."

"My name is James. You're free to use it."

"So you've said." Becky dipped her head to hide her smile. She shouldn't take pleasure in irritating him, but he could be so heavy-handed at times that she hadn't been able to resist.

Before long her back ached and her hands screamed for relief, but she kept on.

She'd been at the milking a good fifteen minutes when James's voice made her jump.

"Lean into her side. It helps."

She did as he suggested and felt the cow's bristly coat against her cheek.

To her dismay, he watched her work for a couple of minutes, and then he peered over her shoulder. "It looks like you're done, so I'll get that." She rose and eased her weary body out of the way. It was a good thing she didn't have to carry the milk, since her bruised ribs were aching.

"Let's go." He freed the cow's tail and hefted the pail.

She followed him out of the barn, took one look at the orchard and came to a standstill. The sun had crested the horizon, stretching its far-reaching fingers to caress each blossom. "I thought it was beautiful yesterday, but this…" She flung her arms wide. "It's breathtaking. Just look at all those trees with their loose petals floating in the air. It might seem silly, but I could see myself dancing in them." He was clearly not amused, so she shoved her fanciful musings aside. "How many trees are there?"

He stood at her side. "About thirteen hundred currently bearing fruit, and five hundred more that I've started in the past three years." Pride dripped from his every word. "I plan to add some more each year until I have all fifty acres planted."

"I love the soft colors of the flowers, but I noticed yesterday when I took a short walk that some of the trees don't have any blooms. Why is that?"

She tore her gaze from the apple trees and was rewarded with a sight sweeter than any fruit. The first rays of sunlight had illuminated James's face, revealing a smile so filled with warmth she could bask in it.

"Those with the white flowers are Rome Beauty and Esopus Spitzenburg, my late-season apples. The pink blooms are my Winesaps. The Jonathans and Baldwins already bloomed and will be ready for harvest earlier."

"When you're not so busy, I'd love for you to show me which is which. I want to learn all about the apples, the trees and how you take care of them."

His expression changed to one of wonder. Or was it disbelief? "You would?"

Disbelief, definitely. "I love apples and know very little about them. Other than how tasty they are and how to bake with them, that is."

"You're the first woman I've met besides *Mutti* who's shown an interest. Neither my sister nor my—my friend..." He glanced from Becky to the house and back. "You'll be busy with *Mutti*, but perhaps we could fit in a lesson now and then."

"Thank you. I'd like that."

He stared at her for several seconds, his face a study in conflicting emotions. Surprise. Curiosity. And was that admiration?

Color crept up his neck, and he shook himself. "I'm sorry. I didn't mean to stare at you like that. I should, um, get this inside." He took off in such a rush that he sloshed milk over the edge of the bucket.

She watched his retreating figure. James might be a bit brusque on occasion, but he had a softer side, too.

Perhaps in time she'd figure out how to get him to reveal it more often.

Not that she'd be here any longer than necessary. Thanks to Dillon, she'd have to change locations frequently to avoid having him find her.

Even so, she welcomed this opportunity to learn all she could about the apple trees. If she happened to enjoy the company of the intriguing man who cared for them, so be it.

Chapter Five

"Shh! If anyone catches us, I could get in trouble."

The copper-colored dog nuzzled Becky's side. She knelt and petted him. "I've spent way too much time out here, Spitz, but I'll be back this afternoon. I'm fixing steaks for dinner, so I'll have some nice bones for you." Since *Mutti* had only picked at her food the past week, there were sure to be some mashed potatoes and a biscuit or two, as well.

The unmistakable squeal of the barn door rollers brought the visit to an abrupt close. She'd have to send the dog away and get back to the garden plot quickly.

Footfalls coming around the corner of the empty cabin startled her. She froze. Her gaze came to rest on the toes of two dusty leather boots. Small boots. She looked up and heaved a sigh of relief. "Oh, Quon. It's you. I was afraid it was James."

She shot a glance at Spitz and back at Quon. "I know this handsome fellow's not supposed to be here, but I'll be going into town tomorrow. While I'm there, I'll ask around to see if I can find him a home. He's a nice dog and would make a fine pet."

"Yes. He nice dog. Look good." Quon dropped to one

knee and ran his hand over the dog's silky fur. "I put food in dish. He like to eat."

"You knew about him and have been feeding him, too? But what about James? If he finds out I've encouraged the dog to stick around..."

Quon scanned the area, looking everywhere but at Spitz. "I not see anything."

She was so grateful to the older man that she fought the urge to give him a daughterly hug. "Oh, Quon, I can't thank you enough, but I don't want you to get in trouble."

He smiled. "It no trouble, Miss Becky. You wait. Boss will let dog stay."

"I want to believe that, but when James makes up his mind about something, it's hard to change it." If she'd learned one thing the past week, it was that he had his way of doing things and didn't take kindly to anyone questioning him.

Quon rose. "You go to garden. I send dog off and come soon. Tomato plant here. We finish work."

Becky stood, too. "The plants are here? That's wonderful." She smiled. "You've taught me so much. I feel like a real gardener now."

"You good student." He tapped his head. "Smart. Learn fast."

"My brother always said I was slow."

"Brother not nice." Quon frowned. "He hurt you?"

Becky's hands went to her cheeks before she could stop them. The bruises were gone, but the pain in her ribs lingered. "He said hurtful things sometimes, but I'm sure all brothers do that. Doesn't Chung?"

Quon laughed, and his dark eyes twinkled. "Chung smart. He know big brother is boss. He not—how you say?—pick fight."

She did her best to shove aside the painful memories

of Dillon accusing her of setting fire to the factory where they'd both worked and striking her when she'd protested. "I'm glad you get along. It must be wonderful to have a brother who's your friend. I never had many friends."

"You have friend now." Quon jabbed a thumb at his chest. "I your friend."

When she'd left Chicago, she never would have imagined that she'd make friends with someone from a culture so different from hers, but Quon was right. He was her friend. The kindhearted man had even been keeping her secret. "Well, my friend, I'd better get back to the garden. I'll be waiting for you."

True to his word, Quon met her a few minutes later with the flat of tomato plants. Their neighbor Mr. Stratton had given them to James as a token of appreciation for his work repairing the broken water pipe. Becky and Quon spent the next hour getting the leafy plants in the ground.

She'd seen no sign of James since breakfast. The past week he'd spoken to her only when necessary. Considering the number of times she'd thought of him since that memorable morning milking the cow and admiring the trees afterward, his absence was probably a good thing.

Even though he'd been keeping his distance from her, he showed *Mutti* kindness, noting her needs and helping her without being asked, and that was what mattered. The tender kiss on the cheek he gave her each evening before she headed to bed showed how much he loved her.

Watching his mother's decline was hard on him. Just yesterday Becky had caught him blinking rapidly after he'd given *Mutti* her nightly buss.

If only he didn't feel the need to shoulder his burden alone, but he'd rebuffed Becky's offers of sympathy. She wanted to help ease his pain, but finding ways to do so would be a challenge.

She removed her work gloves and admired the large plot. "It will be a wonderful garden. I can't wait to see everything come up. Thanks again for all your help, Quon."

He grinned. "I only talk. You do all the work."

"It wasn't work. It was fun." She couldn't remember the last time she'd enjoyed herself that much. Quon had spent hours wielding a hoe as he taught her. He loved learning as much as she did and had encouraged her to tell him about her life back East. She did, reminiscing about her parents but saying little about her bully of a brother.

"I have more work. Must go. Goodbye." Quon pressed his palms together and bowed.

Becky returned the gesture and strolled back to the house. She opened the front door as quietly as she could so she wouldn't wake *Mutti*, but the kindly woman sat in her rocking chair, working on her embroidery.

"I didn't expect to see you up already. Did you have a good nap?"

"It was all right, but it's hard to get comfortable. I feel every lump and bump these days. It never used to be like that. William used to say I could sleep through anything. But enough of my complaints." She patted the seat of Kate's puffy purple chair. "Tell me about the garden. What did you plant today?"

Becky sat and filled *Mutti* in on the morning's activity, minus any mention of the dog.

"I'm not surprised you like Quon. He's a good man. He's definitely more outgoing than his brother. Chung tends to be more reserved, like you, but he's just as eager to please." *Mutti* laid her embroidery in her lap. "What does surprise me is how much my boy intimidates you. When James is around, you say very little."

"He doesn't intimidate me. I just don't know what to

make of him. Sometimes he— No, I shouldn't say any more. He's your son, and I know how much you love him."

"He's my son, yes, but he's not perfect. Go ahead. Tell me what you were going to say. Keeping the lid on a pot can cause it to boil over."

Becky twirled a piece of embroidery floss around her finger. "He can be thoughtful one moment but ignore me the next. Sometimes he even appears to be upset with me. I'm doing my best not to annoy him."

"You don't like him ignoring you, but it seems to me you're doing the same thing. If you'll give him a chance, you'll see he's not the ogre you seem to think he is. You'll try to get along with him, won't you? It hurts me to see you two at odds."

She would do almost anything for *Mutti*, but that was asking a great deal. James was the one making things difficult. If he weren't so gruff, Becky would welcome his company. In the meantime, she'd have to make an effort to be sociable—at least when *Mutti* was around.

James shoveled in the last bite of his cheesecake. If he had room, he would seriously consider having another slice. Becky turned out mighty tasty desserts.

She'd kept her focus on her plate ever since returning from helping *Mutti* to bed. He might as well be alone for all the conversation he was getting out of her.

Although she'd shuddered in his arms during the milking lesson, understandably repulsed by him, he was curious what filled her thoughts. "You've been awfully quiet."

"I'm not very ludicrous."

She rested her fork on her plate, smiling as though

pleased with herself for pronouncing the last word correctly.

Her disjointed reply took him aback. Although she hadn't intended it to be, her misuse of the word *was* amusing. "No, you're not very talkative. I'm not loquacious myself, but I wondered what you've been thinking."

She groaned in a most unladylike fashion and smacked a palm to her forehead. "*Loquacious.* Yes. That's what I meant." She lifted her head and actually looked at him for a change. With the bruises almost gone, the dusting of freckles on her round cheeks was more visible. "I was thinking about the trip here."

"You said that was your first train ride. Did you enjoy it?"

"Very much. I had no idea how big our country is. I saw mountains and valleys, plains and deserts." She laughed, a light, airy sound free of her earlier self-condemnation. "Why am I telling you? Since you drove trains, you know that."

"Drove trains? Where did you get that idea? I never did that."

Her forehead furrowed. "But Dr. Wright said in the telegram that you were a railroad engineer before you became a fruit grower."

James hid a smile behind his napkin. "I see. You thought I was a locomotive engineer. I was actually a civil engineer, helping build the railroad over the Sierras."

She nodded. "That makes sense. *Mutti* told me you went to college. It must have been wonderful to receive such a fine education. When I was six, Chicago's first high school opened. I dreamed of going to it one day. I applied every year—until my mother took ill and I began caring for her—but I wasn't one of the few students granted admission. Even so, I try to learn everything I can on my own." A faraway look in her eyes bespoke a yearning for what she'd been denied.

"That's commendable."

She reached for his empty dessert plate and set it on top of hers. "Why did you decide to become an engineer?"

"When I was young, Papa took me to Sacramento City. I got to meet Theodore Judah. He told me about his dream of building a railroad over the Sierras that would connect the country. I decided then and there that I wanted to work with him. When I finished school, my parents sent me to New York to attend the Rensselaer Polytechnic Institute where Judah had gone."

"Did you work with him?"

"Not for long. I graduated with my civil engineering degree in '62. I was only nineteen at the time, but I got a job with Charles Crocker's company, which was overseeing the construction. Work started the following January. Judah headed for Washington that fall to get backing so he could buy out the owners and do things his way, but he died on that trip."

He stared out the window at the deepening shadows, the heartache he'd felt upon hearing the news assailing him anew. He'd done his best to go on, but his enthusiasm had waned. And then came the accident that had shattered his dreams. "A part of me died, too."

Becky laid her hand on his. "I'm sorry."

He jerked his arm away. "I didn't mean to go on like that. I need to see to the animals."

"Yes, of course. I understand."

Her crestfallen look said otherwise, but he couldn't spend another minute with her probing into his past. Perhaps if he put enough distance between them, he could forget the pity he'd seen in her pretty blue eyes.

James took his time in the barn, grateful for the warmth of his overcoat. The temperature had dropped steadily all day. Not a good sign, since the trees were in bloom.

When he reached the house, Becky had already retired, as he'd hoped. With a long night ahead of him, sitting up and checking the thermometer mounted on the porch, the last thing he needed was to have her dredging up memories best left buried. He hung his overcoat in the lean-to, threw another log on the fire, settled into his armchair and reached for his well-worn copy of Dickens's *Great Expectations*.

Sometime later he was jolted awake by an insistent scratching at the door. He stood, the book in his lap falling to the floor, and stepped onto the porch where a dog sat, its breath creating a misty cloud that hung in the chilly air.

Panic seized James, squeezing so hard he couldn't breathe. He raced to the thermometer. The mercury had fallen even farther, hovering in the midthirties, far too close to freezing. If it went any lower, he could lose his entire crop.

He had to take action. Now.

A nudge to the shoulder woke Becky, and she opened her eyes to find a shadowy figure looming above her. A scream lodged in her throat.

"It's all right. It's me. James."

How dare he scare her out of her wits like that? She shoved his arm away, tugged the covers to her chin and whispered, making no attempt to keep the irritation out of her voice. "What are you doing in here?" Her fuzzy head cleared, and reality returned with full force. "Is *Mutti*—"

He leaned close and spoke beside her ear. "She's fine,

but I need your help. Meet me in the kitchen right away."
He slipped out.

Propelled by a mixture of fear and curiosity, she
dressed quickly and hastened to meet him. "What's
wrong?"

"It's a late frost. I've got Quon and Chung setting fires
under the trees to keep the buds from freezing. I know
your ribs haven't healed yet, but do you think you could
carry wood?"

"Yes."

"Good. You'd better wear this again." He shoved his
sister's cloak into Becky's arms. "I must warn you. It's
coldest just before dawn, so it will be a long night."

"I understand." She followed James to the orchard.
Quon and Chung had already set two rows of fires, which
glowed red beneath the apple trees.

All through the early morning hours they worked.
Thick smoke swirled around her, stinging her eyes and
burning her lungs as she trudged up and down the rows
along with the men. Her ribs ached, but she ignored the
pain and carried on.

James had said the entire apple crop could be lost if
the buds froze. She couldn't bear to see him face such a
loss when he was already dealing with his mother's impending death. He was a strong man, but if her efforts
could help spare him additional pain, she'd be grateful.

Just before dawn, she stumbled as she moved from one
fire to the next, her vision blurry and her legs leaden. She
returned to the wheelbarrow, ready to move on, when a
cry rang out.

"Stop, Becky! Your skirt!"

She blinked her gritty eyes, glanced at her dress and
shrieked.

Her skirt was on fire!

Chapter Six

Becky took off running. She had to get the fire out. Now.

"No, Becky! Stop!"

She froze. Where was the water bucket? If she could find it—

James grabbed her and gently lowered her to the ground. "Lie still. I'm going to roll you over."

She followed his instructions without question, too cold and numb to do anything else. He turned her over twice, stopped and stomped out the last of the flames.

"Oh, Becky." He plopped down beside her, pulled her into his lap and rocked her. She didn't have the strength to resist. Not that she wanted to. Having his strong arms around her helped calm her fears, although being cradled to his broad chest did nothing to slow her racing heart. "Are you all right? Did you get burned?"

"Yes. I mean, no. See?" She tugged her ruined dress and scorched petticoats to her knees, revealing stockings that were blackened but not burned. "I'll be fine. Just give me a minute."

She drew in a series of deep breaths. Smoke filled her lungs, setting her to coughing. Pain shot through her. She covered her mouth with one hand and clutched her aching midsection with the other.

"What have I done?" His voice came out raspy. "Your ribs haven't even healed yet. I should never have asked you to help."

She wanted to protest, but she couldn't speak. Thankfully the spasms subsided quickly.

"Here, boss. This help her." Quon held out a pail of water.

"Drink, Becky." James filled a tin cup and pressed it against her lips, sending the soothing liquid down her parched throat. She drank every drop.

"More?"

She nodded.

He dipped the cup into the pail again and brought it toward her, his hand shaking. She placed hers over his, drawing the cup to her mouth. "Thank you, James."

Sated, she left the comfort of his arms and stood.

"Where do you think you're going?"

"Back to work." As soon as she could get her wobbly legs to cooperate.

He jumped to his feet, restraining her with a firm grip on her arm. "Oh, no, you don't."

"But the trees. If we don't keep the fires going, you could lose your crop." She wouldn't let that happen. Couldn't let it. Somehow she must fight her fatigue and— She took a step, swayed and reached for him.

With no warning, he scooped her into his arms and set off for the house at a brisk pace. "Quon and Chung can see to things until I get back. I'm taking you inside. No arguments."

Bone-tired, she surrendered without a fight, resting her head against his shoulder. She closed her stinging eyes and succumbed to sleep's call.

A familiar voice filled with concern roused Becky. She blinked several times to bring *Mutti*'s face into focus. "The poor girl is very dirty. I will get a bath ready for her."

"She's too tired for that." James held her so close that his breath caused the loose hairs at her temples to flutter. "Just spread an old blanket on her bed, and I'll clean her up a bit."

Her eyelids slid shut. Sounds faded in and out, followed by some jostling. And then softness. The quilt he'd laid her on smelled of cedar. Something brushed her cheek, and she forced her eyes open.

He hovered over her, his face visible in the lantern light. He was a sorry sight, with ash and soot covering every inch of him. She must look just as bad, but he was right. She needed sleep. Lots and lots of it.

"Rest a minute. I'll be right back."

He returned shortly and placed a basin on the bureau by the lantern. Her mattress sagged as he sat beside her and removed Kate's oversize cloak. *Mutti* entered, carrying an armload of toweling. He inclined his head toward the bureau. "Put it right there, please. And then if you could rustle up a cup of tea, I'm sure she'd like that."

"*Ja.* I will." *Mutti* shuffled from the room.

James turned toward Becky with a smile on his face, his teeth stark white against his soot-covered skin.

"You look happy. Did we save the crop?"

"I think so, at least most of it." He plunged a washcloth into the steaming water, wrung it out and took one of her hands in his, holding it tenderly as he dabbed at the layers of grime. "You finally called me James."

Had she, in the midst of her fright, forgotten herself? "I did?"

"When you thanked me, yes." He grew serious. "I'm so sorry I put you in danger."

"I wanted to help. I just wish I could have done more."

"You did more than you realize. I'd accidentally dozed off and would have kept right on sleeping, but a dog woke me."

A chill raced over her, and she shivered. "A dog?"

"Not just any dog. A beautiful red Irish setter. In all my years I've only seen one other."

Red? Spitz must have returned. "About that. He's the dog we saw in Placerville. The poor thing followed *Mutti* and me here. I couldn't turn him away, so I cleaned him up. I've been feeding him. Just table scraps. Nothing else. I plan to find him a home. You don't have to worry. I'll take care of him."

"Oh, you'll take care of him, all right. He'll be your responsibility. You don't need to feed him behind the empty cabin, though. Just see that he doesn't bother the chickens."

She wasn't sure she'd heard him correctly in her fuzzy-headed state. "You knew?"

He rinsed out the cloth and lifted her other hand. His lips twitched, as though he were holding back laughter. If only he would let loose. He was far too serious for his own good. "I know *everything* that goes on at my place."

She shouldn't be surprised. He'd proven to be quite observant. "And you're not sore at me?"

"Your dog helped save my crop. So tell me. What do you call him?"

"Spitz."

James did laugh then, a rich sound that rumbled in his chest. "You adopted an Irish dog and gave him a German name? Why?"

"Whenever I send him off, he runs straight for your

Esopus Spitzenburg trees. I shortened the name, and it seemed to fit. After all, it means *pointedly* in German."

"You've got pluck, defying me the way you did." His voice, low and deep, held admiration, not the anger she'd expected.

He draped the soiled cloth over the side of the basin, wet a fresh one and set to work cleaning her face, each slow stroke of her cheek sending tingles from her head to her toes. No man had ever touched her like that. Not that he was actually touching her, but even so, the act seemed intimate and...romantic.

James O'Brien wasn't a rogue at all. He was a hero— her hero—having raced to her rescue once again.

He brushed the hair from her forehead with his fingertips and swiped her brow. "You don't have anything to say for yourself?"

"Hmm? Yes, I did defy you, didn't I? I had my reasons for doing so, and you must admit they were good ones."

"Huh! I'll admit no such thing." His playful tone belied his scowl. "This is my place, and I expect those who work for me to respect my wishes."

"Oh, but I do." She couldn't resist teasing him. "I respect your need to have a loyal watchdog who will see that no harm comes to you, your mother or your orchard."

He wiped the other side of her face, looking deep into her eyes as he worked, his own a warm brown with a hint of mischief. "For a tired woman, you have an impressive amount of spunk."

It had taken impending danger followed by relief to bring out a more lighthearted side of James. Now that she'd seen it, she was no longer afraid of him. Quite the contrary. She would do whatever it took to be there for him in his hour of need, as he'd been there for her.

Maybe they could become friends. Anything more

was out of the question since she'd have to leave town as soon as she'd earned enough to pay him back.

For some reason, the idea of never seeing him again didn't sit well.

James shifted the brown paper packages in his arms, crossed the porch and stood in the open doorway. His shoulders were sore after the half-mile trek home, balancing his unwieldy load. If he'd known when he'd left how much he was going to buy, he would have driven the wagon, but his plan hadn't taken shape until he'd spied the shelf full of fabrics in Mr. Harris's shop.

Mutti saw James first and chuckled. "*Ach, Sohn.* Did you leave anything for others?"

Becky wiped her flour-coated hands on her apron and rushed over. "Here. Let me help." She grabbed the parcel teetering on top of the stack, set the bulky package on the dining table and watched wide-eyed as he plopped the ones containing the foodstuffs she'd requested beside it. "I know my list was rather long, but this is more than I expected."

"I added a few things."

Her eyebrows and her voice rose. "You did?"

"You don't have to sound so skeptical. I've seen to the shopping for some time now. Why don't you take a look? Start with this one." He shoved the large parcel she'd rescued toward her.

She reached for the kitchen shears, snipped the twine and peeled back the brown paper. Tilting her head, she stared at the contents, saying nothing.

His chest tightened. He'd been sure she would like his choices. After all, he'd taken his time selecting the items, going so far as to seek the opinions of the female customers in the shop. Providing Becky with a new wardrobe was the least he could do after putting her in danger during the frost scare the week before.

Mutti shuffled over to the table and took her seat to the right of Becky.

At long last Becky nodded appreciatively and shifted her attention to *Mutti*. "How nice. James has gotten you some lovely new things."

Becky pulled out the straw bonnet one of the women had said was quite fashionable, followed by a pair of kid gloves, six pairs of stockings, brightly colored material for dresses and plain muslin for nightwear and undergarments—everything the customers had said a young woman would need.

Mutti patted Becky's arm. "My dear girl. He did not get them for me. They are for you."

"No. That can't be. He wouldn't…" She held the bonnet in one hand and fingered the dove-gray ribbon ties, a color the women had said would go well with the fabrics he'd chosen.

"*Mutti*'s right. They're yours."

Becky gave her head an emphatic shake, set the bonnet on the table and pushed the pile of items toward him. "No. You must take them back."

"Come with me, please." He took her by the elbow and led her onto the porch. "What's wrong? Don't you like them?"

"I can't accept a gift like that. It would be improper."

He had to make her understand because he wasn't about to have her wearing that dingy dress of hers any longer. She deserved better. "It's not a gift. Think of it as…your uniform. You've only got one dress since the other's burned, and it's unacceptable."

She bristled. "Unacceptable? What do you mean?"

He touched the sleeve of her faded black mourning

gown. "I know what lies ahead, and so does *Mutti*, but there's no need for her to be reminded at every turn. I realize you're mourning your father, but due to the circumstances, I thought you might be willing to break tradition. I got light colors that will make *Mutti* think of spring."

Becky's irritation evaporated. "That's a wonderful idea." She gave him one of her warmest smiles but quickly sobered. "While I appreciate your intentions, I still can't accept such a lavish display of generosity. If you insist on me having all of those lovely things, you'll have to add the cost to what I owe you for the train ticket."

Relief flooded through him. She liked what he'd picked out. "Agreed." At this rate, she'd be working for him a long time. Not that the idea bothered him as much as it should.

While Becky wasn't as worldly wise as someone like Sophie or his sister, Kate, she possessed common sense and a willingness to work. Even though she'd been in pain, she had trudged up and down the rows, adding wood to the fires without a single word of complaint. "If you still want to learn about the trees, I'll give you a tour later."

Glee shone from a pair of blue eyes as clear as an alpine lake. "Would you really? I mean—" she attempted to stifle her smile, but failed "—thank you, James. I'd like that."

Becky had a way of making him forget his sorrows, if only for a while. He recalled the playful banter they'd exchanged while he'd washed her face and hands after her dress caught fire and the way she'd looked at him, as though he were a whole person again. Perhaps keeping his distance wasn't as important as he'd first thought.

* * *

Diamond Springs was bustling the following Saturday.
Becky had looked forward to the trip all week. Although
the small town had far fewer businesses than Placerville,
she was eager to see what they carried.

She entered Mr. Harris's shop in the Lepetit building. The strong scents of tobacco, lye soap and coffee
beans greeted her.

The owner of the general store appeared. "Good morning. What can I do for you, miss?"

"I have a list of items I'd like." She handed him the
paper. "My employer, Mr. O'Brien, asked that the bill be
added to his account."

"Certainly. I'll fill the order and have it ready for you
in, say, fifteen minutes."

"Fine. I'll come back then."

She left, caught a glimpse of herself in the shop window and smiled. Nothing lifted her spirits like wearing a
pretty dress in a bright color after being clothed in black
for so long. The lavender lawn she'd completed the night
before looked lovely, as would the robin's-egg-blue calico
and sunny-yellow gingham James had chosen.

He'd been so kind and gentle when he'd carried her in
and cared for her after her skirts had caught fire. His
teasing, although unexpected, had been wonderful. And
then he'd gone out of his way to buy her an entire wardrobe. She'd never had three new dresses all at once in
her entire life. And six pairs of stockings? She felt like a
queen. Even though his gesture was motivated by guilt,
it was nice to think of him taking time to make such
thoughtful choices.

What wasn't nice was thinking about the expense.
At the rate her debt was mounting, she would still owe

him money even when her nursing skills were no longer needed.

She spent the next quarter hour exploring the shops. The shopkeepers welcomed her warmly, and passersby smiled as she strolled along the wooden walkways. As Jessie and Callie had said, coming to California had given her the opportunity to put the past behind her and create a new life where no one knew any more about her than what she chose to tell them.

"You there! Miss. Please wait." A tall woman wearing a tall hat darted across the street. She reached Becky, clutched the hitching post and caught her breath.

Becky's gaze was drawn upward. She tried not to stare, but the top hat covering much of the woman's wiry gray hair was ticking. An oversize black pocket watch had been affixed to the front. The white clock face was surrounded by a ring of twelve buttons bearing Roman numerals, one for each hour. A motley collection of hands, gears, springs and other things decorated the wide brim of the masculine-looking hat.

The woman patted the unique creation. "Ah, yes. I always forget what a novelty Big Ben is."

"It reminds me of the White Rabbit in *Alice's Adventures in Wonderland*."

The woman's eyes widened, and her mouth fell open. She snapped the latter shut with such force her teeth clicked.

Her words gushed out with great speed and rather unladylike volume. "You understand. I'm quite impressed. Most people have no idea why I decorated my hat this way. The few who have read Carroll's amazing tale usually think I was out to depict the Mad Hatter and not the harried hare. But enough of that."

She sliced the air with a wave of her hand and continued in a hushed tone filled with compassion. "What I wanted to know is if you're the one caring for my dear friend Mariela?"

"Yes. I'm her nurse."

"Very good. Very good, indeed. I was heartbroken to hear of her diagnosis and surprised to find out that reclusive son of hers sent for someone. I'm glad the boy finally came to his senses. Mariela's been doing too much, and I told him so. I suppose I can't blame him for being hesitant to admit the truth, but it must be faced. Her days are numbered, and she needs help. What a relief it is to see that she has it now. When did you arrive, Miss...?"

"Becky. Just Becky. I've been here a little over a week."

"It's a pleasure to meet you, Becky. I'm Lizzie Brown. *Miss* Lizzie Brown, that is, although most people hereabouts call me Betty, as in Bizarre Betty. You may call me whatever you'd like." The older woman's smile faded. "Dear me. I've gone and shocked you again, haven't I? Don't mind me. I mean no harm."

"Why would they call you that?"

The woman looked down her long nose at Becky. "Because I am a bit odd. Or, as I prefer to think of it—" she winked "—unique."

Becky understood how much it hurt to be called names. Dillon had been jealous of her close relationship with her father as far back as she could remember and had coined some cruel nicknames. *Papa's Pet* wasn't too bad, but the one that had cut her to the core was *Brainless Wonder*. Her brother knew how much she regretted not having a better education and used that against her. She shuddered at the memory. "That's terrible. I'm so sorry, Miss Brown."

"Lizzie, please. And don't be. I take it as a compliment. I wouldn't want to be deemed commonplace. How dreary that would be." She chuckled but quickly sobered. "Enough chitchat. I want to offer my services for those times you need a break. I was a nurse during the war and have worked with some of Dr. Wright's patients before. I'm spending most of my time down in El Dorado with a kindly old gent right now, who spent too many years crushing ore in a stamp mill and developed miner's asthma. I'm free every other Saturday, Sundays and the odd evening when one of his daughters sits with him."

"Sundays? I'd love to attend worship services." Becky had missed two already. "Of course, I wouldn't want to keep you from going."

"That's not a problem. I can go to church in El Dorado and get to the orchard before the minister travels to Diamond Springs for the service here. So I'll see you tomorrow, shall I?"

"I'll have to ask Mr. O'Brien. I don't know if he'd be willing to pay—"

"He doesn't have to." Lizzie clasped Becky's hands in hers. "It will be my gift to a treasured friend. I'd welcome the opportunity to spend time with Mariela."

"I'm sure she'd love to see you. I'll be returning in a few minutes, if you'd like to go with me."

Half an hour later, Becky parked the wagon in front of the house. James stepped out onto the porch, took one look at them and frowned. "Miss Brown," he said drily, "to what do we owe this…pleasure?"

The intriguing woman didn't seem to notice his rudeness. Either that or she chose to ignore it. She climbed from the wagon and faced James. "I made the acquaintance of this charming young lady in town today and have offered to sit with your mother when Becky goes to church. I'm here to pay Mariela a visit."

He folded his arms and narrowed his eyes. "You know what I think of you and your methods. I won't have you giving *Mutti* false hope by touting the curative powers of those oils you put such stock in."

Lizzie crossed her arms, too. "I'm a trained nurse, Mr. O'Brien, and am well aware what Mariela is facing. I wouldn't dream of misleading her, but I can—and I will—offer my friend a measure of comfort, provided she's amenable to the idea. Dr. Wright has seen the benefits of my treatments, so you'll get no argument from him."

James relaxed his stance. "I don't appreciate you patronizing me, but I did promise Becky some time to herself, so I'll allow it. However, if I hear about any shenanigans, I'll put an end to this arrangement faster than you can say *frankincense*."

Lizzie strolled over to where Becky sat on the driver's seat and spoke in an exaggerated whisper. "Don't let him fool you. He may have a hard shell, but there's a nice young man hiding inside. Let's hope having a sweet gal like you around will soften him up a bit." She sidestepped James and swept into the house.

He hefted the crate of groceries from the wagon bed. "Be careful of the company you keep, Becky. That woman has some strange notions."

She summoned her courage, which had an annoying tendency to falter when he glared at her the way he was now. "I like her. She's not afraid to say what she thinks."

His eyebrows shot toward his hairline. "You're mighty quick to come to her defense. Not that she needs defending. She has so much nerve she could lead a charge against an entire squad single-handedly and come out the victor."

"Is that respect I hear?"

"I respect my enemies all right. Doesn't mean I agree with them."

"What do you have against her?"

He shifted the crate, the tin cans inside clanking. "She puts far too much stock in those oils of hers. Just because they were used in Biblical times doesn't make them cure-alls. I prefer modern medicines."

"She said Dr. Wright approves of them, so I figure they're worth exploring. Since I'm *Mutti*'s nurse, that would be my call, wouldn't it?"

James's eyes glinted green, as they did whenever he was upset. "You've become quite presumptuous, haven't you?"

"If that means I'm willing to do whatever it takes to see that your mother's comfortable, I suppose I am a bit—" she slowed her speech in order to get her tongue around the unfamiliar word "—*presumptuous*."

"The definition is 'insolent or overbearing.' What it means is that you're overstepping your bounds."

Becky gripped the reins so hard her knuckles turned white. She'd feared James would interfere, but she hadn't expected it to happen so soon or for him to take issue with something so minor. "*Mutti* is my patient. It's my duty to do everything I can to help her."

He stared at her, a muscle in his uninjured cheek twitching. "We'll talk later, and I'm sure you'll see things my way." He spun around and marched inside.

What an unreasonable man! And to think that a little over a week ago he'd held her in his arms and tended her with such gentleness.

They certainly would talk, and he'd find out she wasn't as pliable as he seemed to think.

Chapter Seven

Sunlight streamed through the stained-glass window over the altar, splashing the walls of the small church with color. Becky sat in the back row, drinking in every word of the minister's sermon. He brought the verse from the Second Epistle to the Corinthians to life in a way that spoke to the broken places inside her.

"'Old things are passed away.' There's nothing in our pasts Christ can't overcome. If we've admitted our wrongdoings, we're forgiven. We can let go of what's gone before. '*All* things are become new.' Every one of us who has accepted His gift is a new creation.

"What troubles me, dear sisters and brothers, is that I see many laboring under loads He wants to lift. We cling to memories of past wrongs, condemning ourselves. As we close today, I invite you to live the new life He wants you to experience, one full of freedom, joy and abundant love. Shall we pray?"

She bowed her head and pondered the minister's words. Although she'd had nothing to do with the fire that had leveled the small clothing factory where she and Dillon had worked, she wasn't free. Instead of living a life of joy, she was forced to spend the rest of her days moving from town to town, being careful not to reveal too much about her past. If Dillon was to find her, she had no doubt he'd make her pay for her defying him—and for the blow to the head. She'd grabbed the coal scuttle, swung it around and hit him hard enough to knock him out, giving her time to escape.

But she wasn't in Chicago anymore. No one here knew about the blaze Dillon had started or that he'd insisted she lock up the factory that night in his place, thus throwing suspicion on her. Lashing out in anger was his way. When their boss had threatened to dismiss him for showing up to work drunk, her brother had vowed to make him pay. She'd overheard that conversation with his cronies and challenged him, deepening the resentment he harbored toward her.

As long as she didn't let anyone here get too close or learn too much about her, she would be safe. For a time, anyhow.

"May we pass, miss?" She'd been so lost in thought she hadn't realized the prayer was over.

"Forgive me. I'm leaving." Roused from her reverie, she joined those making their way to the rear of the sanctuary, where the kindly minister greeted each person as they filed out of the church.

He turned to her and smiled. "Ah, a new face. I'm Mr. Parks, and who might you be?"

"*Mr.* Parks? I thought you were the reverend."

"I am, but I don't use the title. I find it's easier to relate to others if I live as they do."

"That's different, but I like it. I'm Becky Martin." The familiar twinge of guilt returned at the use of her modified name. How would the Lord feel about her misleading a minister? "I'm working as Mrs. O'Brien's nurse."

Sorrow filled his eyes. "Dr. Wright told me the sad

news. I'm so sorry. Mariela's a beloved member of our little family. I'll make it a point to see her before I return to Placerville later today, provided that's not a problem, Miss Martin."

"Not at all. I'm sure she'd love to see you. In fact, if you want to come for dinner, there's plenty. And please, call me Becky as she and James do."

"Since you prefer that, I'll count it an honor to use your Christian name. Thank you for the invitation. I'll be along shortly."

Two hours later Becky gathered the last of the empty dessert plates. She couldn't remember a more pleasant mealtime. Mr. Parks was a wonderful storyteller and had kept them entertained.

The only sour spot was James. Normally, he appreciated her desserts, but instead of enjoying the lemon custard tart, he looked as if he'd chomped into the acidic fruit itself. He'd hardly said a word, speaking only when someone asked him a direct question. If she didn't know any better, she'd think he didn't like the friendly minister. But that made no sense. James was a God-fearing man who prayed before meals.

Mr. Parks laid his napkin on the table. "Thank you for the invitation, Becky. It's been nice visiting with all of you. I'm sorry I have to leave so soon, but it takes me a while to walk to Placerville."

"You walk all that way?" She couldn't imagine doing so. "It's over three miles, much of it uphill."

He smiled. "That's how the Lord traveled, and I figure if it was good enough for Him, it's good enough for me. Besides, I enjoy the opportunity for an extended prayer time." The auburn-haired minister rested a hand on *Mutti*'s shoulder. "I'll continue to lift you before the throne, Mariela. Do you have any special requests?"

Her gaze flitted to her son and back to Mr. Parks. "The usual one. And I would ask that, the good Lord willing, I have energy for a while longer. I do not like having to ask so much of Becky while she is still recovering."

"Very well. And now I'll bid you and your son a good day. Becky, would you be so kind as to see me off?"

She followed him outside, her curiosity mounting with each step. He eased it as soon as she'd closed the door.

"Your job as Mariela's nurse will be a demanding and ultimately heartbreaking one. It's important that you take care of yourself, too. Is there anyone who can spell you, or would you like me to make inquiries?"

"Miss Brown offered to sit with *Mutti* from time to time. That's who was with her while I was at church."

"Ah, yes. Lizzie. The woman has a heart of gold, but I think it's important you understand that James and she have some differences of opinion." Mr. Parks was certainly tactful.

"I found that out when she came to see *Mutti* yesterday. James and I talked afterward, and he made it clear he doesn't agree with Lizzie's methods, although I think they're worth exploring. He'd be the first to deny it, but I think what's really troubling him is watching *Mutti*'s decline and not being able to do anything about it."

He nodded. "I would agree. We men like to feel in control and fix things. When we can't, we feel helpless. I suggest you look for ways to include him in Mariela's care as often as possible. If he feels useful, that could make a difference. Now, I really should be going. Thank you again for the delicious dinner. Good day, Becky."

She bid the minister farewell and returned to the house with a heavy heart. Witnessing *Mutti*'s decline over the months ahead would be hard enough without battling James along the way. He had a surprise coming if he thought she would quietly surrender. Her former self, Rebecca Donnelly, might have cowered, but Becky Martin was stronger and wouldn't give in as easily.

The chickens rushed up to Becky, eager to devour the potato peels she tossed them. Two hens ran toward the same piece. The larger one scolded the smaller until she gave up and backed away. She ran toward one peel after another, each time being shoved aside by bigger, bolder birds.

Becky could relate. For much of her life, she'd been hesitant to stand up for herself. But not anymore. Just that morning she'd listened to Lizzie explain the properties of several oils used in Biblical times. If galbanum could bring *Mutti* relief, Becky would use the strong-smelling oil. If all went well, she'd prove to James that it had medicinal value.

"Here you go, girl." She dangled a brown curl over the little chicken's head. The hungry hen snatched it. "Let's see how many eggs you ladies have laid."

Mutti's energy had waned the past week, requiring her to accept assistance getting around, so Becky hurried through her task. Her search of the nests yielded a dozen eggs, enough to make a sponge cake. She would add strawberry jam between the layers. While this dessert wasn't as fancy as those she'd fixed the past few days, *Mutti* might enjoy it more because it wouldn't be as heavy. James would likely have a couple of pieces, leaving plenty for her to share with Quon and Chung.

Footfalls on the hard-packed earth drew her attention. The three men strode toward the barn and disappeared inside. Judging by their haste and James's barked orders, something was wrong. She rushed into the house and set the basket of eggs on the dining table.

Mutti stopped rocking and rested her embroidery in her lap. "I heard James hollering, but I couldn't make out what he said. What's going on?"

"I don't know, but I'm going to find out."

Becky crossed the yard, entered the barn and jumped back to keep from running into a wooden crate in her path, one of many. Quon and Chung were moving all the crates from a huge stack stored in the corner, and James was examining each of them inside and out.

"What are you looking for?"

He didn't stop his frenzied search. "Cocoons."

"Why? Are caterpillars a problem?"

"Tent caterpillars are, but they're the least of my concerns. I was putting wire mesh around the whips—the young trees—to protect them from critters, but I had to drop everything when Chung noticed a codling moth cocoon on a mature tree." He flipped the crate over to study the bottom. "That pest can spell the end of an orchard. I have to find out how it got here."

Mutti would be content to work on her embroidery for a while, freeing Becky. "I could help."

"You?" He shoved that crate aside. "No offense, Becky, but you wouldn't even know what to look for. The best thing you can do is to keep my mother from finding out what's going on. I don't want to worry her."

He reached for the next crate on the stack, but she held on to it, forcing him to look at her. "It's too late for that. She heard you hollering. If you'll tell me what I can do—"

"It's not your problem, so let me do my job, and you do yours."

"Fine." She left him to his frenzied search. James might be college educated, but he hadn't taken time to think things through.

She returned to the house, determined to hide her concern, but she failed miserably.

Mutti's rocking chair creaked to a stop, and her embroidery hoop fell in her lap. "It's bad, isn't it?"

"I'm not sure yet. He's worried about a moth of some kind damaging the trees, but instead of looking at them, he's tearing through a mountain of packing crates."

"Codling moths?" The panic in *Mutti*'s voice told Becky all she needed to know about the seriousness of the situation. She wasn't about to alarm *Mutti*, but she wouldn't hide the truth from her, either. "I believe that's what he said, but he didn't say he'd actually found any. If you don't mind keeping an eye on dinner, I want to do some research so I understand the situation better."

"Certainly." *Mutti* shuffled to the kitchen and peeked inside the pot of soup simmering on the stove.

Becky sat in James's wing-back armchair and inhaled the fresh, clean scent of his Pear's shaving soap that clung to the fabric. She rummaged through the pile of books on the side table and located the one on apple growing—*American Pomology*. The next ten minutes flew by as she learned everything she could about the apple orchardist's most feared pest and how to battle it. A plan took shape.

With paper and pencil in hand, she questioned *Mutti*, who had returned to her rocker. "Could you tell me the names of the other apple growers in the area and where their orchards are?"

"Certainly, but why?"

"I want to pay them a visit and see if any of them are dealing with this moth."

Mutti ceased her stirring. "I don't think James would like you getting involved in this."

"He won't, but I believe I can help."

"So you're going to defy him, are you? Well, if you're brave enough to take on my son, I won't stop you."

Armed with her list, Becky spent the next two hours visiting the owners of the apple orchards bordering the O'Briens' place. She stood on the porch of a small cottage in desperate need of repair, the last place on her list, and knocked. She'd all but given up hope of solving the mystery of the moth when a spindly gentleman leaning on a cane opened the door.

The stoop-shouldered man blinked his rheumy eyes and smiled, revealing several missing teeth. "It ain't every day a purty young thing like you shows up on my stoop. What can I do for you, missy?"

"I work for Mr. O'Brien. He's found a codling moth cocoon on his property, and I wanted to alert you."

"Codlin' moth, you say? Them's terrible things. Can ruin a man's crop."

"So I've heard. I wondered if you've seen any cocoons on your trees."

He scratched his head, causing his long white hair to stick out every which way. "Cain't say as I have, but then I ain't been able to get around so good lately. My grandson was lookin' after things, but he met a gal and hightailed it outta here just afore the harvest last year. Hated to lose the fruit, but I weren't about to hire a crew. With my measly five acres, it wouldn't pay."

"Are you saying your apples fell to the ground?"

"Reckon they did."

A mix of excitement and dread filled her. "May I take a look?"

He flung an arm in the direction of his orchard. "Help yourself."

It took a mere ten minutes to confirm her suspicions, less than five to secure the proof she needed and only one to decide her next course of action. James would snarl a bit, but once he calmed down, he'd come around. At least she hoped he would.

Chapter Eight

"You left *Mutti* alone and went traipsing through the neighborhood after I told you to let me handle this?" James hadn't intended to speak so sharply, but Becky seemed bent on disregarding his wishes.

Mutti glanced over the back of her rocking chair. "It is fine, *Sohn*. I was happy to help."

"That may be, but I made it clear I wanted her to stay out of this." He leaned against the kitchen counter with his arms folded and shifted his attention to Becky. "What were you thinking?"

She grabbed a handful of silverware and began setting the table. "There's no need to snap. I was doing you a favor. While you were busy inspecting your packing crates, I found out where the codling moth is coming from."

"Am I to understand that you, who have no education or experience in apple growing, figured that out by yourself?"

She set the last soupspoon on the table, spun to face him and spoke with the exaggerated patience of a schoolmarm explaining something to a slow-witted student. It took every ounce of restraint he possessed not to interrupt.

"The moth found its way to Mr. Oldham's property. His health is failing, and he hasn't been able to care for his orchard. His last crop was left to rot. He hasn't removed the bark on the trunks of his trees for three years, so there are cocoons on them."

"How do you know? You've never seen a codling moth or its cocoon."

"Yes, I have. I'll show you." She stepped onto the porch, came back inside and placed a Mason jar in his hands. "See?"

He held up the clear canning jar and stared at the three cocoons inside. Despite the warm spring day, he shuddered. "It can't be. How could Mr. Oldham let things go like that? He's endangered every orchard in the area. Something has to be done about this—and fast."

"I might not be well educated like you, James, but I do know how to read." Becky inclined her head toward his pomology book, which lay facedown on the end of the table. "It didn't take long to learn what a serious problem you're facing, but you needn't worry. Everything's under control."

"What do you mean?"

The smile she shot him was filled with such sweetness his teeth hurt. It would be easier to justify his anger if she weren't being so reasonable. "As soon as I showed the neighboring orchardists the jar, they agreed with my plan to meet at Mr. Oldham's place this afternoon to inspect his trees, destroy any cocoons they find and burn the remains of his crop."

"*Your* plan?"

"Yes, mine, and they think it's a good one." She opened the oven, filling the room with the mouthwatering smell of freshly baked bread, but his appetite had long since fled. She tossed her next comment over her shoulder. "By the way, they're expecting you to join them."

He worked to keep his tone level. "You said I'd be there without checking with me?" He could imagine what his neighbors must think of him, sending a woman to solve the problem instead of seeing to things himself.

But he hadn't sent her. Becky had gone without consulting him. "You should have come to me first."

"I did, but you told me to go away. I figured you wouldn't want me bothering you again."

He couldn't argue with her on that.

She turned the loaf out on a platter and set it on the table to cool. "The way I see it, if the source of the codling moth isn't dealt with, the threat would still be there, and you would have to inspect your trees over and over again. Wouldn't you?"

He gave a halfhearted shrug. "I suppose you've got a point." A good one, as much as it galled him to admit it. "But that didn't give you the right to take matters into your own hands."

"*Ach, Sohn.* Do not be so...so..." *Mutti* grimaced. "I forget. What do you say when someone will only do things his way and is like a mule?"

Becky chuckled. "Stubborn?"

"*Ja.* That is it. Do not be so stubborn, James."

"I'm not."

Mutti tottered toward him, grasping the furniture to steady herself. "I do not like it when you two fight. I will be in my room until dinner is ready."

He caught a whiff of something that made his stomach churn. "Wait a minute."

Mutti stopped and clutched the edge of the dining table.

"What's that grassy smell?"

Becky froze with the butter dish in her hands and a challenge in her eyes. "It's galbanum. Lizzie left it for us."

"One of those oils? You used it even though you know what I think?"

"*Mutti* was experiencing some pain when she woke this morning, and the oil relieved it. Isn't that good news?"

It wasn't good news at all. His mother wasn't supposed to be in pain, and she certainly wasn't supposed to have cancer. Codling moths he could fight—and he would— but there wasn't a thing he could do about the detestable disease that had attacked his mother.

He rushed to *Mutti*'s aid. "Here. Let me help you." He wrapped an arm around her waist, escorted her to her room and returned to do battle with Becky.

She bustled about, seemingly oblivious of him. He waited, but she said nothing. No explanations. No apologies.

Silence hung in the air, and he could take no more of it. In three strides he crossed the room and stepped into her path. "Why didn't you tell me she was in pain?"

"Because she asked me not to. You've got so much to deal with, and she doesn't want to add to your burden. Besides, the pain isn't too intense yet."

"She's not a burden. She's my mother." He dropped onto the bench, propped his elbows on the dining table and leaned his scarred cheek into his upturned palm.

"I'm sorry, James." She rested a hand on his shoulder, her soft touch surprisingly reassuring. "I know it's hard, but she's strong and very brave. I'm doing what I can for her, but I could use your help."

How could Becky show him such kindness when he'd snapped at her? "I apologize for my outburst. I—I don't know what came over me." He swallowed the apple-sized lump in his throat. "It kills me to think of her hurting. The hardest part is knowing it's going to get worse."

She pulled her hand away, and he missed the warmth that had flowed from her into him, chasing away the icy fingers of dread. "We'll do everything we can to ease her pain. If that means using some of Lizzie's oils, then I will. I know you don't approve and doubt the oil's ef… effi…" She made the cutest face and groaned with frustration. "I can't remember the word. It's like *effectiveness*, but better, fancier."

He found her desire to use highfalutin words endearing. "*Efficacy*?"

"Yes. That's it." She rewarded him with a warm smile. "The thing is, it doesn't really matter whether or not the oil actually works. What matters is that *Mutti* thinks it does. And the galbanum really seems to have eased her pain, so I'm willing to deal with the odor and hope you can, too."

He stood. "Well, I suppose I could. But for the record, I still don't like it."

"There." She gave a brisk nod. "I knew you were a reasonable man. You're also talented. Could you fashion a cane for *Mutti*? I'm sure you've noticed how unsteady she's gotten."

At last. Something he could do for his mother. "A cane? Certainly. I'll start on it right away."

"After you help do away with the codling moths, right?"

"After we've *eradicated* them, yes." His use of the more specific term earned him another smile. With her rosy cheeks and shining eyes, Becky was a far sight prettier than when she'd arrived. Why hadn't he noticed before? "You know, I may have misjudged you. You're more capable than you appear."

"And I misjudged you. You snarl at times, but you know when to back down." She sent him a saucy smirk that told him all was forgiven. "Dinner will be ready in ten minutes. Since you have a busy afternoon ahead of you, I suggest you show up on time."

"Yes, ma'am." He saluted, executed an about-face and headed for the barn with his step and his heart lighter than they'd been in weeks.

Becky had outsmarted him. He'd been so shocked to find a codling moth cocoon in his orchard he hadn't stopped to think about the possibility that it could have come from someplace else. Instead of listening to her, he'd spent the better part of three hours inspecting every crate and packing barrel on the place to see if the pest had wintered in them. He had her to thank for discovering the source of the pest—and he would. But how?

A contented sigh slipped from Becky. Helping James protect the orchard from a possible codling moth infestation had eased some of the tension between them. He'd begun teaching her about the trees and all that went into caring for them.

She watched with fascination as he started the steam engine to test his irrigation system. The clicking and hissing reminded her of the train that had carried her to the West. His fellow orchardists relied on gravity to get the water to flow in open furrows, but not James. He'd used his engineering skills to design something more complicated—and clever. His innovations never ceased to amaze her.

He stooped and twisted a handle, sending water flowing through the system of copper pipes that stretched down the rows in the orchard. He'd drilled a series of small holes in the pipes, from which water burbled at the base of each tree.

A satisfied smile crinkled his scar. She rarely noticed the discoloration anymore, but he'd rubbed the spot on the right side of his face several times while he worked—until she'd realized he was self-conscious about it and had moved to look over his left shoulder. He needn't have worried. When she looked at him, all she saw was a ruggedly handsome man.

James stood and dusted off his hands. "This pump produces some serious pressure, so if you ever tend to this chore, be sure you only give the spigot a quarter turn. Chung gave it four full turns the first time he tried it, and water shot so high it looked like it was raining."

"I'll remember that." She followed him to the end of the row, where water had soaked the soil at the base of every tree.

"Looks like the system's in good shape, so I can shut the pump down."

She glanced toward the backyard, visible in the distance, and heaved a sigh of relief.

"Is everything all right?" He headed toward the pump.

"It's fine. I was just checking to see if *Mutti* needs me. She agreed to hang her red tablecloth on the line if she does. Having a signal will allow me to work outside without worrying. It's not there, so I'm free to spend some more time outdoors, which is nice. It's such a glorious spring day."

"That it is, but it won't be long before we see our last storm of the season and I have to start irrigating. It's rare to get any rain from now until late September."

"It stops raining in mid-May? No wonder you have to water the trees."

"We might get another storm or two, but I wouldn't

count on it." He rubbed his cheek again, caught her looking at him and pursed his lips.

"I'm sorry. I didn't mean to—"

"Stare?" He gave a dry laugh. "I'm used to it. People do it all the time."

"You misunderstand. The only reason I took notice is that you keep touching your face. That reminds me of something Lizzie said. She has an oil that's supposed to help reduce...well, scarring."

"She's got an oil for everything, doesn't she? You and *Mutti* may believe in their supposed curative powers, but I don't." His hands hanging at his sides formed fists. "There's nothing that can be done for me."

Becky ached to put his mind at ease, but short of telling him she found him so attractive that he'd become a distraction, albeit a delightful one, she couldn't come up with a suitable response.

They reached the pump, where he cranked the handle closed with such force she was afraid he might have damaged it. He straightened. "Why don't you just ask how I got it? It's obvious you want to know."

"I do, but it would be rude to pry."

His foot tapping, he pierced her with a penetrating gaze. "I don't have all day, so go ahead and spit it out."

She extended her lower lip and exhaled, causing the tendrils around her face to flutter. "Fine. If you insist. How did it happen?"

"It's a short story. There was an accident while I was working on the railroad. Some nitro exploded before it was supposed to. I was hit with—" he winced "—shrapnel. It left a scar. The end. Are you happy now?"

His sarcasm bit, but she saw it for what it was—an attempt to avoid reliving the pain of what had to have been a horrific experience. As much as she longed to sympathize, he'd rebuffed her previous attempts. Sticking to facts would be more prudent. "*Mutti* said you returned to the orchard and have been here ever since. Do you miss the work?"

He rested a hand on the pump and stared at the hills to the east. "At times. I enjoyed the challenges, but I've got plenty to keep me busy here." He grabbed the wrench he'd used to tighten a loose fitting. "You've seen how I irrigate the orchard. I've got other chores waiting, so that's the end of today's lesson."

And clearly the end of their discussion. Since neither James nor *Mutti* was likely to say any more about the accident, she'd have to satisfy her curiosity some other way.

She fell in step beside him as he headed toward the barn. They'd just cleared the trees when she spotted a large red cloth draped over the clothesline.

"*Mutti!*" She took off running with James on her heels.

Chapter Nine

Dr. Wright set his black leather bag on the kitchen table. "I'm sorry, James. I know it's difficult."

Becky reached across the dining table and squeezed James's hand, an impulsive gesture she immediately regretted. Before she could pull it away, he squeezed back. His unexpected response warmed her clear through.

He cast a glance at the bedroom where *Mutti* napped. "I knew the time would come when she'd require morphine, but I'd hoped it wouldn't be so soon."

The episode the day before was the worst so far. When Becky had seen the red tablecloth flapping in the breeze, a wave of guilt had washed over her. While she'd been enjoying her time outside, *Mutti* had been inside battling pain so intense it had wrung tears from her eyes. Strong though she was, she was no match for the cancer relentlessly pursuing her. Becky despised few things, but cancer was one of them.

Dr. Wright pulled a syringe and an orange from his black leather bag. "I'll teach both of you to give the injections."

The color drained from James's face. "You said it's

going to be one in the morning and another at night. Becky can see to that."

Dr. Wright nodded. "True. But later on the amount of morphine I've prescribed won't be adequate. As the tumors grow, there can be times when the pain will spike, as it did yesterday. She'll need more of the drug then, and I recommend that either of you could administer it."

Half an hour later Dr. Wright prepared to leave. "You both did well. I know it's hard to undertake such a task, but you'll be relieved to have a way to ease her pain."

Becky saw the kindly doctor out. Compassion shone in his eyes. "Your job is challenging, Miss Martin. Not only are you overseeing Mariela's care, but you're also the person on whom James is forced to rely. I don't envy you the task."

His consideration touched her. "Thank you, Doctor. And please, call me Becky. I prefer it."

He hesitated, looking from her to the open doorway and back.

"Was there something else?"

He stood so close she could smell his lime-scented shaving soap. "I feel partially responsible for putting you in this situation. I hope my haste in sending the telegram hasn't caused you undue difficulties. I had no idea James would change his mind the way he did. I trust all is well."

She took a step back. "It's fine. Everything has worked out for the best."

"I'm glad to hear that. I just wish I could make things easier for you—for everyone." He gazed into her eyes for several seconds, started as though he'd realized he was staring and resumed his professional manner. "If you need anything, please don't hesitate to let me know. I can't always make it over from Placerville right away, but I'll come as soon as I'm able. Good day…Becky." He doffed his hat, climbed aboard his buggy and was off.

Her duties called, so she didn't have time to ponder the surprising interaction with the courteous doctor. She returned to find James staring at the bottle of morphine and syringe. The fear in his eyes was understandable. The thought of giving *Mutti* an injection left Becky feeling weak-kneed. But she would do what was necessary, just as he would. She'd do her best to spare him that ordeal, though.

He held the objectionable items out to her. "Here. Put them away. Please."

She slipped the bottle in her pocket and placed the syringe in a pan of water heating on the stove. Dr. Wright had heard from Lizzie that horsehair sutures, which were boiled to soften them, had led to fewer infections among soldiers during the war than silk ones, which were not boiled. He'd since become a firm believer in sterilizing his equipment and had seen a reduction in the number of infections. Since an infection could be deadly, Becky would follow suit.

James sat in his customary spot on the bench, wordlessly watching her while she spread the fabric for the last of her three new dresses on the far end of the kitchen table. She had just enough time to cut out the dress before she needed to start dinner.

"Thank you again for everything you got me. I know I might have seemed ungracious, but I really am grateful. I love my new dresses." She swept a hand over the sunny yellow-and-white-checked gingham she'd completed the week before.

He shook his head as though clearing it. "Hmm? Oh, yes. I'm glad you like what I chose."

A full five minutes passed before he spoke again. "Why did your brother hit you?"

Her jaw dropped, and the straight pins she'd held between her lips fell to the table. "Wh-what?"

"You said he was grieving and had been drinking, but something must have triggered his actions."

Busying herself retrieving the pins, she avoided his gaze. She opened the tin and put them inside. It was so quiet as James awaited her response that one really could hear a pin drop.

Memories of that horrid evening rushed in. Her brother had grabbed her by the wrist with the intention of dragging her to the police station, where she was to admit to having been the last one in the factory before the fire started, spreading from the storeroom in minutes and consuming the entire building in a short time.

She *had* locked up, but Dillon had gone back a short time later and set the fire, a fact the drunken fool admitted when he'd arrived home afterward. When she'd refused to take the blame as he'd ordered her to do, he'd panicked and grabbed her.

Because his coordination had been off, she'd been able to slip out of his grasp. He'd still managed to get in two stinging blows and shove her into the sideboard before she'd knocked him out. She'd gathered her meager possessions and raced to the church. Reverend and Mrs. Hastings had offered her refuge, bless them.

Now she was here in Diamond Springs on a secluded apple orchard. Safe. Or so she hoped.

She debated how much to tell James and decided being as honest as possible was her best choice. "Dillon set fire to the factory where we both worked. He intended to frame me for it, but I got away before he could do anything."

James scowled. "Oh, he did something, all right. He struck you, his own sister. If I ever see him…"

"You don't have to worry about that. I didn't tell him where I was going, so there's no way he could find me here." She'd remembered to give Becky Martin as her name when she'd bought her ticket rather than Rebecca Donnelly, which is what everyone back East had used.

"That's a good thing, because if he were to show his face, I would have a hard time being civil. I can't abide a man who would lay a hand on a lovely young woman like you."

"Glory be, James! That's the nicest thing you've ever said to me. If you keep that up, I'll have to revise my opinion of you." She chuckled.

Her attempt to lighten the mood had no effect. He was as stony-faced as before.

"I'm not as bad a sort as you seem to think I am, Becky. Once upon a time I was a decent fellow. At least some thought so."

She plopped herself on the bench across from him and gazed into his eyes, hoping he could see earnestness in hers. "I know we've clashed at times, but you're a fine man, James—a real-life hero."

He shook his head.

"Oh, but you are. I asked Quon and Chung about the accident, since you didn't say much. You forgot to mention the part about saving their lives that day. If it weren't for you, they wouldn't be here. They said you saw the man carrying the nitroglycerine slip, realized the danger you would be in if he fell and jumped in front of them before the blast, shielding them from the debris. That makes you a hero in my book." He'd also come to her rescue. Twice. The day she'd arrived and rushed after the dog, and the night her dress had caught fire.

He slammed a fist on the table, causing her to jump. "You're wrong! A man died that day. A good man." Memories of that horrific day pinched his features. "I tried to reach him in time, but I failed."

Becky longed to lift the burden of guilt he'd shouldered. "That's not true. You did your best. There's nothing more a person can do."

"I don't appreciate flattery."

"I'm just stating the obvious. I know you don't believe it, but I'll pray that you will…in time."

He got to his feet. "Pray all you want, but it won't change a thing. The facts stand." He left the house without another word.

Becky grabbed a pair of tongs and took the syringe out of the boiling water. Thanks to Dr. Wright, she had a way to help relieve *Mutti*'s pain.

If only she could figure out how to help James deal with his.

Lizzie breezed through the front door and joined Becky in the kitchen. "James is back on schedule, so we can proceed as planned. Mariela will be quite surprised."

"I hope so." Becky added the final swirl to the frosting. *Mutti* wouldn't be able to eat much, if any, of the cake, but a birthday wasn't complete without one.

"How long did he say it would take him to do his part?" Lizzie dipped into the bowl of frosting and licked the pilfered treat from her finger.

"He asked me to keep her occupied for half an hour."

Lizzie grimaced. "That's a long time to have her out in this heat, but it can't be helped. It could be worse. I've seen it reach one hundred by Independence Day in years past."

Becky didn't want to think about temperatures that

high. The low nineties they'd been experiencing the past
month were bad enough. She'd taken to wearing a single petticoat to keep from sweltering. At least she didn't
have to deal with the humidity as she had in Chicago.
"It's cooler under the trees, and I'll take plenty of water
so I can dab her face as needed."

"I'll let him know we're ready for him to unload the
wheelchair." Lizzie marched toward the barn, a woman
on a mission. Becky smiled. Her new friend put her all
into everything she did.

Minutes later *Mutti* leaned on Becky and made her
way to the front porch. James pushed the wheelchair up
the ramp he'd created by laying planks over the stairs.
"Are you ready to take a ride, *Mutti*?"

She stared at the chair for several moments. When she
finally spoke, her voice shook. "I cannot believe it has
come to this already."

Lizzie supported *Mutti*'s other side. "It's a wonderful chair, Mariela, and will enable Becky to take you
outdoors whenever you'd like. Come. We'll take you for
your first ride."

With Lizzie's help, *Mutti* was soon seated in the wicker
chair, her feet propped on the wooden footrest. Becky
grasped the wheelchair's high back and headed down the
ramp. The small third wheel behind the two large ones
flanking the seat made steering the chair easy.

James planted a kiss on *Mutti*'s cheek. "Have a nice
time."

"You are not coming, *Sohn*?"

"Not today. I'll let you lovely ladies enjoy your walk,
but I'll be here when you get back. We have a birthday
to celebrate, and I want a big slice of that chocolate cake
I've been smelling."

Afraid she would return before James had completed

his preparations, Becky inclined her head toward the apple-shaped dinner bell that hung over the porch railing. "You could always grab the striker and ring that to let us know if you miss us too much."

He nodded knowingly. "I'll do that."

Becky and Lizzie took turns pushing *Mutti* into the orchard as far from the house as they could get. *Mutti* bore the trip bravely, but it was evident the exertion had tired her. Becky wouldn't have planned such a lengthy outing if they hadn't needed to keep *Mutti* away from the house in order to give James time to complete his work, but the trek would be worth it.

"This has been nice," *Mutti* said, "but I would like to go back."

Before Becky could think of a stalling tactic, the dinner bell clanged. She lifted a silent prayer of thanks. "Certainly."

When they neared the house, she suppressed her excitement. "Close your eyes, *Mutti*, and don't open them until I say. We have something special to show you."

She obliged, and Becky dashed off to find James. She found him in the barn putting away his tools. "We're back. Come on."

He followed her to the front of the house, where Lizzie had parked *Mutti*'s chair. "All right, *Mutti*. You can open them."

She took one look at the house, smiled and launched into German, something she rarely did when nonspeakers were present.

Becky translated. "She said the window boxes with the geraniums are very pretty and are just like the ones on her house when she was a child."

Lizzie rested a hand on *Mutti*'s shoulder. "James has been planning this surprise for weeks. This is the real reason he made the trip to Sacramento City last week. He wanted to pick out the flowers himself."

Mutti gazed up at James, tears glistening in her eyes. "*Sohn*, you could not have given me anything I like more. They are—" she gestured toward the window boxes that hung at every window, green like the shutters and brimming with bright red geraniums "—*wunderbar*."

He squatted and grasped the arm of her wheelchair. "I can't take the credit. It was Becky's idea. I made the boxes, but she painted them. She suggested I get the chair while I was down the hill so you wouldn't know we were up to something."

His kindness in mentioning the small part she'd played sent a wave of gratitude surging through Becky. She shot him a smile.

He returned it. "We make a good team."

While she'd never thought of them as a team, she liked the idea. Her opinion of James had grown steadily over the past three months. He worked from sunup until sundown caring for the orchard, but he would do anything for *Mutti*, no matter what time of day or night a need arose.

He'd gone beyond taking Becky's suggestions and had found other ways to help his mother, putting his many skills to work. He'd added a wider base on *Mutti*'s cane so it offered more stability and had built a footstool to help her get in and out of bed.

But the most amazing thing he'd done was design a system to heat the bedrooms come fall so *Mutti* would be warm day and night. The hot air currents in the chimney would spin fan blades, which would turn a pump and force heated water down copper pipes he'd installed beneath the floorboards. The water would cycle back to be reheated, ensuring that the rooms would be warm as long as there was a fire in the fireplace.

Mutti smiled. "It makes me happy to see that you two are friends now. It is much better to get along, is it not?"

Becky agreed, but she hoped she and James could become even closer friends. He'd hidden behind a wall of bitterness far too long. She was determined to discover what had caused him to retreat. One day she would, and when that happened, she'd do everything she could to help him heal. In the meantime, she would treasure the rare moments when he dropped his guard and gave her glimpses of the man he used to be and, Lord willing, would be again.

Before Becky knew it, fall had arrived with its frenzy of activity. The harvest was under way. Extra workers filled the orchard, busy with their various tasks.

James supervised, but he also worked alongside the pickers, climbing up and down the tall A-shaped ladders. When the canvas pouches the pickers slung over their shoulders were full, they lugged them to the waiting wagons, where they unhooked the bottoms and allowed the ripened fruit to gently roll into the crates.

As often as she could, Becky slipped outside to watch the pickers working in the distance. She'd just hung the last of the laundry when a wagon with a load of apples rumbled up to the sorting station beside the barn. The sweet scents of Jonathans and Baldwins filled the air.

The workers lugged crates from the wagon to the makeshift tables, where the sorters waited. Blows of hammers hitting nails rang out as Quan and Chung, who were in charge of packing the apples, sealed another barrel of the marketable fruit.

Her chore complete, she headed inside to check on her patient. The disease had taken a toll on *Mutti*. Now bedridden, she weighed very little and was as fragile as an apple blossom. Although Becky was no stranger to nursing, she blinked back tears at the thought of losing this precious woman who'd become a second mother to her.

She peeked into their bedroom. "Oh, you're awake."

Mutti patted the mattress beside her. "Come. We must talk. I don't have much time left, and there are some things I have to say."

Becky sat. "Hush now. There's no need for that."

"Please. Listen. I need you to promise me something. Will you do that?"

She nodded. "If it's something I can do, yes, of course."

"I knew the moment I met you that you were just what we needed. James couldn't see it, but he will, in time. I know he can be difficult, but he's like an apple tree. The strong bark protects the heartwood inside."

Mutti grasped Becky's hands and held them more tightly than she would have imagined possible for one so weak. She drew in a raspy breath and continued, intensity unlike any she'd ever shown before lighting her eyes. "My dear boy has done his best to shut out the world. I fear that once I'm gone, he'll close up entirely. You mustn't let that happen. Promise me you'll stay until the trees bloom again and will check on him."

There was no way she could turn down *Mutti*'s plea, not when she, too, longed to help James escape the prison of his past. He would have no need of her once his mother was gone, but she would still owe him money, giving her a valid reason to remain in Diamond Springs a few more months. "I'm not sure I'll be here then, but I'll stay as long as I can."

All she had to do was figure out how to support herself once her present job ended.

And how to keep Dillon from discovering her whereabouts. The longer she remained in one place, the greater the chance of him finding her. She couldn't let that happen.

The sounds of the harvest workers in the distance carried on the still, hot air. Becky looked toward the orchard with longing. How she'd love to get a lesson in apple picking—maybe even do some herself. Alas, she was needed elsewhere.

At least she got to spend a few minutes in the garden each day gathering the ripe vegetables. The weeds had taken over, but there was nothing she could do about that. She couldn't be away from *Mutti* for long.

Becky picked up her basket of produce and started for the house. She couldn't complain. She got to be with *Mutti* while James had to work in the orchard every day, knowing his mother had very little time left.

Dr. Wright had visited the day before and said it was just a matter of weeks. James had put on a brave front, but he hadn't been able to hide the sadness in his eyes.

She must support him, give *Mutti* the best care possible and not say one word about her challenges. How could standing over a hot stove compare to his heartache?

Although she needed to go inside and prepare supper for the workers, she paused to watch two men coming toward the house. Something about their gait seemed unusual.

As the men drew near, she saw that their neighbor Mr. Stratton was supporting James.

She set down her basket of produce and met them. "What's wrong?"

Chapter Ten

James gave Becky a weak smile. "I'm fine."

"You don't look fine." His face was flushed and his eyes glassy.

Mr. Stratton staggered under his load. "Don't listen to him, miss. He kept working even though he was feeling poorly. At one point he got so wobbly we were afraid he was going to fall off his ladder. He refused to stop, so I had to near pin him down."

"He can be a bit ornery at times, can't he? Let me help you get him inside." She slipped under James's other arm and wrapped one of hers around his waist.

Together she and their neighbor got James onto his bed. She felt his forehead. "He's burning up. Mr. Stratton, could I ask you to help him into his nightclothes? I'll get a basin of cool water. I've got to get his fever down."

When she returned with the water, James was in bed with the sheet over him and his eyes closed. She followed Mr. Stratton out. "Do you think it could be influenza? Have you heard of anyone else in town who's ill?"

"Charlie Coulter and Jack Higgins didn't show up today. Got word they're sick abed. Leaves us awful short-handed, what with James out, too. What do you want us to do? Keep on as we were?"

She'd have to talk with James, but his overriding concern was getting the crop harvested before the first rain fell. "Yes, please do."

After a quick check to be sure *Mutti* was asleep, Becky perched on the edge of James's bed.

He opened his eyes. "The harvest. I have to get back out there." He tried to sit, but she pushed him back into his pillows.

"Your men will take care of everything until you're better. You must rest."

"But they need to know what to do."

She plunged the cloth into the cool water. "You've hired good people. They can do this."

A coughing spell overtook him. It passed, and he rubbed his throat. "I feel awful."

She smiled. "You've looked better."

Her jest went unnoticed, which wasn't surprising. James had one thing on his mind. His livelihood depended on that crop.

He spoke in a voice growing raspier by the minute. "The workers would never take orders from Quan. They won't like having a woman over them, either, but you're the best person for the job."

She wrung out the cloth and dabbed his forehead. "Me? I'm flattered, but I think the fever must be getting to you. If you recall, you weren't too happy with me the last time I took charge."

"I wasn't. Not at first. But I apologized. I also said you were capable, and you are. You're bright and have a lot of common sense, too. You can do this." He reached for her hand and gently squeezed, making it almost impossible to concentrate. "Please, Becky. I need your help."

As much as she appreciated his compliments, she didn't know the first thing about harvesting apples or supervising a crew of workers. Not that she would let that stop her. Despite her doubts, she would do everything in her power to see that things went well and put his mind to rest. "All right. But before you get any sicker, tell me everything I need to know."

He released her hand far too quickly. She gave him her full attention as he explained the basic steps of the harvesting process, relishing the opportunity to gaze at his handsome face openly. The minute he finished croaking out the information, he closed his eyes and fell asleep.

How she got through the afternoon, Becky didn't know, but somehow she was there when *Mutti* needed her, bathed James's flushed face three more times and had supper on the makeshift table in the yard when the workers arrived.

She'd rushed out to the orchard to see the harvest in action and had come up with a plan. Before she did anything else, she needed to talk with the men—all of them.

As soon as the workers were seated, she addressed them, explaining that James had put her in charge. She waited until the murmuring subsided before continuing. "Since I'll be discussing some new procedures I'll be putting in place, I've invited Quan and Chung to join us."

One man jumped up. "Oh, no. I'm not sharing the table with—"

"Fine. Leave." She wouldn't tolerate such behavior.

The disgruntled worker stared at her, and she stared back. He threw his napkin down and stormed off.

"Anyone else who feels the same way can join him." The remaining workers eyed her warily, but they shifted to make places at the table for the Lees.

While the men shoveled in their supper, she shared

her plan. "So are you willing to continue under the new terms?"

The men exchanged some dubious looks, but they didn't contest the changes. She was certain that rearranging the various stations, employing the men's wives and children and redistributing the workload would speed things up while cutting costs.

When the men came for their wage packets that evening as the sun was setting, many of them said they'd return the next day with the additional workers, ready to put her plan into action.

Five days later James woke feeling much better. He was eager to get out to the orchard. The workers had left two days before when they'd finished harvesting the early-ripening varieties ahead of schedule, but they were back to pick the Winesaps, Rome Beauties and Esopus Spitzenburg.

He entered the kitchen and found Coleen Stratton and her daughters fixing dinner. Becky was nowhere to be seen.

The door to *Mutti*'s bedroom was ajar, so he peeked inside. Lizzie occupied a chair at his mother's bedside. The eccentric woman jumped up at the sight of him and whispered. "They're both asleep."

"Both?" He craned his neck to see over her shoulder. Sure enough, Becky lay on her bed. With her face resting in the crook of her arm and her pleasingly full lips slightly parted, she looked quite fetching. He could gaze at her for hours.

"Enough gawking." The take-charge nurse chuckled, took him by the elbow and ushered him into the kitchen, pulling the door closed behind them. "It's high time you took notice of that selfless gal. Not only has she worked tirelessly overseeing the harvest by day, but she was also up several times during the night helping your mother, although you won't hear her utter a single word of complaint. I sit with Mariela every morning now, so I insisted Becky get a nap."

Coleen, a Scottish woman with an accent as thick as the stew she was stirring, spun around. "Aye. A wee rest will do her good. The sweet lass was fair puggled."

He raised an eyebrow. "*Puggled*?"

"Tired, ye would say."

Lizzie nodded. "We'll tell her you were asking after her."

Coleen shook her wooden spoon at him and smiled. "Off with ye, Mr. O'Brien. Me girls and I have a dinner to make."

James held up his hands in mock surrender. "I know when I'm not wanted." His house was full of women. Bossy but well-meaning women. Better to get outside with the men.

He stepped onto the front porch and came to an abrupt stop. Where was the sorting station? He'd set it up in front of the barn, but it was nowhere in sight.

A wagon creaked to a stop beside the barn—Stratton's wagon with Ralph's oldest son on the driver's seat. How odd. James went to investigate.

The young man smiled. "Good to see you up and about, Mr. O'Brien. Pa said you might be joining us today."

"That I will."

Two teenaged boys, sons of another worker, hopped off the back of the wagon. The strapping young fellows hefted a loaded packing barrel to the ground and rolled it over to where the others were stored under the eaves of the barn.

James tromped through the orchard. Voices rang out in

the distance. He frowned. If he wasn't mistaken, that was childish laughter. What were children doing here? The men knew his views on such things. He made straight for the commotion.

When he reached the hub of activity, he stared in disbelief. Never in all his born days had he seen such a sight.

The men picked, the older children carried the full pouches to makeshift tables where women sorted the apples and the young children gathered the culls into bushel baskets. Chung and Quan had filled a barrel, which they sealed and loaded onto a wagon with Charlie Coulter's son on the driver's seat.

James had always done things the way his father had, hauling the apples to the barnyard for sorting and packing, all the work being done by men. Someone had radically altered things. Although he didn't like to admit it, the changes improved the flow and sped up things considerably. No wonder the harvesting of the early varieties had been finished ahead of schedule.

Who was behind the changes? Quan perhaps? Or maybe Ralph and Charlie? His neighbors had worked the orchard every harvest season and might have given Becky some suggestions.

Chung spotted him and waved. "Boss, you back. Good see you."

James strode over to the Lees. "It's good to be back. I see things are being done differently. Was this your idea?" He waved his hand toward the workers.

Quon removed his hat and swept a sleeve over his brow. "It was Miss Becky. She is a smart lady."

This was Becky's doing? He knew she was an intelligent and capable woman, but he hadn't realized how much so. The woman was downright clever. She had things running more smoothly than ever before.

He'd meant to thank her for her help with the codling moth but had yet to purchase the gift he had in mind. He would remedy that right away. Since Kate was finally making the trip up from San Francisco to say goodbye to their mother, he would ask his sister to bring the item.

Glancing out the kitchen window, Becky spotted James. He stood in the barnyard, admiring the stacks of packing barrels ready for his buyers.

She left *Mutti* in the care of Kate, who'd arrived earlier that morning, grabbed her new cloak and hurried out to join him. The sweet smell of apples mingled with the musty odor of damp earth.

As Becky stood beside James, a sense of pride filled her. The past two weeks had been challenging but rewarding. Instead of being upset with her for altering his system, he'd thanked her repeatedly.

Even more surprising were the times when she'd served the men their meals and caught James watching her with what resembled attraction in his expressive eyes. Such a thought was foolhardy. What she'd seen was more likely appreciation on his part, brought about by weariness on hers.

He spoke, returning her to the present. "I would never have expected the harvest to be completed four days ahead of schedule. If it weren't for your improvements, there would still have been fruit on the trees when the rain came yesterday. We'd have been forced to wait until the apples were dry to finish the job."

"I was happy to help." She would do anything in her power to lighten his load.

"You did more than help. You brought about a complete transformation. You've instituted processes and procedures that enhanced and expedited the harvest, so much so that the work was completed well under projections. You reduced my expenses, too, hiring the women and children at lower wages. What you accomplished was an admirable and laudable feat."

"Not so fast." She chuckled. "If you continue using such big words, I'll need my dictionary."

"What I'm saying is that you made things better, and I'm proud of you."

She basked in his praise. "I knew you were worried about getting the harvest in with so many men out sick, so I tried to think of ways to make it faster. That's all."

"You went above and beyond your duties, Becky. Something you've done many times. I want to thank you properly, which is why I asked Kate to do some shopping for me."

"I appreciate that. The cloak is wonderful." She ran a hand over the charcoal-colored wool, grateful he'd insisted she accept it as a gift rather than allowing her to add the large sum he must have paid for it to her mounting debt.

"That's not what I mean. I had her get that because I was tired of seeing you swallowed up in her old one. Come inside, and I'll show you what else she brought."

There was more? She followed him into the house where Kate sat at the kitchen table, her hands wrapped around a steaming cup of tea. Clad in the most exquisite gown Becky had ever seen, with her hair expertly coiffed, Kate was a rare beauty. Unshed tears shimmered in hazel eyes so like her brother's.

Compassion filled Becky. She reached around Kate and enveloped her in a hug. The floral scent of her expensive perfume tickled Becky's nose. "I'm so sorry. I know it's hard to see her like this."

Kate stiffened. "I'm fine." Apparently, she was as restrained as her brother.

Becky removed her pretty new cloak, hung it on its peg in the lean-to and returned to find James smiling. He pushed a large brown-paper parcel across the table toward her. "Here. This is for you. Open it."

His uncharacteristic eagerness piqued her curiosity. He must be proud of what was in that package. She snipped the string, peeled back the paper, saw the book inside and squealed.

Doing her best to compose herself, she read the words on the spine aloud, her voice shaking despite her attempts to remain calm. "'*An American Dictionary of the English Language* by Noah Webster.' I can't believe this amazing book is for me. It's so big." She hugged the massive dictionary to her. "And heavy." She plunked the four-inch-thick volume on the table, where it landed with a thud.

Kate tapped the brown cover. "It's the latest edition. *Webster's Unabridged*, the clerk called it."

James grinned. "With one hundred fourteen thousand entries, you should have plenty of words to learn."

"Yes, indeed. This is the most amazing present anyone's ever given me. I can't begin to tell you how much your magnanimous gesture means to me." Overcome by his thoughtfulness and generosity, she rose on her tiptoes and planted a kiss on his cheek.

His dazed look indicated he was every bit as shocked by her impulsive display of affection as she was. Heat flooded her cheeks.

Kate laughed. "I'd say she liked it, Jimmy."

Eager to change the subject, Becky seized the opportunity Kate had given her. "I've never heard anyone call him that before."

"He isn't fond of the nickname, but he limits his displeasure to a scowl rather than actually snarling." Kate gave an airy laugh.

He was scowling at his sister, but he didn't look the slightest bit upset. Quite the contrary. His eyes weren't the usual green they became when he was irritated. Instead, they were the deepest shade of brown Becky had ever seen, the color they turned when he was happy about something. Like having his sister here at long last.

Mutti called Becky's name, and the atmosphere in the room changed instantaneously. She headed for the door, eager to see what her precious patient needed—and to keep from being alone with James after her exuberant display of gratitude—but Kate stopped her.

"I'll go this time."

"Are you sure?" Kate wasn't exactly dressed for nursing.

"It's time I face the truth." She left with a swish of her silk skirts.

Overcome with a sudden rush of shyness, Becky opened the dictionary and flipped through the pages, attempting to slow her hammering heart by drawing in slow, steady breaths. "First the cloak, and now this. You really surprised me."

He leaned against the kitchen counter with his arms and ankles crossed, looking far too appealing. "There's a lot of that going around."

His meaning couldn't be any clearer. "I'm sorry about that. I was overcome and wasn't thinking."

"No apology needed. I didn't mind." A smile danced at the corners of his mouth.

She felt a glimmer of hope. "You didn't?"

"What man would turn down a sisterly peck on the cheek?"

Her hope faded. Why would he be interested in her, a

plain, uneducated woman? She shouldn't be entertaining such thoughts, anyway. Not when she would be leaving as soon as she'd repaid him.

If Becky hadn't insisted on taking Kate to meet the stage, James would have made the trek. Instead, he faced the task of meeting *Mutti*'s needs.

She'd been drifting in and out of sleep. All he'd had to do so far was give her a sip of water. That he could handle, but if she needed anything else… He refused to look at the syringe Becky kept washed and ready.

He wandered aimlessly through the great room, unable to stay in one place. Normally, he could lose himself in a book, but he'd stopped trying after reading the same paragraph four times and being unable to recall anything in it.

Kneeling in front of the fire, he added a log. Flames shot up, licking the sides of the oak. The blaze snapped and crackled, sending sparks shooting up the chimney. He warmed his hands.

He stood and looked around for something to occupy him until Becky's return, when he could head to the barn and work on his latest project. He spotted her dictionary. She hadn't moved it from the far end of the dining table. Whenever she had a spare minute, her face was buried in Webster's massive volume.

His gift had certainly made her happy. Reaching up, he brushed a hand over his cheek where she'd left that whisper-soft kiss. She'd been so close that he'd smelled a hint of lemon from that lotion she rubbed on her nose, presumably to remove her freckles. He had half a mind to toss the stuff and tell her she didn't need it. The dusting of spots added to her charm.

He didn't know how he would have made it through

the past five months without her. Becky had a way of making the dark days more bearable. She'd proven to be a hard worker, an excellent cook and a good friend. He didn't like to think about her leaving once her nursing skills were no longer needed. Life wouldn't be the same. He'd miss her sunny smile and cheery laugh, but most of all he would miss her companionship.

Enough! He'd gotten downright morose of late, and that had to stop. What was to come would come, and he needed to accept that.

A sound out front had James bolting for the door. The jangle of harnesses had never been more welcome. Becky was back!

He stepped onto the porch, a broad smile on his face. "Am I ever glad to see you."

She sat on the driver's seat, the reins clutched in her hands, her shoulders shaking with laughter.

No. Not laughter. She was sobbing.

He vaulted over the porch railing and was at her side in an instant. "What's wrong?"

"It's…" She rocked back and forth, a torrent of tears rendering her speechless. She drew in a series of shuddering breaths. "It's terrible."

Terror settled in his stomach, setting its contents to roiling. "Kate? Is she…?"

Becky shook her head. "She's fine. She's gone. And s-s-so is my home."

"What do you mean?"

She turned, revealing swollen and splotchy cheeks and a red nose. "It's all gone, James. Chicago is gone." The reins slipped from her fingers as she reached for him.

He grasped her waist, lifted her to the ground and nearly stumbled as she flung herself at him. His arms went around her before he'd even formed a thought. She buried her face in his chest and sobbed as though her heart were breaking.

As much as he wanted answers, they would have to wait. Sweet, selfless, self-sufficient Becky needed him. And he would be there for her no matter what.

Chapter Eleven

As James completed a turn on the winding road leading to Placerville, Becky released her grip on the wagon seat and sighed. "No matter how many times I think about the extent of the damage, I still can't believe it. Three and a half square miles of the city burned to the ground. Hundreds are presumed dead. Tens of thousands are homeless. It's inconceivable."

"That it is." As he had ever since she'd told him the news, he listened patiently while she recounted the facts and struggled in vain to make sense of them. The house she'd lived in, the church she'd attended, the shops she'd frequented—they were all gone.

When she'd first heard about the Great Conflagration after seeing Kate off, she'd shrieked, drawing the attention of everyone within earshot. When they'd learned she'd spent most of her life in Chicago, they had attempted to console her. All she'd been able to think about was getting back to the orchard, the only home she had left.

James had been such a dear, holding her upright as she soaked his flannel work shirt with her tears. She hadn't intended to throw herself at him, but when she felt his hands on her waist, her knees had turned to applesauce. If she hadn't clung to him, she would have collapsed. His strength was all that had gotten her through the first agonizing hours.

She gazed at the oaks stretching their gnarled limbs toward the sky. "At church Sunday I heard that even though the O'Learys' barn, where the fire started, burned, their house is still standing. That's hard to believe, isn't it?"

James slowed the wagon as they began the descent down Sacramento Hill. "I'll never understand the way God works. Some people suffer, while others rejoice."

How could she have forgotten what he was going through? *Mutti* had a week left at best, but he'd set aside his pain in order to take Becky to the Benefit for the Chicago Sufferers being held in Placerville. He'd even arranged for Lizzie to sit with *Mutti*.

Becky's heart swelled with gratitude for his sacrifice. She rested her hand on his arm. "Thank you for being such a good friend. I'm sure I'll be better able to cope after the meeting."

At times she wondered what it would be like if she and James were more than friends. Whenever she found her thoughts traveling that path, she quickly steered them back to the present. Allowing herself to imagine a future with a husband, children and a home of her own would only lead to disappointment. A woman on the run had to keep her feelings in check.

She had James to think about, too. He was already hiding from the world. If he suspected she cared for him, he would retreat further, and she couldn't bear that.

In an effort to lighten the mood, she changed the subject. "Now that the harvest is behind you, how do you prepare the orchard for winter?"

They spent the rest of the trip discussing pruning, planting and grafting.

She wasn't likely to see James perform the tasks, though. She'd only be staying in Diamond Springs long enough to earn the money she needed to pay him back. Unless Dillon discovered her whereabouts first.

They arrived in Placerville, and another wave of sadness washed over her. She blinked away tears.

James parked the wagon on Reservoir Street behind the Cary House and helped her down. They joined the crowd headed up Main toward Sierra Hall. Although it had opened as a roller-skating establishment the month before, tonight the doors had been thrown open for the benefit. He kept a hand at the small of her back as he led her to the door, where he paid the fifty-cent admission for each of them.

A young boy pointed at James. "Look, Mama. What's wrong with that man's face?"

The woman pushed the lad's hand down. "Shush, son." She sent James an apologetic smile.

He gave her a polite nod of acknowledgment, but Becky could tell by the twitch in his jaw that the interaction had affected him. She could understand. She remembered all too well the stares of strangers when her cheeks had been bruised.

Once inside the hall, James found them places on a bench shoved against a wall, which was quite a feat, given the turnout. Because of the limited seating, she was forced to sit so close to him that their shoulders touched. Under normal circumstances, she would have been concerned about propriety, but not tonight. She was grateful for his comforting presence. Being the gentleman he was, he would have accompanied anyone in her situation, but she could pretend he was there for her alone.

Mr. Parks stopped to speak with them, leaning close in order to be heard over the hubbub. "My heart goes out to you, Becky. This tragedy must have affected you deeply."

"It has. So much was lost. What's worse is that I don't know the fate of my brother or my friends. I've read all the articles in the newspapers, but it will be some time before everyone is accounted for."

"I'll keep you and your loved ones in prayer."

The kindly minister shifted his attention to James. "And how is your sweet mother?"

"She's home resting. Thank you for asking." His curt reply delivered, he turned to speak with the gentleman on his other side.

Becky could understand that James didn't want to face the harsh reality that they could lose *Mutti* at any time, but he didn't have to ignore Mr. Parks. She took up the conversation. "The end is near, but I think *Mutti*'s ready to go home. Her daughter, Kate, came to see her, and they said their goodbyes. She'd been waiting for that and has been at peace ever since."

"I'll stop by tomorrow. I'd like to see Mariela one last time. She's such a precious soul."

Mr. Parks excused himself and took his seat on the dignitaries' platform. James had grown quiet and sullen so Becky watched the Philharmonic Society take their places. Having never heard an orchestra play before, she couldn't wait. As the musicians tuned their instruments, the medley of discordant notes whetted her appetite for their performance. The elderly gentleman beside her noted her interest and pointed out the various instruments.

Minutes later the program got under way. The master of ceremonies thanked everyone for coming out to support such a worthy cause. Mr. Parks said the opening prayer, and a lecture called "America and the Americans" followed. The speaker lauded the resiliency of the Chicagoans. Even though the fire had been extinguished only nine days before, tales were already being told of the spirit of renewal evident in the city.

An enthusiastic round of applause followed the uplifting address. Men and women alike had been moved. Only by recalling the good memories of her childhood spent in Chicago's Bridgeport neighborhood had Becky managed to keep tears from tumbling down her cheeks.

The conductor stepped onto his platform, raised his baton and waited until every musician's eyes were on him. A hush fell over the room, and she held her breath.

With one flick of the baton, the orchestra began playing, filling the hall with sounds far sweeter than any Becky had ever heard. Light, airy notes from the violins and violas blended beautifully with the deeper notes of the cellos and basses. The brass and woodwinds joined in, creating a feast for the ears and chasing away the sense of hopelessness that had enveloped her ever since she'd heard about the fire.

When the concerto came to an end, she clapped so hard her palms stung. Dropping her hands to her lap, she had the feeling someone was watching her and turned to find Dr. Wright flashing a smile her way. But not just any smile. If she wasn't mistaken, he was attracted to someone. She cast sidelong glances in each direction. No other woman was on the bench. She peeked at him from beneath her lashes, and he nodded at her.

Glory be. The dignified doctor was smiling at her. She flicked open her fan and ducked behind it to hide the color sure to be staining her flaming cheeks.

James chose that moment to brush a hair from her shoulder, his hand lingering longer than necessary. His forehead was creased, and his eyes were a deeper green than she'd ever seen, a sure sign he wasn't happy about something.

What could have upset him? Perhaps he resented being away from *Mutti* and had been too kind to say anything. Well, there was nothing she could do about that now. It would be rude to leave in the middle of the performance, so she would just enjoy the music and be ready to depart the minute the program was over.

All too soon the last note faded. The reverend gave a stirring benediction, and the room filled with the buzz of conversations. Becky stood, slung her lovely new cloak over her shoulders and joined the throng making its way to the door. Before she'd gone five feet, Dr. Wright called her name. After their puzzling interaction earlier, she hoped her cheeks weren't crimson.

The dignified doctor rested a hand on her forearm, and she resisted the urge to draw back. An ordinary girl like her didn't deserve the attentions of a learned man like him any more than she did James. Surely a doctor would want a cultured woman, not someone who'd worked in a factory and fled her abusive brother.

Dr. Wright gazed at her with the same compassion she'd witnessed when he sat at *Mutti*'s bedside. What a ninny she'd been to think he was interested in her. Her uneasiness fled.

"I can't tell you how sorry I am, Miss Martin. I didn't call Chicago home as long as you did, but I made many friends when I was at Lind Medical School. Did you lose…?" He shifted his hat from one hand to the other. "That is to say, have you learned the fate of your former home?"

"My entire neighborhood is gone."

"I'm sorry to hear that." He raked a hand through his

neatly trimmed blond hair. "It's times like these I wonder how those without a firm faith in the Lord deal with life. We don't understand why these things happen, but we do know He's in control."

James made a sound low in his throat that resembled a growl. He continued to bristle whenever someone suggested he rely on the Lord. If only he could find solace there, his burdens wouldn't seem as heavy.

Dr. Wright shifted his attention to James. "How is your mother?"

"There's been no significant change since your last visit, but she's growing weaker by the day. Isn't there anything else we can do for her?"

The doctor's shoulders rose and fell as he drew in a breath and released it. "I'm afraid not. Are you able to keep her comfortable?"

"Yes, but Becky's had to increase the dosage and frequency of the injections in order to control the pain."

"Unfortunately, that's what's required. Take every opportunity to talk with her whenever she's lucid. It won't be long until she's unable to communicate."

James gave a curt nod. "Thank you again, Doctor, for all you've done."

"I wish I could do more. And now, if you could spare Becky a moment, I'd like to have a word with her."

James pressed his lips together, scraped a hand over his scar and spoke in clipped tones. "Fine, but please don't tarry, Becky. We need to return home."

"I'll be quick." She'd be faster than that. She had no intention of spending more time alone with the doctor than was necessary, not when James was so eager to get back to his mother.

Dr. Wright held out a hand to the vacated rows of

chairs. She stepped between two of them, and he followed suit, clutching his hat in his hands.

He cleared his throat. "I couldn't help but notice how enamored of the music you were. We have several musical groups in the community. You might enjoy their performances, too."

"I'm sure I would." Not that she could attend them. She hadn't a penny to her name and wouldn't until she'd repaid James.

Dr. Wright opened his mouth to reply, glanced at something behind her and closed it. An agonizing few seconds passed, but she didn't know what else to say.

"I could tell you about upcoming concerts, if you'd like."

"That would be nice."

"Very well, then. I know you need to be going, so I won't keep you. But before you do, I have something for you. It's a letter...with a Chicago postmark."

"Oh!" Had Dillon found her already?

He held out a gray envelope. "It was sent to my office. I hope it contains good news."

She clutched the letter to her and avoided looking at the handwriting, afraid she'd see Dillon's bold scrawl. "Thank you."

"I'll be on my way, but don't hesitate to send word if you need me." He bowed and left.

A familiar voice from behind caused Becky to spin around. "Callie!"

"Oh, Becky, it's so good to see you." Callie threw her arms around Becky and gave her a sound squeeze.

Drawing back, Becky drank in the sight of the friend she'd made on her trip West. "What are you doing in Placerville? I thought you were going to Georgetown to search for your brother."

Callie's face bore traces of recently shed tears. "I'm staying there for the time being, but when I heard about the benefit, I couldn't miss it. The house where I lived was spared, but so many of those we knew lost theirs. I hope yours wasn't one of them."

"I'm afraid it was."

"That's terrible. I know you weren't planning to return, but it must be so hard to think about everything you remember being gone." She didn't wait for a response but shook herself and produced her characteristic smile. "The talk was quite inspiring, don't you think? They'll rebuild, and Chicago will rise from the ashes, bigger and better than before."

Callie's optimism didn't surprise Becky. Her new friend could find something positive to say about a tooth extraction. "Are you any closer to finding your brother?"

"I know a number of places he's not, so that's progress. I'll find him. It's just a matter of time." Callie inclined her head toward James. "I take it your rescuer the day we arrived in town was none other than Mr. O'Brien?"

"Yes. I would introduce you to him, but we're in a hurry. His mother's failing and won't be with us much longer."

"Is he always so serious?"

Becky shook her head. "He's a very nice man...once you get to know him."

Callie brushed an errant curl from her face and studied James, who stood with his arms folded, scowling. She pinned Becky with a knowing look. "Well, now, this is an interesting development. You've gone and fallen for him, haven't you?"

"No! It's not like that."

"Don't bother denying it. It's as clear as the scar on his face."

Becky bristled. "His scar doesn't matter. He's a hero who got it saving lives. Besides, it just makes him look more rugged."

Callie grinned. "Oh, my. It's worse than I thought. You're smitten. Admit it."

"I'm not. We're just friends. That's all we can ever be."

"Why?"

Becky lowered her voice. "I can't stay here. My brother could find me, and…"

"I hadn't thought of that." Callie checked to see that no one was around and leaned close. "I don't mean to be blunt, but do you know if he survived? I've heard there were casualties."

"I haven't seen Dillon's name in the papers, so I assume he's all right. He is homeless, though. What if he comes looking for me?"

"Do you really think he would?"

"I wouldn't put it past him." The truth tasted bitter, but as much as Becky wanted to ignore it, she couldn't. "He's *not* a nice person."

Compassion filled Callie's eyes. "I'm sorry. I need to be going, but here's a word of advice. Don't give up hope, my friend. God loves you and will keep watch over you. And who knows? Perhaps things with Mr. O'Brien will turn out well." She gave Becky a quick hug and disappeared out a side door.

Footfalls sounded on the wooden floor. James made no attempt to contain his irritation, but it wasn't as if she'd planned to talk with the doctor or Callie. "Are you finished?"

"I'm sorry for the delays. We can go now."

"What did the doctor want? Is there something about *Mutti* he's not telling me?"

"It wasn't about her. It was…personal."

His eyes glinted green. "I see. Let's go." He placed her hand in the crook of his arm, drew her to his side, held her close—very close—and hurried her toward the wagon. They passed Dr. Wright, but James didn't even acknowledge him. If the idea weren't preposterous, she would think he was jealous.

Just as they reached Quartz Street, a man with an all-too-familiar build staggered out of the Arch Saloon next door, the gaslights revealing hair the same shade of brown as her own. She buried her face in James's overcoat.

He wrapped an arm around her. "What's wrong?"

She pulled away from him, her heart racing. Her breath hung like wispy clouds in the chilly air. "It's nothing. I thought I saw Dillon, but I was mistaken."

She lived in fear of her fist-wielding excuse for a brother finding her, but she was letting her imagination get the best of her. She had to read that letter, whether she wanted to or not.

With trembling fingers, she turned the envelope over and held it up to the gaslight. She'd never been happier to see Mrs. Hastings's handwriting. Relief turned her legs into limp noodles. She clutched a post supporting the balcony overhead.

James was at her side in an instant. "Are you sure you're all right?"

She nodded. "Dr. Wright handed me a letter after the benefit, and it's from our reverend's wife. I trust this means they're all right. Would you mind if I stepped inside and read it?"

"Not at all." He held the door open for her, and followed her into the lobby of the Cary House hotel.

Becky sank onto a settee, pulled a pin from her hat and slit the envelope. It contained a single page, which she unfolded and read from start to finish as rapidly as possible, her heart racing all the while.

October 11, 1871
Dearest Becky,
As I'm sure you've heard, much of Chicago has been destroyed by the fire that swept through the city. The church and parsonage are gone, but the reverend and I are safe. We spent the first night in Lincoln Park. Thanks to some kind friends, we were able to secure transportation and get to my sister's place in Evanston the next day. She's assured us we can stay with her as long as we need. The good Lord willing, we'll be able to rebuild soon. People will need a place of solace after this tragedy.

Sadly, your house didn't survive. I don't know what's become of your brother, but he paid us a visit shortly before the conflagration. He wanted to know where you'd gone. Of course, we said nothing.

You were wise to leave. He's been spreading lies. It pains me to tell you, but word is the police have begun searching for you. It seems you're wanted for questioning. I've yet to see your name in the paper, but I expect it to appear before long. Arson is taken very seriously here, as you would expect.

I'm sorry to be the bearer of such sad news, but I felt you needed to know the situation. You're innocent, and I trust that truth will prevail. Even so, I urge you to be discreet in your dealings and to stay where you are for the time being. If I hear anything more regarding your situation, I'll contact you through Dr. Wright.
Faithfully yours,
Hortense Hastings

James sat beside her. "You're frowning. Is there more bad news?"

"I knew the church and our houses were gone, but it's hard seeing it in writing."

"I haven't asked before, but since you no longer have a home there, I'm guessing you won't be going back. Or will you?"

"I can't." She was a wanted woman. "My brother has succeeded in convincing the police that I'm a suspect. If I were to return, I could be hauled in for questioning."

The one good thing about the Great Conflagration was that it had kept the pleas for information on her whereabouts from making the newspapers. For now, anyhow.

She had a reprieve. But how long would it last?

Chapter Twelve

Early the next morning Becky came in from gathering eggs to find James in his armchair, staring at the crackling fire. He didn't even look up when she bumped into a pile of firewood dumped in the middle of the floor and did a jig to keep from dropping the basket. It wasn't like him to leave anything out of place.

Had the end come? No. She could hear *Mutti*'s labored breathing through the open door.

Becky set the basket of eggs on the table, put the pieces of oak in the wood box on the hearth and wheeled around. Despite the blaze, a chill stole over her.

James held the syringe in his clenched hand.

She knelt in front of him. "I'll take this."

Only when she began to pry his fingers from the dreaded instrument did he loosen his grip. "I didn't think I could give *Mutti* an injection, but the pain was—" his voice cracked "—so sudden. So intense. I had no choice. All I could think about was easing her suffering."

She set the syringe aside and rested a hand on his arm. "I'm sorry I wasn't here, but I knew you could do it. You're a strong man and a loving son."

He shook his head. "I'm not strong enough for this. I can't bear to lose her. What am I going to do?"

His agony ripped Becky's heart to shreds. "We can pray. God will hear us and—"

"No!" He spat the word. "He's taken so much from me. I don't have anything to say to Him."

"It might feel like that now, but He's there for you. He always has been." Just as He'd been there for her, offering comfort when she woke in the wee hours following a nightmare in which Dillon chased her down the main street of Diamond Springs.

Her brother had no idea where she was, but seeing that drunken man who resembled Dillon zigzagging down the dark alley the night before had raised questions she didn't have answers to. What had happened to him now that he was homeless? Would he come after her? Since she'd left without telling him where she was going, her fears made no sense, but that didn't stop her mind from conjuring frightening possibilities. If he could produce the supposed arsonist and free himself from suspicion, she had no doubt he'd do it. Even if it meant framing his own sister.

James scoffed, drawing Becky back to the present. "Where was God when the explosion killed Liang right before my eyes? When I fought for my life afterward? When Papa succumbed to pneumonia, leaving me no choice but to take over the orchard and see that *Mutti* was provided for?"

Becky struggled to hide her shock. In his anguish, he'd revealed the roots of his bitterness. He'd suffered so much loss. No wonder he was ill-tempered at times and had turned from God.

But God hadn't turned from James. The trouble was that telling him so would do no good. He had to return to the Lord on his own, when he was ready. She prayed that would be soon, for only then could he experience peace.

She took her hand away, but he reached for it, threading his fingers through hers. Warmth flowed through her like heated molasses over hotcakes, sweet and good. Very, very good.

"You and God are like this, Becky." He held up their joined hands. "You and *Mutti* have no trouble trusting Him. Even though she's dying, she's still praising the Lord and saying she wants to be with Him." His hold on her hand tightened to the point of pain, but she said nothing. "Why does she want to leave me? I'll be all alone."

"You have Kate."

"Ah, yes. My loving sister." He loosened his grip on Becky's hand, but he didn't let go. She dared not say a word lest he slam the door to his past. "You, of all people, should understand that just because a person is family doesn't mean there is a strong tie. Look at you and Davin."

"Dillon."

"Right." James pulled his hand away.

She mentally kicked herself for correcting him. "I'm sorry. Go on."

"Kate and I were never close, and I don't see that changing. We're too much alike."

"That's not true. She wasn't content with her life here, but you love the orchard."

Silence hung in the air as James focused on the crackling fire. Becky waited for him to continue, but somehow she knew he'd said all he was going to.

Moments later he shook himself and directed his attention to her. "Your knees must be getting sore." He tugged her to her feet and tipped his head toward *Mutti*'s rocking chair.

She settled into the soft cushions. James returned his gaze to the fire. If only he would let her behind that wall he'd erected, she would do whatever she could to comfort him and ease his pain.

Mutti's feeble attempt to call Becky's name made her shoot to her feet. "I'm sorry, James. I've got to check on her."

She raced to *Mutti*'s bedside. "What can I do for you?"

Even though every movement caused her untold pain, *Mutti* reached out a hand. Becky placed hers over it. "Must see James. Say goodbye."

Fear surged through Becky and set her stomach roiling. This wasn't supposed to be happening. Not now. It was too soon.

She willed herself to remain calm. Dr. Wright had said *Mutti* would be comatose before the end. She was talking—or trying to, anyhow—so there was still time. "I'll get him for you."

"First you." *Mutti*'s speech was punctuated by wheezing breaths. "You promised…you would stay…for a while longer. Comfort him. Please. My dear boy…needs you."

"I'll stay and do what I can." Not that it would make much difference. He'd built a wall so thick she couldn't budge it. But for *Mutti*'s sake, she'd keep trying.

"You've been…such a blessing. I love you…Becky."

She blinked several times to clear the sudden moisture in her eyes. "I love you, too." She planted a kiss on *Mutti*'s forehead. "Now let me get James for you." She took a moment to compose herself before leaving the room. It wouldn't do to alarm him.

Pasting a smile on her face, she took the few steps to the half circle of chairs and stood by his. "*Mutti* would like to speak with you."

James rose. "I know what I said about prayer, but if

you were inclined to say one for me now, I wouldn't turn it down."

"I will."

Several seconds passed as he stared at her, emotions flitting across his face with the speed of hummingbird wings. Sorrow. Anguish. Fear. She could empathize.

He trudged to *Mutti*'s room, his shoulders slumped under the weight of the heartrending task before him.

Becky sank into his armchair, bowed her head and prayed one of the most earnest prayers of her life.

Lord, I lift James to You. He isn't ready to say good-bye to his mother. No child ever is. Please uphold him. And Lord, I ask You to find a way to reach into his soul and show him that You're there for him and that You do care. So do I. More than I should. Guide me as I—

A tap on her shoulder caused her eyes to fly open.

James stood beside her. "I'm sorry to interrupt, but *Mutti*'s speaking German. I can usually understand her, but she's mumbling."

"I'll translate." That was the least she could do for him.

"Thank you."

They returned to *Mutti*'s room. He sat facing her and took her delicate hand in his strong, masculine one. He inclined his head, indicating he wanted Becky in front of him.

She perched on the edge of the bed, and he placed his free hand on her shoulder.

"Becky's with me now, so you can talk. I'm listening."

Mutti rasped out two short sentences. The mere effort of talking tired her.

"See what I mean. I can't understand a word she's saying."

Becky whispered, not wanting to draw attention to

herself. "She said she loves you and not to forget that God loves you, too."

He lifted *Mutti*'s hand to his lips and kissed it. "I love you, *Mutti*, more than you'll ever know. I'm sorry I went away. I never meant to make you and Papa work so hard. I was young, idealistic and selfish. Please forgive me."

Once more *Mutti* spoke, her voice faint.

Becky leaned close to listen and supplied the translation. "She said there's nothing to forgive. They wanted to help. You made them proud."

Mutti opened her eyes, an otherworldly glow in them. "*Auf Wiedersehen.*" Her eyelids drifted shut. Within seconds she was asleep, her breathing shallow.

James released *Mutti*'s hand, stood and helped Becky to her feet. He smoothed the blankets, cradled his mother's face in the palm of his hand and bent to kiss her forehead. "Sleep well." He straightened.

Becky tiptoed to the door, but he was at her side instantly, his hand on her elbow, ushering her from the room. He'd touched her more in the past few minutes than he had in the entire six months she'd lived there.

He led her to the kitchen, where he leaned against the counter, standing with his feet spread and his arms folded. "It won't be long, will it?"

"I'm afraid not. She's ready to go. It'll be easier on her if you let her."

"What do you mean?"

"Tell her you'll be all right, and that she can answer the call."

He drew in a breath and exhaled slowly, his broad chest rising and falling. "If that's what she needs, I'll do it the next time she's awake."

Becky did her best to telegraph the urgency with a grimace and a slight shake of her head.

"I see. It's now or never, is it? Well, then." He crossed the kitchen in three long strides, squared his shoulders and entered the bedroom.

She longed to spare him the pain, but as much as he wanted to hold on to *Mutti*, letting her go was the greatest gift he could give her.

Shadows stretched as that seemingly endless Saturday afternoon wore on. The sun shouldn't be shining so brightly when his world was black as a moonless night.

James dragged his gaze from the leaf-strewn ground and threw a stick for Spitz. The spirited dog bounded after it and returned, his tail wagging wildly, eager for another toss. Over and over again James sent the knobby branch sailing. Each time Spitz let loose with an excited bark and streaked toward the prize, never tiring of the pursuit.

Unlike the beautiful Irish setter, James was weary. Every hour of the thirty-three that had passed since he'd given *Mutti* permission to leave her cancer-riddled body behind and go to her heavenly home had been at least a month long. Even though he wanted time to stand still, he didn't know how much longer he could bear the watching and waiting.

Mutti was ready. Becky knew it and had said as much. He knew it, too, although he hated admitting it, even to himself.

Every time he thought of *Mutti*'s strong faith and eagerness to see the Lord, his conscience dealt him another blow. He'd shoved God aside, no longer going to church and praying only when forced to.

He'd silently rejoiced when *Mutti* no longer joined them for meals, figuring he could forgo asking the traditional blessings beforehand, but Becky had the same expectations. He'd managed to produce prayers that sounded fairly convincing. If she knew what a fraud he was, she'd probably pray for his salvation.

Spitz returned, dropped the stick at James's feet and sat on his haunches, his tail swishing and his tongue lolling. James squatted, petted the loyal dog and received a slobbery kiss in return. "Thanks, pal. My face needed washing." He ran his palm over his damp cheek.

"James!"

Fear coursed through his veins, and his muscles tensed. There could only be one reason Becky would holler his name at the top of her lungs. He sprinted for the house, reaching it in record time.

She met him at the back door. "Hurry."

"No." He braced a hand on the door frame. "I can't face this."

"You must. It's time." She took him by the hand and tugged.

He had no choice but to follow her. Once inside *Mutti*'s room, she let go of his hand. "I don't want to intrude, so I'll leave you to—"

"Don't go! *Please*. I can't do this alone."

"I'm here." She placed a hand on his back and exerted gentle pressure.

It was all he could do to put one foot in front of the other, but moments later he was at *Mutti*'s bedside, looking into that face so dear to him. She was still breathing, each inhalation slow and laborious. A brief pause was followed by one more breath.

And then nothing.

His legs had turned to rubber, and his teeth chattered. He clutched the edge of the bureau. "Sh-sh-she's gone?"

Becky rubbed his back in small circles that radiated warmth. "I'm so sorry, James."

"It's all right. I knew it was coming. I'm fine." He would be. He must be. But the walls were closing in on him. His stomach churned. "I have to go."

She stepped aside. "I understand. I'll see to things—" she inclined her head toward the bed "—and then I'll get supper ready."

How could she think about food at a time like this? He pressed a hand to his mouth, ran from the room and reached the privy before he retched.

As he stepped into the fading light, the world tilted. He staggered to the pump by the garden, rinsed his mouth several times and swiped his chin with his sleeve.

The bright red geraniums in *Mutti*'s window boxes caught his eye. With the first frost due any day, they would freeze. If he took some cuttings, he could winter the flowers indoors and have them ready for spring planting. She would like that.

A stabbing pain nearly doubled him over. *Mutti* was gone. He'd never see her smile again or hear her say his name with that thick German accent of hers.

Without even realizing how he'd got there, he found himself in the barn. He dropped to his knees and lifted his face to the rafters. "Please, God. Help me."

Supper would be a simple affair. Physically and emotionally spent from her labor of love the past hour, Becky didn't have the energy to fix anything fancy. Although she had no appetite, she couldn't let James go hungry.

After his frenzied wood-splitting session, he must be exhausted. And cold. The minute *Mutti* had breathed her last he'd bolted from the house in his shirtsleeves. At least the ringing of the sledgehammer striking the wedge had stopped when the sun set. He'd spent the past half hour piling the firewood he'd chopped beside the barn. As much as he'd produced, the stack must reach the eaves.

Becky pulled a batch of biscuits from the oven and set them on the table, adding butter, honey and an assortment of jams. A platter of cheese and fried ham slices completed the meal. All she needed now was James.

She slung her cloak over her shoulders and dashed out the front door. She stood at the foot of the steps, allowing her eyes to adjust to the dark. The only sound was the whisper of wind through the apple trees. She scanned the area, but James was nowhere to be seen.

A stream of lantern light spilling from the barn revealed his whereabouts. She crossed the yard and slipped through the small opening between the doors. A strange sound like that of a wounded animal sent icy shivers down her spine. The wailing came from the empty stall beyond the milk cow's, where Spitz often slept. Had the dog been hurt?

Becky padded past the horses with their noses in pails of oats, past Buttercup contentedly munching her supper, reached the vacant stall and ground to a halt.

Spitz sat at James's feet. The dog was fine, but James wasn't. He was leaning on the top rail, his head resting on his crisscrossed arms, his shoulders shaking.

His sobs tore her heart into a thousand pieces. The poor man was in agony.

In a heartbeat, she was by his side. As if of its own accord, her arm encircled his waist.

He tensed. "No, Becky. You can't see me like this."

"It's all right. I understand. I loved her, too."

Turning away, he pulled a bandanna from his pocket and scrubbed his face. "Go inside. Please."

"I'm not leaving you." She stepped in front of him.

He took a step back, and she took a step forward. He

took another and another, and she followed, step for step, until he was pinned in the corner of the stall.

She reached up and caressed his damp cheek.

He stood as still as a statue, his gaze locked with hers, making no move to stop her.

Emboldened by his acceptance, she trailed a finger over the scar that had once scared her but now just added an element of ruggedness to his handsome face.

The sorrow in his eyes drew her to him. James needed her, and she would be there for him, just as she'd promised *Mutti* she would be.

She lifted her right hand and stroked the other side of his face with her fingertips.

He cupped her shoulders and pulled her toward him. Ever so slowly, he lowered his head.

Her heart slammed against her corset. James was going to kiss her!

Blood rushed in her ears, drowning out all other sounds. Her eyes drifted shut.

He murmured against her cheek, deep and throaty. A single word that turned her bones to whipping cream. "Becky."

She placed her palms on his broad chest to keep from sinking to the floor. The small part of her brain that was still functioning said she shouldn't allow herself to enjoy his tender touch, but her heart ached for him. For his loss. For hers.

The pull was too strong, the moment too sweet, to put a stop to it. She tilted her head and waited, not sure what to expect.

His lips found hers at last. The kiss started slowly and grew into something more wonderful than she could ever have imagined. Her girlish notions of what it was like to be kissed were nothing compared to the surge of pure joy filling the empty places inside her.

All too soon he leaned back and looked into her eyes. His were a warm cocoa-brown. He smiled. "You have an interesting way of consoling a fellow. Not that I'm complaining."

Reality returned full force. He'd kissed her, and she'd done nothing to stop him. Not that she'd wanted to. But her moment of weakness was a mistake. She couldn't get close to him—to anyone. Not when she was a woman on the run. "I shouldn't have done that."

"Why? You wanted it as much as I did."

Even though he was right, that didn't change things. His grief had mingled with hers, and she'd dropped her guard. But she couldn't let it happen again. Wouldn't let it.

She stepped back, out of his reach. "I—I can't stay here any longer. I need to go. Your supper's waiting."

"I couldn't eat now. Not with her…you know." He looked through the barn door she'd left open at the house beyond.

She could understand his hesitation. The task before her would be difficult, but she would do whatever she could to spare him the heartache. "I'll set your plate to the side, then, and see to the arrangements."

Two hours later the undertaker left, and Becky made her second trip to town that evening. This time she wouldn't be returning to the orchard. Propriety demanded she leave.

If she weren't emotionally spent, she would have said goodbye to James. But in her present state, she hadn't trusted herself to see him again, so she'd left a note, instead.

She needed time to make a plan before she spoke with him. And she needed sleep. Lots and lots of sleep.

If she happened to dream of a handsome apple orchardist and the heart-meltingly sweet kiss he'd given her, so be it.

Chapter Thirteen

Something wasn't right. James blew into his hands to fend off the chill. The heating system should have kept his room warmer. He must see to the fire right away. *Mutti* would be cold.

Reality washed over him, as bone-chilling as the air in the room.

She was gone. The hard fact had been driven home when the undertaker's wagon had rumbled into the yard the night before. He'd stayed in the barn and left the arrangements to Becky. After her difficult day yesterday, she must have been so tired that she'd overslept, too, and had yet to get a fire started.

He dressed quickly and went to the fireplace, where a few embers glowed. He'd have a blaze going in no time. And then he would think about what to say when she appeared.

When he'd finally come inside last night, he discovered that she'd eaten supper without him and barricaded herself in her bedroom, which was fine with him. He hadn't been ready to face her then.

Not that he was now.

He'd made a fool of himself, crying like a baby, and

she'd caught him. She'd gazed at him with compassion in her bright blue eyes. And what had he done? Taken advantage of her kindness, that's what.

She'd only meant to comfort him, as she had when she'd let him hold her hand after he was forced to give *Mutti* the injection. He'd been so hungry for more of Becky's tender touches that he hadn't made a move to stop her—even when she'd traced his ugly scar with a fingertip.

He'd let things get out of hand. He should have put an end to it, but she'd reached out to him again, so trusting. He'd betrayed that trust, giving her what must have been her first kiss, based on her wide-eyed wonder afterward.

But what a kiss. It was apple pie, chocolate cake and gingerbread all rolled into one. A generous helping of sweet with a welcome side of spice.

In that moment he'd felt whole again. He'd been tempted to go back for seconds, but Becky had smiled, her innocence and inexperience evident in her shining eyes. She'd never looked more beautiful, with her lips swollen from his kiss.

But then she'd backed away, wariness creasing her lovely brow. She shouldn't have had to put a halt to things. That was his place, and he'd failed her.

The realization of what he'd taken from her had smacked him upside the head, packing such a punch it had knocked some sense into him. He couldn't give her the wrong impression. He had no desire to court her—or anyone, for that matter.

The moment she came out of her room, he would apologize. They could put the incident behind them and move on.

Before long the fire was snapping and crackling. He stood with his back to the blaze, warming his hands, when it struck him that there wasn't a fire in the cook-stove, either. He would start one so Becky could fix breakfast once she was up. Since he'd eaten little supper, he was ravenous. A pile of her fluffy hotcakes with eggs and bacon would silence his rumbling stomach.

Once the stove was heating up, he headed to the barn to take care of the animals. Buttercup's lowing greeted him. The poor girl was overdue for her milking.

He grabbed the stool, set it beside the uncomfortable cow, filled her feedbox with hay and reached for the tail holder, as Becky called his invention. He could still hear her squeal of delight when he'd given the elongated wooden S-shaped device to her. She'd declared him a genius. He wasn't any smarter than she was, but she had a way of making him feel appreciated. He appreciated her, too, more than he could say.

The past months would have been unbearable without her. He would apologize for his lapse in judgment, and then he would figure out a way to properly thank her, although he'd be hard-pressed to find something she would like more than the dictionary he'd given her.

As soon as the milking was finished and the horses were fed, he hefted the pail of frothy milk and returned to the house, ready to make things right. If all went well, she would forgive him, and he'd finally be able to eat.

Warmth greeted James when he entered the house, but Becky wasn't bustling about the kitchen. He set the milk pail on the counter, grabbed napkins and silverware and set two places.

Something was missing. Her dictionary. She kept it on the far end of the table, but the only thing there was a piece of paper with his name on it. A sense of foreboding settled over him. He gulped and unfolded the note.

James,
Before I left, I took care of the arrangements we'd discussed. If you'd like to make any changes, just let the undertaker know. Otherwise, I'll see you at *Mutti*'s funeral Tuesday afternoon.

   I know I still owe you a considerable sum. You needn't worry. I'll find a way to repay you as soon as possible.
Becky

He stared at the brief message, his mouth agape. She'd said she couldn't stay any longer, but he'd thought she meant in the barn. With him. Obviously, he'd been wrong.

   She couldn't be gone, could she? She had nowhere to go. She'd arrived penniless, and every cent she'd earned since then had gone toward repaying her debt. He'd suggested she keep some of her earnings for herself, but she'd refused.

   Bracing himself, he opened the door to *Mutti*'s room. Relief whooshed the air from his lungs. Instead of sickness and galbanum, the room smelled of lye soap and lemon wax. Becky had assured him she would see to everything, but she'd surpassed his expectations. A quick perusal revealed that she'd changed the sheets on both beds, removed all the medical paraphernalia and emptied the wardrobe and drawers of her things, as well as *Mutti*'s.

   Only a handful of *Mutti*'s personal items remained—those Kate had said she'd like to have. Becky had arranged the keepsakes on top of the bureau.

   Closing the bedroom door, he faced facts. He was alone. Completely alone. He'd have to figure out what to do. The first order of business was clear. If he wanted breakfast, he would have to make it.

Forty-five frustrating minutes later he sat down to one of the worst meals he'd ever eaten. He'd given up on fried eggs after three failed attempts and settled for scrambled. Although edible, they had the consistency of shoe leather and about as much flavor. He'd burned the bacon as well as the toast. The latter he buried under mounds of preserves. The former he washed down with a cup of too-strong coffee. Why hadn't he accepted *Mutti*'s offer to teach him how to cook a few simple meals?

At least he could wash dishes, which he did, all the while berating himself for his foolishness. The kiss had been wonderful, but his self-absorption combined with his lack of consideration for Becky had caused her to run away. The one thought that consoled him was that without any money, she couldn't have gone far.

Or could she?

He opened the pantry and pulled out the empty cocoa tin where he kept a small amount of money. He'd given Becky permission to use what she needed for minor household expenses and asked that she record how much she took and what she'd spent it on.

Flipping open the ledger, he scanned the recent entries. She'd made no notations in the month of October, having bought everything she'd needed on his account at Harris's grocery. In that case, the amount in the tin should match what was in the ledger.

A quick count had him shaking his head. Becky had taken two dollars but left the rest. He didn't begrudge her the small amount, but why had she taken so little? She couldn't go far on that.

Which meant she must still be in town. And he knew just where to find her.

He marched to his room, threw open his wardrobe and pulled out his Sunday best.

* * *

The congregation rose for the singing of the closing hymn. Lizzie leaned toward Becky, her whispered comment covered by the flipping of hymnal pages. "You won't believe who's in the back pew. Your erstwhile employer."

Unable to resist the urge to turn around, Becky did so as discreetly as possible, peering from beneath the brim of her bonnet. Sure enough, James stood in the far corner with his scarred right cheek resting in his hand, his gaze downcast. Although he'd driven *Mutti* to services when she was still able to go, he hadn't set foot inside a church since the explosion four years before. "Good. I can speak with him after the service."

The thought of talking with him set Becky's knees to quivering, but she had no choice. The plan she'd formed depended on him.

The trouble was that she wouldn't be able to look at him without reliving the thrill of being in his arms with his lips pressed to hers. Or the hollowness in her chest when she'd realized the ramifications of what she'd done and was forced to retreat.

She'd worked hard to be his friend, but her boldness in reaching out to him had jeopardized that. She'd rarely felt as ill at ease as she had at that moment—or as disappointed in herself. She'd been tempted to grab her things and flee right then, but she'd promised to spare him the pain of seeing to the arrangements. As hard as it had been to perform her duties, she'd lived up to her end of their bargain.

Although she'd run away from her brother, she wouldn't run from James. She'd have to leave before too much time passed, though, but she'd pay back every cent she owed him first.

In the meantime, she'd do her best not to dwell on the kiss, although her efforts so far had met with little success. The kiss had been wonderful. Sweet at first, but changing into something deeper, richer. What was that word she'd just learned? *Fervent.* Yes, that was it. He'd needed her, and she was happy to offer him what comfort she could.

No! She mustn't think about the kiss. She would concentrate on the service.

"Ladies and gentlemen—" the reverend held up a hand "—I feel led to change the final selection. Please turn to hymn twenty-four, instead, 'O, For a Thousand Tongues to Sing.' We'll sing the first, third and fifth verses."

Becky knew Charles Wesley's stirring hymn by heart. She had a good idea why Mr. Parks had chosen those particular verses. The third spoke of Jesus' name bidding our sorrows cease and the fifth of mournful, broken hearts rejoicing. Perhaps the words would minister to James.

She didn't like seeing anyone suffer. His precious mother had, and now he was. Thoughts of the pain *Mutti* had endured caused Becky's eyes to mist. She blinked to clear her blurred vision, focused on the stained-glass window over the altar and joined the others in song.

The moment Mr. Parks finished the benediction, Lizzie grabbed Becky by the arm and ushered her to a secluded spot at the front of the small sanctuary. "I know you intend to catch up to James, but I don't think talking to him in your present state is a good idea. You've suffered a great loss. After your…encounter in the barn, you're vulnerable."

Becky stole a glance at the back of the church and groaned inwardly. He was nowhere to be seen. "I'm fine."

Lizzie scoffed. "That young man didn't show up here because he felt a sudden need to worship. More than likely he woke up this morning expecting to find you in the kitchen as usual. When you weren't there and he was forced to feed himself, he came to his senses, realized it was Sunday and hightailed into town, knowing right where you'd be. I don't think he's here to woo you. I'm guessing he's out to convince you to return as his housekeeper."

"That's what I'm counting on. If all goes as planned, he'll let me continue to work for him—on my terms."

Concern creased Lizzie's brow. "Do you think that's wise? Things between you have changed. There's no denying it."

Becky shook her reticule, but there was no reassuring clink of coins. The drawstring bag held nothing but a handkerchief, her comb and a spare hairpin. "What choice do I have? I don't have a cent to my name, and yet I still owe him a good deal of money."

"You owe him money, yes, but you don't have to earn it working for him. You're a bright, talented young lady with many skills. I'm sure you could think of other ways to earn a living."

"I have, and he's going to help me do it. He just doesn't know that yet."

Lizzie smiled. "I like the sound of that. Tell me more."

Becky outlined her idea. "So that's the business I have in mind. Now I must convince him it would be a wise investment."

Hopefully, she'd sounded more confident than she felt. She couldn't impose on Lizzie any longer. Although her friend had welcomed her last night, despite the late arrival, Lizzie's cottage was no bigger than a pat of butter. They'd had to share the one bed.

"Suppose he agrees? It's as clear as the clock face on Big Ben—" Lizzie patted the ticking timepiece on her hat "—that you've developed a soft spot for the fellow. Keeping your distance might be more of a challenge than you think."

"You don't have to worry. I can handle myself."

Lizzie folded her arms and frowned. "You're a grown woman, but I hope you know what you're doing."

"I do." Perhaps if she said it enough times, she'd believe it. "I'd best go before he leaves."

Determination put a spring in her step. She rushed down the aisle, bid the reverend a hasty farewell and scanned the churchyard.

James stood off by himself beneath a gnarled oak with yellowed leaves. He tugged at his collar and adjusted his cravat. His uneasiness overcame her own.

She pasted on a smile and marched up to him, crisp leaves crunching under her feet. "Good morning, James. What a nice surprise to see you here."

He rubbed his scar, further evidence of his discomfort. "You left."

In the past she would have taken pity on him, possibly even reached out to him. No more. She must remain strong and businesslike, lest he think the kiss had meant something special to her. "I spent the night at Lizzie's."

"Why?"

"It wouldn't have been proper for me to stay there without *Mu*— without a chaperone."

"I hadn't thought of that." He fidgeted with his watch fob. "I noticed you borrowed some cash from the tin. Not that it's a problem," he added quickly. "If you need more…"

Caught up in the busyness of the past few weeks, she'd forgotten about the money she'd taken. She'd planned to tell him about her special purchase once *Mutti* was gone, but with things between them uncertain, now was not a good time. Unfortunately, her oversight could make the timing of her request problematic. "I should have said something, but you needn't worry. I'll pay it back, along with the rest."

"I know you will, but two dollars won't go far."

"True, which is why I have a proposition for you."

He leaned against the trunk of the massive oak. "I'm listening."

She lifted her chin and gave her best impression of her forthright friend, Jessie. "In order to finish repaying you, I need a job. In order to eat decent meals, you need someone to prepare them. You'll need help with the laundry and other household chores, too. I'd be willing to see to all that in exchange for my meals and the use of the extra cabin. It would be strictly a business arrangement."

"Sounds fair enough." He nodded. "You've got yourself a deal."

He'd agreed in a hurry. That was a promising start. "I'm not finished. When my work is done, I'd like to use your kitchen to prepare pies, cakes and such, which I'll be selling in town."

His brows dove into a V, sending her confidence into hiding. "Go on."

She moistened her lips and forged ahead. "I'll need supplies, so I'd like to buy them at Harris's grocery on your account and have the amount added to what I owe you."

There. She'd done it. She held her breath and awaited his response. If only she had a backup plan in case he turned her down, but she didn't. Her livelihood and her future were in his hands.

Chapter Fourteen

The last thing James needed was for Becky to lick her lips like that. He was having a hard enough time keeping his thoughts from straying to that amazing kiss they'd shared. The rosy glow in her cheeks and sparkle in her eyes didn't help, either. If she knew the effect she was having on him, she might decide not to come back.

With effort, he maintained the scowl he'd feigned. "You've already added two dollars to your debt. Are you sure you want to increase the amount?"

"In order to establish my business, I would require an initial investment. I don't think it would take me long to repay it, though."

"How much are we talking?" Not that it mattered. He'd gladly give her whatever she needed, although he knew better than to offer. She had a hard time accepting gifts from him.

She toyed with the fringe on her handbag. "I'm not exactly sure. I hadn't calculated it yet, but to start off I'll need—" she ticked off the items on her fingers "—a barrel of flour, a sack of sugar and a couple of gallons of molasses to make brown sugar, along with baking soda, vanilla and some spices. I'd say thirteen dollars would do."

That was all? He'd expected at least twenty. "Hmm. That's a considerable sum. How do I know you'll make enough money to repay me?"

Her fidgeting ceased, and she lifted that pretty round chin of hers. "There are a number of bachelors who don't have anyone to bake for them, so I'm sure I could convince Mr. Harris to sell my wares. And I would see if the hotels would be interested in them, too."

One taste of Becky's delectable desserts, and the owners would be eager to have her supply them. "Since I know you're a hard worker and can bake better than anyone I've ever met, I would be willing to loan you the money—on one condition."

A hint of a smile lifted the corners of her mouth. "You want to be my taster?"

He scrubbed a hand over the lower half of his face to hide his grin. "That goes without saying. In exchange for the use of my kitchen and all the milk, eggs and butter you would need, I'd like your help with some tasks in the orchard on occasion."

"You weren't all that eager to have my help in the past. Before the harvest, anyhow. Why now?"

"There are some tasks you would be well suited for."

Wariness creased her brow. "Would I be working with you?"

That was the idea, but it was clear that didn't appeal to her, which was understandable after last night. "I would have to instruct you, but you'd be on your own after that."

"I'll agree, then—on one condition."

"And that is?"

Her cheeks turned Rome Beauty–red. "About that scene in the barn…"

BUSINESS REPLY MAIL

FIRST-CLASS MAIL   PERMIT NO. 717   BUFFALO, NY

POSTAGE WILL BE PAID BY ADDRESSEE

READER SERVICE

PO BOX 1867

BUFFALO NY 14240-9952

NO POSTAGE
NECESSARY
IF MAILED
IN THE
UNITED STATES

Send For
2 FREE BOOKS
Today!

I accept your offer!

Please send me two free novels and two mystery gifts (gifts worth about $10). I understand that these books are completely free—even the shipping and handling will be paid—and I am under no obligation to purchase anything, ever, as explained on the back of this card.

102 IDL GJ2X/302 IDL GJ2Y

Please Print

FIRST NAME

LAST NAME

ADDRESS

APT.#   CITY

STATE/PROV.   ZIP/POSTAL CODE

Visit us online at
www.ReaderService.com

▲ Detach card and mail today. No stamp needed. ▲

"Yes?" He couldn't wait to hear what she had to say.

"It can't happen again."

He rushed his reassurance, infusing it with a full measure of sincerity. For some reason it had become essential that he convince her to stay. "It won't. Our arrangement will be strictly professional."

A flicker of pain clouded her eyes, but she blinked twice and fair weather returned. If he didn't know better, he'd say his response had disappointed her. But that made no sense. Perhaps he'd only seen what he wanted to see when what she was really after was a promise. "I give you my word, and you know how much I value honesty."

A different kind of pain wrinkled her brow. She twirled the ribbon ties of her bonnet around her finger and said nothing for several seconds.

At length she dropped her hand to her side. Her mouth was pressed into a firm line. Not a promising sight.

He had to lighten the mood. "Do you have a name for your business?"

She shook her head. "Not yet."

"What about Becky's Baked Goods?"

The color drained from her normally rosy cheeks. "It's nice, but I can't use it."

"Why not? I thought you'd appreciate the alliteration."

"I do, but…" She twisted a button on her gloves so hard it was a wonder the pearl-like thing didn't pop off. "There's something you need to know."

His stomach soured.

Honesty was every bit as important to Becky as it was to James, and yet she'd been living a lie. She could call it whatever she wanted—a falsehood, a fib or a fabrication—but that didn't change anything. She hadn't been entirely honest with him.

He'd agreed to finance her business, so he deserved to know the truth. Perhaps not the whole truth, but enough of it to grasp the gravity of her situation. He might be angry about her deception, but she'd just have to endure his outburst. Once he calmed down, she could explain things to him. Surely he'd understand why she'd felt it necessary to keep certain information to herself.

But would he agree to keep her secret? Or would he insist she leave?

There was only one way to find out. She must take a risk and trust that James would see things her way.

She took three short steps across the churchyard, the carpet of oak leaves crunching beneath her feet, leaving just two feet between them. A quick glance showed they were alone, but even so she lowered her voice. No one else could hear what she was about to say. Not even Lizzie.

"When I arrived you asked me who'd hit me, and I told you it was my brother. I told you later why he did it. Do you remember?"

He pushed away from the tree trunk he'd been leaning against, stood with his feet spread and arms folded. "Of course I do. You said he'd set fire to the factory where you both worked, and that he'd convinced the police to question you." Skepticism creased his brow. "That was the truth, wasn't it?"

"It was, but there was more to it." The words tumbled out. "He was angry with me. Although he committed the crime, he set things up so it looked like I was the culprit. He lit the fire on a night when I'd locked up, intentionally throwing suspicion on me. When I figured that out, I challenged him. Things got ugly, and he raised his hand to—" She took a steadying breath. "Everything happened so fast. I didn't see it coming."

He punched a fist into his other hand. It landed with a smack, and she jumped. "It's worse than I thought. Your brother is a— No. I can't say it."

Relief pushed the air from Becky's lungs in a noisy sigh. He was angry, but not at her. Perhaps he could be trusted with her secret. "Dillon's not the nicest person, that's for sure. I'm afraid he'll try to find me."

James rubbed his scar in an agitated manner. "That's why you were so scared when you thought you saw him after the benefit, wasn't it?"

She nodded.

"But you said you didn't expect to see him again. Has that changed?"

He was making this easier than she'd thought it would be. "In the letter my minister's wife sent she said Dillon had been looking for me. I'm afraid he might seek retaliation."

James frowned.

"That is the word, isn't it? It can't be *revenge* because I didn't do anything wrong. All I did was protect myself. He threw the first punch."

"Are you saying you hit him?"

She hadn't meant to say anything about that. "I, um, smacked him pretty hard with the coal scuttle. The blow knocked him out. That's how I was able to escape."

A smile crinkled James's scar. "You're even spunkier than I thought." He sobered. "Do you really think your brother can find you?"

"It would be hard. I used a different name, but even if I hadn't, there would be no record since the rail station where I boarded the train was destroyed in the fire."

"Becky Martin isn't your real name?"

My, but he was observant. "It is, and it isn't. Back in Chicago everyone knows me as Rebecca Donnelly. Martin was my mother's maiden name, and she used it as my middle name. I adopted the nickname Becky when I left and dropped Donnelly."

His brow furrowed. "If you were that worried, why didn't you use an entirely different name?"

"I don't like misleading people." Especially him. For some reason his approval meant a great deal to her. "I wouldn't have done it, but I had to conceal my identity or risk having him follow me."

"That makes sense. So does your concern about using Becky in your business name. We'll have to think of something else."

"We?"

"I'm financing your venture, so I figure I have a say. Wouldn't you agree?"

She hadn't expected James to show such interest, but she liked it. What she didn't like was increasing her debt. She would just have to make a success of her business so she could repay him quickly and be free to move on as soon as she heard from her minister's wife.

If only she didn't have to live life on the run.

Mariela O'Brien had been a beloved member of the community, as evidenced by the pews filled with her friends. James sat up front with his sister, Kate, her husband, Artie, and his five-year-old niece, Lottie.

When Becky had sent the telegram, she hadn't expected Kate and her family to attend *Mutti*'s service, but she was glad they'd made the trip from San Francisco. James and Kate needed one another, even if they were too stubborn to admit it.

The funeral was short and simple, in keeping with *Mutti*'s wishes. Mr. Parks delivered a stirring eulogy, and those gathered sang three of *Mutti*'s favorite hymns, concluding with one written by Martin Luther that had been translated from German to English, "A Mighty Fortress is our God." Becky sang it in German. Her eyes misted when she reached the last verse that contrasted one's mortal life with God's enduring kingdom. *Mutti* had looked forward to entering her heavenly home.

At the conclusion of the service, James and Kate stood at the door and thanked those who'd come to pay their respects. He stood as stiff as his starched collar, whereas his sister appeared more approachable than Becky had ever seen her, graciously accepting kisses on the cheek from several older women with tear-streaked faces. If Kate had been able to make her peace and move beyond the past, perhaps James could, too.

Becky caught a whiff of lime. Dr. Wright must be nearby. She glanced over her shoulder and spotted the doctor's blond hair beyond Lizzie's hat. Her friend stepped aside to speak with someone, and the doctor closed the gap.

He spoke in hushed tones. "I hesitate to say good morning at such a time, so I'll ask how you're doing, instead. I'm sure the past few days have been difficult."

"It hasn't been easy, but I'm managing. *Mutti* was very dear to me, and I miss her something fierce. My consolation is that she was ready to go and is no longer in pain. At the end, it was hard to keep it under control, even with the morphine."

"Unfortunately, that can be the case."

They made their way to James and Kate. She spotted Becky and gave her a hug. "I can't thank you enough for everything you did for *Mutti*. You were a godsend."

Dr. Wright added his praise. "Your mother couldn't have had a better nurse. Becky could make a living helping others like Mariela."

James brought his conversation with one of *Mutti*'s friends to a close and joined theirs. "She has a job. She's working for me, and—" he looked almost smug "—she's starting her own business. Gold Country Confections is sure to be a huge success."

His abrupt announcement surprised Becky, but if it had shocked Dr. Wright, the cultured gentleman didn't let it show. "That's wonderful news." He flashed her a smile. "Although I haven't had the privilege of sampling your desserts, I've heard great things about them."

Kate chimed in. "We're going to have a small gathering at the house after the family graveside service. We'd love it if you would join us for dinner, Doctor. Wouldn't we, James?"

His reply was far from enthusiastic. "Of course."

"Thank you both. I would count it an honor. I'd been hoping to have a word with Becky, so I'll escort her to the house." Dr. Wright held out his arm, and she had no choice but to take it.

James turned away, but not before Becky saw his narrowed eyes glint green. As flattering as it was to think of him being jealous, he'd made it clear he had no romantic interest in her. Even so, she couldn't shake the memory of the amazing kiss they'd shared.

Spending a few minutes in the company of the easy-going doctor would help her forget about James and his capriciousness. She smiled. How nice it was to have a wonderful dictionary that yielded such an apt word for his changing moods.

Dr. Wright led Becky down Main toward the livery, where he'd left his buggy. They walked in companionable silence, giving her time to make a mental list of pastries she could sell.

"Will you be making cream puffs? They're my favorite."

The doctor's comment took her aback. "The timing of your question is uncanny. I was just thinking about my selections."

He grinned. "So was I. I have a fondness for sweets and look forward to sampling your wares. Might I hope you'll be serving dessert after the meal?"

"I will. Three kinds, actually, that are variations on the usual fare. You'll be one of those subjected to my experiments."

"A more willing subject you'd be hard-pressed to find."

She chuckled. "Your flattery will ensure that you get hefty portions, Doctor."

"Matthew, please."

Shock glued her feet in place. Her thoughts were such a jumble she couldn't form a response. Was he interested in her? What would she do if he was? He was a nice man, but she had no romantic feelings for him.

He came to a stop, too. "I've startled you, haven't I? Do forgive me. Spending time with you reminds me of being in the company of my dear sisters, so I was eager to dispense with the formality."

"You have sisters?" She hadn't conversed with a gentleman about personal matters before, other than James. This glimpse into the doctor's life was intriguing.

"Yes, two. They took pity on their older brother, who was too engrossed in his studies to have a social life, and would cajole him into being their escort at various functions. I found I enjoyed attending plays, concerts and the like, and have done so ever since. Since you appreciated the Philharmonic Society's music, I'd hoped you would consider joining me at such functions on occasion. Would you?"

His comments at the benefit made sense now. He needed a friend, and so did she. The trouble was, she couldn't accept his offer. "I would love to, but I'm afraid I can't."

"And why is that, might I ask?"

"I haven't anything suitable to wear to a formal affair." She swept a hand over the black crepe she'd worn when she'd first met James. "I have only this and three simple day dresses."

"Please don't let that stop you. I realize many put stock in such things, but I don't. You look lovely no matter what you wear." Dr. Wright placed her hand on the crook of his arm, gave it a reassuring pat and resumed their stroll down the walkway.

"You're too kind, Doctor, er, Matthew. I don't know that I'll be as satisfactory a companion as your sisters, but I'm eager to learn new things and enjoy new experiences." She might as well enjoy herself while she could since such opportunities weren't likely to come her way very often.

"Your company will be most appreciated. The Musical Society over in El Dorado held its fall concert at Rutledge Hall earlier this month. Their performance was wonderful, as usual. I'll secure two tickets for their winter performance, which takes place the last Saturday in January. I'll let you know about other events, too."

Minutes later Becky was seated beside Matthew in his buggy. Conversation flowed freely as they recounted their days in Chicago. Since status and appearances didn't seem to matter to him, she relaxed and enjoyed talking with this unpretentious man who seemed to regard her as an engaging companion.

They reached the edge of the orchard where several birds perched in the apple trees, their assorted calls creating a pleasant chorus. Gray clouds scudded by, and a breeze fluttered the ties on her bonnet. The predicted storm would arrive before dinner was over. Thankfully, the doctor's buggy had side curtains. He would need them to protect him from the rain.

Since she'd agreed to continue working for James, she would need to protect herself from the deluge of emotions bombarding her. His might be changeable, but hers were confusing. She found herself thinking about him with increasing frequency and fondness, and that would never do.

Strong and steadfast. That was what she would be. And she'd keep her distance, too.

At least she'd try.

Chapter Fifteen

At last everyone had gone. James stood on the porch, the brisk wind running its fingers through his hair and ruffling Spitz's fur. The carriage Artie had rented from the livery disappeared down the long drive. James should be happy Kate and her family would return at Christmas, but all he wanted right now was to be left alone.

It didn't help that Kate had invited Dr. Wright and Lizzie to share their meal. He knew what to expect from the outspoken nurse, but the doctor had acted strangely. Instead of his professional manner, he'd been friendly. Overly so.

How could *Mutti*'s physician sit in the house where she'd breathed her last just three days before and lead such a lively conversation? It didn't help that the others had encouraged the doctor, laughing at tales of his sisters' futile attempts to educate him on women's fashion when he was younger. Becky had taken quite an interest, smiling at him openly. Almost as though she'd taken a shine to him.

Voices carried from beyond the barn. Becky appeared with Dr. Wright at her side. He carried a small brown paper parcel and seemed oblivious to all but the charming woman at his side. Not that James could blame the doctor. Becky grew lovelier with each passing day. Now that the strain of caring for *Mutti* was gone and Becky enjoyed uninterrupted sleep, her pretty round cheeks had taken on a healthy glow. She walked with a spring in her step that James hadn't seen in a long time.

There were her warm smile and cheery laugh again, two things he'd had a hard time coaxing out of her since the kiss they'd shared. Around him she was all business— when she was actually around.

She prepared delicious meals, but she took her portion to her cabin before he came in to eat. If he wanted to talk with her, he had to stop work early and catch her before she left or make a point of visiting her when she was in the middle of her baking. He'd tried both, but she busied herself with her chores, rarely making eye contact with him.

Perhaps she just needed some time to herself. She did have a lot to adjust to, what with *Mutti* gone, moving into her own place and starting a business. If hard work alone could make a success of her new venture, she was sure to succeed.

The squeak of a buggy's springs as Dr. Wright climbed aboard drew James's attention. The doctor set the package he'd been carrying on the seat and turned toward Becky. While James couldn't hear their conversation, he could see them. She used to look at him the way she was looking at the doctor, as though captivated by his every word, and he wanted that again.

Spitz loped over. James stooped to rub the friendly dog's silky fur and was rewarded with the swipe of a wet tongue across his cheek. "As much as I enjoy your company, boy, your kisses leave much to be desired. What

I would like is for you to put in a good word with your mistress. Tell her I'm not such a bad fellow."

The doctor drove away, and Becky returned to the house, passing James without a word. He followed her inside.

"I'll have things cleared up in a jiffy and leave you be." She began clearing the table.

"Aren't you going to bake?"

"Not today."

Disappointment slumped his shoulders. He sat at the table watching as she stacked the dirty dishes on the counter. She hummed a hymn but made no attempt to start a conversation.

The storm that had been threatening struck with a vengeance. Wind rattled the south-facing windows, and rain drummed on the metal roof. She peered out the front window. "I hope Kate and her family boarded the stagecoach before this hit. I pity poor Matthew. He has that three-mile drive back to Placerville ahead of him. At least he's heading north, so hopefully he'll be able to stay dry."

Since when had she taken to using the doctor's first name? Things between them seemed to be changing rapidly. Overcome with a desire to protect her, James couldn't keep quiet. "It looked like you took the doctor to your cabin. Is that wise?"

She whirled around, her blue eyes snapping. "I might not be as cultured as you are, but I know better than to invite a man into my home. The doctor is a gentleman and waited on the porch while I got a package for him."

"What was in it?" The moment the words were out of his mouth, James wished them back.

She folded and refolded a soiled napkin. When she finally spoke, her characteristic compassion resurfaced. "As much as I'd like to tell you it's none of your business, that would be untrue. I knew how hard it would be for you to see the medicine bottles, syringe and such, so I removed them that night and returned everything to Matthew today."

"I shouldn't have said that, but when I saw you two together, I assumed…"

"I enjoy Matthew's company. I see nothing wrong with that."

So his suspicions were correct. It appeared she intended to encourage the young doctor. She'd certainly gazed at him with warmth and interest. The way she'd looked at James moments before he'd leaned in for the unexpected kiss that had emblazoned itself in his memory.

Enough! Dwelling on the past did no good. If he wanted things between them to return to normal, he needed to think about the future. A good place to start would be convincing her to linger a while instead of bolting at her earliest opportunity.

"Let me take that for you." He reached for the napkin, and his hand brushed hers.

"Oh!" She dropped the checkered cloth. "You startled me. I was woolgathering."

She'd no doubt been thinking about Dr. Wright. No, not Dr. Wright. *Matthew.*

She scooped up the napkin, gathered the others and scurried to the lean-to, where she deposited them in the laundry basket. She reemerged with her head held high, filled the washtub and set to scrubbing the dishes so energetically that she sloshed water down her front, soaking her apron and likely the dowdy black dress beneath it.

He approached cautiously, careful not to startle her again. "Slow down, Becky. Please."

"I want to finish so I don't disturb you any longer than necessary."

"You're not disturbing me. You'd be doing me a favor by keeping me company."

Her hand froze midswipe. "I thought you'd want to be alone."

"I've spent too much time alone. The house is so quiet, so empty. If you were here baking, the walls wouldn't close in on me the way they have been."

"It seems disrespectful to go about my business as usual, but…" She glanced at *Mutti*'s room and caught her lower lip between her teeth, a gesture he found quite distracting. "All right, I'll stay. But if you change your mind, you must promise to tell me."

"Agreed." She had no need to worry. He wanted her there, humming while she worked and chasing away the gloominess with her own brand of sunshine.

He sat in his armchair, *Mountain Democrat* in hand, pretending to read last week's edition of the newspaper. Tasks awaited him in the barn, but he didn't have the heart to tackle them. He'd leave the work to Quon and Chung and concentrate on restoring the bond he'd shared with Becky before that memorable moment in the barn.

She finished the dishes in short order and pulled out her baking supplies. He ambled over and leaned against the kitchen counter. "You don't mind if I watch you work, do you?"

The topmost apple in the pyramid balanced on her splayed palms threatened to topple. Using her chin to hold the Rome Beauty in place, she prevented it from tumbling to the floor. "Why would you want to do that?"

"Two reasons. One is that as your initial investor, I want to see how you're utilizing your supplies. The other is that I'm curious what you're making today."

"Apple soufflé. That is, if you don't mind me using

some apples." She gestured toward the pile now resting on the counter.

"You may use all you want—" he grinned "—provided I get to perform a taste test."

Her answering smile didn't reach her eyes, but he took it as an encouraging sign nonetheless. "I would think you'd be full. You tucked in a fair amount of dessert after dinner."

"Don't worry. I'll find room for more." He moved farther down the counter, out of her way.

Watching her bake was a sight to behold. She wielded the tools of her trade with confidence. Joy oozed from her, as thick and creamy as the egg whites she'd whisked into white-capped perfection. He inhaled deeply, savoring the aromas of apple, vanilla and hope.

He'd made progress today. If he kept this up, things would be back to normal soon.

Some time later she pulled a tray of baked apples toward her and spooned in the frothy concoction she'd whipped up. The thought of sinking his spoon into one of the tasty desserts made his mouth water.

He tossed an apple in the air and caught it. "I'm curious. You cored and baked Rome Beauties, but you used Esopus Spitzenburg for the filling. Why?"

She opened the oven door, sending a blast of warm air swirling into the room, and slid the filled apples into the oven. Straightening, she blew a loose strand of hair out of her eyes. "The Rome Beauties are larger, and they hold their shape well after baking. When it comes to taste, though, they're rather plain." She lowered her voice, but he was sure she'd said, "Like me."

Before he could think of a way to counter her comment, she continued. "The Esopus have more sharpness to them."

"Like me."

His quick response elicited a genuine smile—and a chuckle. "Their sharpness is what makes them ideal." Even though Becky had erected a barrier, she didn't have it in her to be unkind.

"You seem to have a real understanding of the different varieties. I've been thinking of adding two more. Which would you suggest?"

"Hmm. From a baker's standpoint, I'd choose Northern Spy for its spiciness. I'd like to work with the flavorful Gravenstein, as well. I know the trees aren't as hardy as other varieties, but since the Gravenstein is harvested earlier, you could spread the work out."

She'd evidently done her research. Both varieties had been successfully cultivated in the area. "Good choices. I'll order the cuttings, and you can help me graft them to the root stock when they arrive in January."

"You meant what you said Sunday, didn't you? I wasn't sure, but helping with such chores would enable me to reduce my debt sooner."

"It wasn't intended to be a chore. I thought you'd enjoy learning to graft."

"Oh, I would, but..." She refilled the dish tub, using hot water from the cookstove's reservoir, and added some cold from the tap he'd installed.

As much as he dreaded finding out how thick the wall between them was, he had to know. "But what?"

She poured soap flakes into the steaming tub and swished them around until she'd created suds. Seeking a dry spot on her drenched apron and finding none, she pulled it off, glanced at her soaked front and muttered something about having nothing else to wear.

At long last she answered him. "I don't think it's wise for us to spend extended periods of time together."

It wasn't the work itself causing her to balk. It was the fact that she'd be working with him. He had to overcome her objections. "I didn't take you for a fickle person."

Her eyes widened. "I'm not."

"You told me you wanted to learn all you could about the trees and how to care for them. Now you're saying you don't want to. What else am I supposed to think?"

She turned away, but not before he saw those lovely lips of hers tremble. Her shoulders rose and fell three times before she faced him again. "I've done some calculations. Come the first of March, I'll no longer be beholden to you and will be free to leave. I've already been here longer than is wise."

Although he understood Becky's concern, she herself had said it was unlikely that her brother would find her. As far as he could tell, she'd allowed her fears to escalate beyond reason. "You don't have to do that. I need you—your help." If she left, she'd take the only bright spot in his life with her.

She grabbed a dish towel and dabbed at the wet spot on her black skirt. "I realize my departure will force you to find a replacement, but I can't stay here indefinitely."

"I know what you said about your brother, but it seems to me you're safer here than you might think. If you did decide to leave, what would you do?"

"I'm going to work on establishing my reputation as a baker. If possible I'll locate some customers in El Dorado and Placerville. I should be able to get several letters of recommendation before I have to go, and they would help me get customers elsewhere."

Placerville? That made sense. She'd be able to see Dr. Wright on a regular basis and enjoy his attentions.

James stiffened his spine. He wasn't about to stand by and watch that happen without a fight. She'd given him an idea how he could break through her defenses. She might protest, but he wouldn't let that keep him from pursuing his plan.

Chapter Sixteen

If James O'Brien thought he could force her to extend
her stay in Diamond Springs by foisting more fabric on
her, he was mistaken. The emerald bombazine, purple
poplin and coffee-brown wool would make wonderful
winter dresses, but she wouldn't give in this time, no
matter what he said.

Becky gave the pile of material a lingering look and
marched out of the house. A brisk wind whipped her
skirts. She shoved aside thoughts about how toasty warm
she'd be if she wore petticoats made from the soft flannel he'd bought.

After several minutes spent searching, she found him
on the far side of the orchard where he and the Lees were
plowing and scraping a two-acre section. This must be
where James planned to plant the one-year-old whips
he'd grown in his nursery beds. She dreaded seeing the
small trees uprooted, but now that the last leaves had
fallen, it was time.

She tromped across the field, careful to avoid the rows
of upturned soil left by the plow, and stopped in front of
him. He stood next to an odd-looking contraption with
three legs, notebook in hand. "We need to talk."

He slid the pencil behind his ear. "I take it you found the fabric."

"How could you do that again? I haven't even paid you back for what you bought last spring."

"You don't have to pay me back. It's a gift."

She shook her head. "I can't accept it. I won't. You knew that, but you bought it anyway. Why?"

His answer was a shrug coupled with a grin. Although she was piqued, she couldn't help but notice how handsome he looked with merriment dancing in his hazel eyes, now more brown than green. "Because I'm a generous sort, I guess."

"You can't trick me into staying longer than I think is wise. I'll just have to take everything back." She turned to leave.

"Please don't."

The urgency in his voice drew her up short. She wheeled around.

He dropped the notebook to the ground and closed the gap between them in a single stride. "You know what your problem is, Becky? You help others, but you refuse to let anyone help you. It's not fair."

She pressed her lips into a firm line. She was many things, but unfair wasn't one of them.

"I knew you'd get riled up, but I'm not going to let that stop me. You need warm dresses, whether you want to admit it or not, and so you'll have them."

There were many reasons she couldn't accept such a lavish gift. She grabbed at one he couldn't refute. "I have a dress." She swept a hand over her black gown. "It's warmer than the others, and what's more, it's suitable for mourning, whereas the others wouldn't be."

"There's no need for that. She wasn't your mother."

Indignation straightened her spine. He had no right

to discount the special bond she'd formed with *Mutti*. "How can you say that? I loved her, too, and I miss her. Very much."

"Of course you do, but you don't have to observe mourning. You can wear whatever you'd like, and I'd prefer to see you in pretty dresses."

"You'd prefer? What about me and what I want? Did you even stop to think about that?"

His brow creased. "You don't like what I chose?"

"Of course I do. You have excellent taste, but that's not the point. I want to honor *Mutti*'s memory—and I don't want to owe you more than I already do. I'd be forced to live here until—" she glanced at the orchard while she made a quick calculation "—until the trees bloom."

"Is being here with me so distasteful? You enjoy Lizzie's company. Why not mine?"

"It's different. You're…" Words failed her, and she sighed.

He gave her a long, pained look and held up his hands in surrender. "Not someone you want to be around any longer than necessary, I know. I thought you'd appreciate what I did for you, but I was wrong. You're too independent for your own good."

She clapped a hand to her chest and stepped backward, catching her foot in the furrow. Her arms flailed.

"Careful!" James caught her, his strong hands gripping her shoulders. He gazed into her eyes for the briefest of moments before releasing her, but it was long enough for her to see the depth of his grief.

His accusation stung because he was right. She had been thinking of herself. Her loss was nothing compared to his. "Thank you."

He gave her a halfhearted smile. "See? The words aren't that hard to say."

"I'm sorry. I didn't mean to sound so ungrateful. It's just that I've always been indebted to someone, and I want to make it on my own."

"So it's not really about the clothes? Good. Because I don't want to be reminded of my loss every time I look at you. It's hard enough living here with all the memories. You'll make up the dresses, then?"

She nodded. "I will, but you have to let me repay you. *Please.*"

His lips quirked into the most adorable smirk. "If that means I can enjoy your delicious meals and delectable desserts longer, I'd be a fool to argue. You have yourself a deal." He held out a hand, and she slipped hers into it. Warmth flowed up her arm and wrapped itself around her heart. She'd have to redouble her efforts to remain immune to his charms.

Instead of shaking her hand as she'd expected, he gave it a squeeze before letting go. "Since you're so eager to repay me, I have a surveying job you could help me with."

"How? I know nothing about surveying."

"It doesn't matter." He stooped to pick up the notebook. The top page contained a series of figures. "I attended the Grand Agricultural, Horticultural and Pomological Exhibition held at the Mechanics Pavilion in San Francisco back in August of '70. While I was there, I heard about a hexagonal system that will enable me to plant more trees per acre. Once the Lees and I have the ground leveled, I'll work the transit—" he jabbed a thumb at the fancy piece of equipment "—and you can hold the rod. If you're interested, that is."

Yes. Very. "Perhaps. We haven't settled on a rate of pay for my work in the orchard. I'll expect more than I get for the household chores and cooking."

He named a rate that was more than fair. "Agreed?"

"If you're sure you want my help. You know I'll pepper you with questions."

A grin lit his face. "I'm counting on it."

The next months could prove to be quite a challenge. She'd have to guard her traitorous heart because, try as she might, she couldn't deny her attraction to this remarkable man.

James grabbed the file and wire brush, which he plunked down on his workbench. Where was the oil? He'd left it on the shelf overhead, but it was nowhere to be seen.

The barn door squeaked, reminding him of yet another task on the list of chores that never seemed to get any shorter. Quon stepped inside. "You start work early, boss."

"Have you seen the linseed oil?"

Quon picked up a bottle sitting on the workbench in plain view and handed it to James.

"Thanks." He reached for a shovel and inspected it.

"Miss Becky say this day is hard for you. Chung and me can do chores. Work is not good when heart is broken."

"I'm fine!" He hadn't meant to snap, but things weren't going as planned. Becky had helped him with the surveying, and although she'd asked a passel of questions, she'd kept her distance. Worse yet, she still refused to eat her meals with him. Until today. She'd insisted on making a Thanksgiving feast.

"Leaves are all off trees. Chung and me rake yard." Quon walked backward with his hands in the surrender position. "We will not come in barn."

"Yes, rake. I'll help later, but I'm cleaning the tools now."

"Boss clean. Good." Quon took two rakes and hurried from the barn.

James poured vinegar into a tin and dipped some steel wool in the pungent liquid. He secured the neck of a shovel in his vise and began scrubbing.

Today would be the first day Becky sat at his table since *Mutti*'s passing. But they wouldn't be alone. Despite his protests, she'd invited guests. Who or how many he didn't know, since she wanted it to be a surprise. He was sure a certain doctor would be among them. She'd gone skating with Dr. Wright at the roller rink in El Dorado the week before and had come home with rosy cheeks and shining eyes.

Not that James had been watching for her. He'd heard a noise out front and needed to investigate, that was all. The fact that the sound had resembled the crunch of the doctor's buggy on the blanket of frosty leaves beneath the bare oaks had nothing to do with it.

The barn door squeaked once more. He groaned. "What now?"

"I came to get chicken feed."

"Oh, it's you, Becky. I thought Quon was back."

She looked lovely in the simple green dress she'd finished the day before, just as he'd known she would. The purple and brown ones looked good on her, too. If she didn't balk when he gave her anything, he would shower her with surprises. Someday she would thank him for a gift as enthusiastically as she had the dictionary, and he would rejoice.

"I won't be but a minute." She stole over to the sack and filled the scoop. The grain pinged against the metal sides as she poured it into the pail.

He leaned the shovel he'd been cleaning against the workbench. It slid and fell to the floor with a thump. She jumped and sent chicken feed flying. Dropping to her knees, she snatched at the grain.

His long strides carried him across the barn in no time. He held out a hand. "Leave it."

She refused his help, stood and dumped another scoop into the pail. "I know you're not happy that I decided to fix a big dinner, but ignoring the holiday won't make it any easier. You'll be happy when you see what I've done."

He doubted that.

"Scowl if you like, but I won't let your grumpiness ruin the day for everyone else." She swept out of the barn without a backward glance.

That was for the best. He had work to do. These tools wouldn't clean themselves. He picked up the file and ran it over the blade. With each stroke, the edge of the shovel grew sharper—and so did his thinking.

Becky didn't want *things*. She valued experiences and knowledge. He'd just have to think up something sure to please her.

An idea began to form.

Becky enjoyed the rich texture of the linen tablecloth beneath her fingertips as she smoothed a wrinkle. She'd set four places with the Meissen china boasting delicate yellow flowers that James's grandparents had brought over from Germany. She'd added a bowl of yellow and red leaves as a centerpiece. If all went well, the homey atmosphere she'd created would help James recall wonderful memories of Thanksgiving celebrations he'd shared with his family around this very table.

Everything was prepared, save the biscuits, which were almost ready to come out of the oven. The wild turkey he'd shot was roasted to perfection. The sage stuffing filled the house with mouthwatering scents. Mashed and sweet potatoes, three different vegetable dishes, cranberry sauce and assorted preserves and condiments completed the offerings. All she needed was for her reluctant dinner partners to arrive.

As if on cue, the door to James's room opened. She'd asked him to dress for the occasion, and he'd obliged, donning the brown tweed frock coat, white dress shirt and cravat he'd worn the day she'd met him. She'd been too agitated then to realize what a striking figure he made, but no more. It required restraint not to feast her eyes.

He tugged at his waistcoat. "Everything smells delicious, as usual." His gaze passed over the table. "Only two guests. Lizzie and Dr. Wright, I presume."

She shook her head. "Lizzie's working. Matthew's parents are in England, so he invited his sisters out West to spend the holidays with him."

James didn't attempt to hide his relief. He made no secret of the fact that he didn't care for Lizzie, but he used to hold *Mutti*'s doctor in high regard. Something had changed, and for the life of her, Becky couldn't figure it out. Unless…

She shook her head. James couldn't possibly blame Matthew for his mother's death. The kindly doctor had done everything he could to help her. There must be some other reason.

"Ralph and Coleen?"

Becky hadn't meant for her surprise to puzzle him, but she'd been afraid her shy guests would change their minds if he said something to them. "Not the Strattons. They're celebrating with their children."

"Someone from church?"

"No. The guests I've invited wouldn't be welcome, not that they would attempt to attend services."

"I'll admit I'm flummoxed. You didn't invite some strays off the street, did you? I know you have a soft spot for the downtrodden, but—"

Someone knocked. He jerked his head toward the front door, his features tense.

Doubt about her decision gnawed at Becky. "You don't have to worry. It's just the Lees."

"Really?" He yanked the door open.

Quon stood on the porch wearing a patterned purple tunic and rocking from heel to toe, with Chung behind him in a red version of the beautiful silk garment, the more reserved brother's gaze resting on the floorboards.

A smile lit James's face. "How wonderful to see you, gentlemen." He stepped aside and invited them in with a sweep of his hand.

They removed their pointed wicker hats, and Becky hung them in the lean-to. She returned to find the three men looking equally uncertain, despite the warm welcome James had given the brothers.

"Let me turn out the biscuits, and then we can all take our seats."

Moments later she placed the basket on the table and sat. "Quon and Chung, you may take that bench—" she held out a hand to the one opposite her "—and James can sit beside me."

Once the men were seated, she waited for James to lead them in prayer, but he said nothing. She leaned over and whispered, "Did you want to say grace?"

He cast her a sidelong glance filled with apprehension. "I can't. You'll have to."

She hadn't thought about it before, but he'd dived into the meals she'd left him a number of times without asking a blessing beforehand. Had he ceased praying all together? The thought pinched her heart. *Lord, please give me the words.*

"I'm going to say a short prayer, gentlemen. Please bow your heads and close your eyes." They obliged, and she began, a sense of peace filling her. "Dear Father, it's been a difficult year for all of us, losing *Mutti* as we did, but we have much to be grateful for—a wonderful place to live, the bountiful harvest and special friends. Be with us now as we enjoy the food You've provided for us. In Your Son's name, Amen."

James echoed her *Amen*, cleared his throat and set to work carving the turkey. "You've outdone yourself, Becky. Everything looks wonderful." He served her and turned to the Lees. "Do you want to try this?"

Quon held out his plate. "Yes. Miss Becky is good cook."

Chung nodded. "Much good, yes."

James paused with the carving knife and fork suspended in midair. "When have you eaten her cooking?"

Quon cast a glance at Becky. "You not tell him?"

"Tell me what?"

She picked up a bowl of green beans. "I wanted to try their food, and they wanted to try mine, so we've been sharing some of our meals. Since I don't take more than my share from your table, I didn't think it would be a problem."

James cut a slice of white meat for Quon. "It's not. I'm just surprised...since you don't eat with me anymore."

Chung passed his plate to James. "She here now. Ask us come. Nice lady."

Unwilling to explore the topic further in front of the Lees, Becky changed the subject, identifying each of the items the brothers hadn't tasted before. The conversation drifted to talk about the orchard. She listened, eager to learn as much as possible about growing apples, but she couldn't get James's comment out of her mind. He'd sounded hurt that she didn't dine with him. Perhaps she should reconsider her decision.

The men tucked in seconds and thirds before they were done, heaping compliments on her as they refilled their plates. In spite of all they'd eaten, they didn't want to wait for dessert, so she brought out the pies—apple, pumpkin and mince. The spicy aroma of cinnamon set her mouth to watering.

Quon and Chung had introduced her to green tea, and they enjoyed a pot of it. James reached for the sugar bowl, but she stopped him. "They taught me to drink it without cream or sugar. Why don't you see if you like it that way?"

He stared at her hand resting on his.

She pulled her hand away and tucked it in her lap. "Never mind. Do what you like."

"It's fine. I'll try it." He lifted the cup, blew on the fragrant beverage and took a sip. The face he made was so comical she and the Lees laughed.

Chung caught his breath first. "Boss not like."

Becky smiled. "It takes some getting used to. I'll get these out of the way." She hopped up from the table and began clearing the dessert plates.

The Lees jumped to their feet, and James followed suit.

Quon bowed. "Thank you for good time, boss. Thank you for good food, Miss Becky. We have gift for you. Something Chinese."

Chung flipped open the most beautiful fan she'd ever seen. A Chinese couple had been painted in the center of the white silk, surrounded by red, yellow and purple flowers. While the images were stunning, she couldn't take her eyes off the row of brilliantly colored peacock feathers mounted between the wooden stays.

"Here. You take." Chung handed her the exquisite creation.

She resisted the urge to hug the brothers and bowed instead, as was their custom when expressing gratitude. "Thank you. I've never had anything as fancy as this. It's almost too nice to use."

Quon smiled. "We happy you like it."

Following the Lees' departure, Becky stood in the kitchen with fan in hand. She appreciated their thoughtfulness and generosity, but what meant more to her were the friendships she'd formed with the brothers. Quon had been easy to get to know, but it wasn't until recently that Chung had begun to talk to her.

"You certainly seem happy with your gift."

She looked up to see James watching her, a frown tugging at his mouth. "I am."

"I see. I suppose it depends on who's given it."

His meaning wasn't lost on her. "We're not back to that, are we? I do appreciate all you've done for me, but it's different."

"Obviously."

"They're my friends."

"And I'm not?"

He didn't understand. "You're my friend, too, but—"

"Please. Don't say any more." He drew in a deep breath, released it in an audible puff and unfurled his fists. "I appreciate your hard work. The dinner was delicious. I don't know how you talked Quon and Chung into coming, but I'm glad you did. I've never been able to convince them to join me. Seems no one wants to lately. Now I'll change out of these fancy togs and tend to the animals." He ended with a halfhearted smile.

That was quite a speech he'd given, obviously sincere but revealing. She'd hurt him. "I didn't realize how much you dislike eating alone. If it's that important to you, I could eat my meals here. At least part of the time. Quon and Chung will still be expecting me."

"Do whatever you want. It doesn't matter to me." He spun on his heel and headed to his room, leaving her with a dilemma. Did she continue as she had been, eating elsewhere, which made it easier to fight the attraction that refused to dim no matter how hard she tried to ignore it? Or did she reinforce the wall she'd erected around her heart and dine with James?

Chapter Seventeen

He really should be helping Quon and Chung level the new plot, but when Becky had asked to borrow the wagon to deliver her baked goods to Mr. Harris and the hotel owners in Diamond Springs, James had seized the opportunity to join her. Ever since Thanksgiving, she'd become friendlier. Not overly so, but she had eaten with him five times during the past two weeks.

Watching her interact with her customers brought him a sense of satisfaction. She conducted herself with confidence befitting someone with far more experience. At the rate her business was growing, she'd repay him by spring for sure. He had a short time to convince her that the possibility of her brother showing up was slim and that she didn't need to leave the area once she'd settled her debt. Why it mattered so much, he wasn't sure. But it did.

Becky completed her conversation with the owner of the Washington House hotel and rejoined James, a broad smile dimpling her cheeks.

"You look pleased."

"That I am." Her breath hung in the chilly air. "Mr. Young and Mr. Bird are planning several holiday events at their hotels. Both want lavish dessert displays, and both have hired me to prepare them. I'll have to be creative and expand my selections, because neither wants to serve something the other offers."

James grinned. "I like the sound of that. More experimentation on your part means more sampling on mine."

She gave him a playful swat. "You and your sweet tooth."

He placed her hand on his arm and started down the wooden walkway, rejoicing when she didn't pull away. "Did you see the flier in the window about the Mud Springs Musical Society's concert next month? I thought you might enjoy going to it."

"I will. Matthew's taking me. He enjoys music, too, and says their performances are every bit as good as the concert I heard in Placerville."

James clenched his teeth to keep from showing his disappointment. He should have known the doctor would have asked her already. He seemed to find as many opportunities as possible to enjoy Becky's company. She'd gushed about the poetry reading he'd taken her to the week before.

The thought of Dr. Wright courting Becky appealed to James as much as reliving the nitro explosion that had torn his world to pieces. He'd been plagued by one of his nightmares last night, waking in a cold sweat.

She toyed with her collar. "Matthew's assured me one of my new dresses will be just fine."

"But surely you'd feel more comfortable in a fine gown." If only he could think of a way to give her one, but if he did, she would protest like usual. Unless...

"I'm sure no one will be looking at me." Her overly bright laugh wasn't convincing.

"I think you might be surprised." It wouldn't matter if she wore a flour sack. Gentlemen would still admire her. He could see why Dr. Wright enjoyed having her on his arm. She possessed an inner beauty that added to her appeal.

"Something must have tickled you. You're grinning."

Was he? "I was thinking about how much I'm enjoying some time away from the orchard and its many demands." He had thought of that. Earlier.

"You do seem more relaxed than usual. And here I was sure you were thinking about the company you're keeping." She giggled, a cute sound that did strange things to him. "A man with your penchant for sweets would want to keep on good terms with his baker."

"*Penchant* must be your new word for the week."

"A single word a week?" She chuckled. "I do my best to learn three new words a day. Mr. Young just used that one, and I found a way to do so myself as soon as possible. That way I won't forget it."

"Well, then, how about *predilection* or *proclivity*? Both could be used to express a fondness for something."

She stopped. "How did you do that? Come up with such fitting synonyms so quickly? I'm impressed—and a mite jealous."

"I suppose it's due to my reading."

"It must be wonderful to be so learned. Someday I'll be able to buy books and immerse myself in them. But that will have to wait. First I need to repay you, which reminds me." She opened the small handbag hanging from her wrist, counted out fifteen dollars and handed the coins to him. "I've earned enough to pay you back for the supplies and—" she dipped her head "—the other."

"The other? I don't understand. You only borrowed thirteen for supplies."

She lifted her chin and her gaze. "The money I borrowed from the cocoa tin."

"Oh, that small sum. I'd forgotten about it."

"Well, I didn't. I take my debts seriously. I'll be able to finish paying off my train ticket soon, and then I can work on reimbursing you for the fabric. With the new orders I got today, I might even be able to cancel my debt earlier than I'd expected. Wouldn't you like that?"

Not at all. She'd be leaving then, unless her suitor, Dr. Wright, convinced her to stay. "There's no hurry. You'll want to be sure you have enough to purchase the supplies you need."

"I have." She held up her purse and shook it, the coins inside jingling. "And speaking of supplies, Mr. Harris should have my order ready by now. We can pick up yours, too, and get back home."

"Certainly. I'm sure you're eager to get started on dinner." He held out his arm, and she wrapped her gloved hand around his elbow without hesitation.

"I'm not cooking dinner today. Quon and Chung are. We thought you might be willing to join us so you could sample Chinese food for yourself."

"Really? I'd like that." More than she knew.

He was making inroads. If he kept this up, Becky would trust him again in no time. Then he could figure out what to do about an overly friendly doctor.

Christmas had never been so exciting. Having Kate and her family staying at James's place added to Becky's joy. When Kate insisted Becky join them on their Christmas Eve outing up the mountain, she'd eagerly accepted.

If only James would take advantage of this opportunity to patch things up with his sister, but he was keeping his distance. At least he was enjoying his young niece. Lottie's squeals as he and Artie took turns sledding with the fun-loving girl warmed Becky's heart.

James had grumbled when Kate wrote that Lottie's Christmas wish was to see snow for the first time. Despite his reluctance, he'd spent his free time the past week fashioning a bright red sled for Lottie.

Becky piled the remains of their simple dinner in the wicker basket and set it in the back of the wagon next to the small pine James had felled, which they would be decorating that evening. Her nose tingled from the cold, but that didn't bother her. Some of her happiest childhood memories were of the afternoons she'd spent racing down the hillside on Dillon's old sled.

Kate turned from watching her husband and their five-year-old daughter barrel down the snowy slope. Mischief danced in her eyes. "What's going on with you and James? When I was here before, I was certain romance was blooming, but things seem strained between you now. He mentioned you've been seeing Dr. Wright. Have you developed feelings for the doctor?"

Becky forced a laugh. "I have a handsome, successful man eager to take me places. I'd be a fool to refuse his kind offers, would I not?"

Although she'd begun to suspect that Matthew might have feelings for her, she'd done nothing to encourage him. While he was kind and generous, he didn't set her pulse to racing like— No. She mustn't entertain such thoughts.

Kate persisted. "If the roses in your cheeks weren't brought on by thoughts of Dr. Wright, could it be James who's put the color there?"

Before she could stop them, Becky's hands flew to her face. She lowered them and fought the urge to grimace. "He's a fine man. I have great respect for him."

"Respect? Is that all?" Kate smiled a knowing smile. "While my cantankerous brother is as chilly toward me as ever, the looks he's been sending you are as warm as that hot cocoa you promised us."

"He might have moments when he's testy, but he can be a lot of fun, too." Becky glanced at him sliding down the hill with Lottie snuggled in front of him, a grin on his handsome face. "Look at him now."

"I think he could have more fun if you were to join him." Kate waved a hand and called out, "Oh, James! Becky wants a ride."

She did, but she hadn't planned to ask. This was Lottie's day, and the sled was her brand-new Christmas present.

He came to a stop at the base of the hill and helped his niece get to her feet. Artie suggested building a snowman, lifted his agreeable daughter onto his shoulders and headed off toward a flat area. James grabbed the rope tied to the front of the sled and smiled. "Come on. I'll take you down."

Riding with him was not what she'd envisioned. Although the sled held two people, they would have to sit close. Very close. Resisting his charms required distance and a cool head. Thanks to his offer, she would lose the first, and that would make maintaining the second nearly impossible.

"Um, thanks." She tromped over to him. The snow threatened to crest her boot tops. Putting a hand over her eyes to block the glare from the sun, she scanned the hillside, assessing the surface packed by many who'd gone sledding before them. "I see a perfect spot to start from. Follow me."

"I should have known you'd done this before."

"Yes, but not on a sled as fine as this. Your workmanship is extraordinary."

He shrugged. "Lottie likes it. That's what matters."

By the time they reached the top of the hill, Becky was winded and her hem was wet, but that didn't dampen her spirits. She hadn't had the opportunity to sled in years, and she missed the thrill.

James eyed the slope. "Are you sure you want to do this? We'll pick up a lot of speed going down."

She laughed. "That's the idea. Unless you're scared." With his hands tucked into his armpits and his eyebrows drawn, he did look a bit apprehensive.

His hands fell to his sides. "Of course not. It's just snow." He exhaled, his breath floating between them in a frosty swirl, and inclined his head toward the sled. "After you."

Eagerness put a smile on her face. She grabbed the rope handle and tugged, angling the sled toward the path she'd chosen. Taking care not to expose any more of her petticoats than necessary, she sat on the varnished seat and braced her feet on the front crosspiece he'd added. That feature would make this ride much better than any she'd taken before.

James plunked down behind her, dug his feet into the snow to anchor the sled in place and wrapped his arms around her waist. Despite the layers of fabric between them, a band of warmth encircled her. If things between them were different, his proximity would be a delight. As it was, she'd have to concentrate on the matter at hand to keep from thinking about how nice it was to be nestled on the sled in front of him.

She grasped the rope, and excitement surged through her. "I'm ready whenever you are."

"I, uh, hope you've charted a good course, because I'm at your mercy."

"As long as you hold on tight, everything will be fine."

Everything except her pulse. Thanks to his nearness, it was erratic.

He raised his feet and placed his legs alongside hers. They shot down the hill. Exhilaration overtook her as they picked up speed.

They approached the small mound she'd aimed for. She leaned back, bracing herself for their short flight.

James's face appeared beside hers. They left the earth, his gasp ringing in her ear.

Leaning into the hill, she attempted a smooth landing, but he loosened his hold just as they hit, throwing off her balance and sending them tumbling. The sled bounced its way to the bottom of the hill without them.

Becky performed an ungainly somersault before catching herself, but James rolled a good fifteen feet before coming to a stop. She got up, laughing, and scampered down the bank to him. "Are you all right?"

He stood, brushed himself off and scowled. "I don't like snow."

"Why not? It's such fun to play in."

"Well, it's not fun to work in."

"When did you? Ah, yes. On the railroad." She started down the hill with James tromping along beside her.

"The winter of '66–'67 was the worst. There was one storm after another. Forty-four in all, they said. We battled eighteen feet of snow at times at the summit." He rubbed at his scar.

A chill overtook her, and she shivered. "The explosion. It didn't happen in the summer like I'd thought. It happened that winter. The other worker slipped on the snow. And you slid down a mountainside covered in it, didn't you?"

"I'd rather not talk about it."

"Oh, James. I'm so sorry. I understand now why you

didn't want to come today. But you did it anyway—for Lottie. Bless you."

"Becky, please. Don't make a fuss. Let's just get the sled and try again."

"Of course." She wagged a finger at him and scolded him playfully, "But next time don't let go of me."

He grinned. "Never."

They reached the bottom, where Lottie skipped over to them. "You fell down, Uncle James. Do you need some love? Mama gives me some when I get hurt."

"I'd like that." He dropped to one knee and opened his arms.

Lottie flew into them. She hugged his neck and planted a kiss on his forehead. "There. You're all better. Will you help build the snowman?"

"Sure. Unless anyone else needs some love. Becky did fall down, too." He winked at her.

Shock rendered her speechless. Surely he didn't mean to give her a kiss.

Of course not. He was merely suggesting that Lottie dole out another hug. "I'm fine. In fact, if you'll let me use your nice new sled again, Lottie, I'd like to ride it alone until your uncle is ready to rejoin me."

"You can play with it. Uncle James is gonna help Papa and me." She took his hand and tugged him toward the spot where her father had formed the snowman's base.

Kate sauntered up to Becky and stood beside her while watching the men and Lottie. "My, my. I've never seen my brother flirt before. It appears he's taken quite a fancy to you."

"You're mistaken. There's nothing between us." There couldn't be, not when she would be forced to leave as soon as she earned enough to clear her debt. "The fall just brought up…something." James wouldn't want her telling his sister what had happened.

"It's all right. I know his nightmares have returned. I thought a trip to the snow might help. He hasn't been since that awful day."

"He's here now. That's encouraging."

Lottie pelted James with a snowball. He chased after her, caught her and spun her in circles, her laughter floating on the crisp air.

Kate chuckled. "What's encouraging is seeing him happy again." She grew serious. "I stayed away in part because being around him in his grumpy state was unpleasant. But he's warmer now, like our dear Papa was, and I have you to thank for that."

"I didn't do anything. I just prayed." Daily. Earnestly.

To her delight, God was answering her prayers. While things with James were still strained, he was more amiable. And entirely too attractive for his own good—or hers.

She couldn't form an attachment to him…to anyone, not when she'd be gone before the snow melted.

Chapter Eighteen

The lingering scents of the delicious breakfast Becky had prepared before she'd left for her place combined with the fresh scent of the pine tree James and Lottie had decorated to create a festive atmosphere. His energetic niece and her indulgent father had gone to the barn to pay the animals another visit, leaving James alone with Kate. His sister had her nose buried in the newspaper.

James picked up the family Bible from the table beside his armchair and flipped it open to the book of Luke. Kate had asked him to read the account of Christ's birth, as had been the custom on Christmas morning throughout their childhoods. The difference was that both of their parents were gone now.

For Lottie's sake, he had to shake his melancholy. As he had yesterday, he would get through the next part of their Christmas celebration by keeping his focus on her. Things might turn out better than expected. After all, he'd dreaded going out in the snow and had actually ended up enjoying himself.

There had been that unfortunate episode when Becky had attempted to take the sled over a snowdrift and send it hurtling through the air. Instead, they'd tumbled. Although she'd asked about the explosion at the time, she'd let the matter drop after that—unlike Kate.

His overbearing big sister had said he should go back up to the summit, where he'd come so close to losing his life that fateful day in '68. She insisted that seeing the place under different circumstances might bring an end to his nightmares.

If only he hadn't had one while she was there. But he had, calling out the night before last and waking her. Seeing her face in the shaft of moonlight as she'd leaned over his bed had brought back memories of the many times she'd looked out for him when he was a boy.

Perhaps he'd been too unyielding. She and Artie were happy with their life in San Francisco, as well they should be. They had everything James himself had been working for—a fine house in a good part of the city, friends in the right social circles and respect.

No one looked down on Kate. Of course, no one knew she was the daughter of poor, hardworking immigrants. She'd traded her Irish surname six years ago for Artie's respectable British one. No one maligned an Elliott.

James heaved a sigh.

His sister put the newspaper down, moved from her puffy purple chair to *Mutti*'s rocker beside his armchair and clasped his hand. "I know it's hard, Jimmy. I miss them, too. But we have each other."

He gave her hand a squeeze before releasing it. "Yes, we do. I've been a hardheaded fool. Can you forgive me?"

"If you can forgive me for storming out of here all those years ago. I honestly believed *Mutti* and Papa didn't care about my dreams as much as they did yours, but I know now I was wrong. Becky encouraged me to return and say what I needed to say to *Mutti*. I didn't want to, but I'm thankful I heeded Becky's wise counsel. I don't have to live with regrets."

He glanced over his shoulder to the empty kitchen. "Speaking of Becky, I thought you were going to ask her to stay."

"I did, but she said she didn't want to intrude on our family time."

"She has to be here."

Kate assumed the big-sister manner he knew so well, ordering him about, albeit with a smile this time. "Of course she does. Go get her."

He covered the distance to Becky's cabin in no time, rapped on the door and waited. A flurry of footfalls sounded before she opened it.

Her cheeks were flushed. "Oh, James, it's you. I wasn't expecting company. Not that you're here for a visit, I know." She cringed, and the color intensified. "I'm sorry. You've caught me in the middle of wrapping my gifts. I have a little something for each of you that I'll bring over when I come to fix dinner."

"You can bring them yourself. Now. We'd like you to join us."

Her hand flew to her throat. "Are you sure? I'm not family."

"We want you there. All of us." No one more than him. Without her, the celebration would be incomplete. "Please. It would mean a great deal to me—to us."

She smiled. "In that case, how can I refuse?"

"Good. I'll wait on the stoop until you're ready."

"I can't ask you to do that. It's cold, and you're not wearing your overcoat." She tipped her head from side to side as though weighing a decision. "If you won't accuse me of being forward, you can step inside while I finish wrapping Lottie's gift. It won't take long."

He should insist on remaining outside, but a desire to see her place overruled his good judgment. "Thanks. I appreciate the offer."

"Do come in, then." It wasn't like Becky to get flustered, but she looked decidedly ill at ease.

He stood just inside the door of the one-room cabin, taking in the sparse surroundings. He hadn't been inside in years. The only furniture was a bed covered with *Mutti*'s cast-off bedding, a table where Becky's dictionary lay open and a single bentwood chair. No bureau, washstand or wardrobe. Not even any hooks for her dresses. They hung on nails haphazardly driven into the wall. The rest of her clothing must be in the crates stacked in the far corner.

He wouldn't ask a man to endure such stark conditions, and yet Becky had been living there the past two months without a word of complaint. He would have to make amends for his oversight right away.

Becky folded a pair of mittens inside a fabric square, wrapped a piece of brightly colored string around the small package and tied a bow, chattering as she worked. "The embroidery floss was *Mutti*'s, but she told me I could use any of her supplies I wanted. I hope you don't mind."

"Not at all." Guilt left a sour taste in his mouth. Becky was as thoughtful as he was neglectful. But he had a couple of surprises in store for her that would make her happy. Or so he hoped.

Sitting in *Mutti*'s rocking chair with Kate to her left, James to her right and Artie at the far end of the semicircle, cradling Lottie in his lap, Becky couldn't help but feel out of place. James had insisted she join them, so here she was, even though her conscience had screamed at her all the way from her cabin to the house.

The way he'd watched her every move as she'd wrapped the final package, with his eyes wide and pupils so large the hazel was all but hidden, she'd been powerless to refuse his request. The simple act of tying a bow had become a near impossibility as she stole glances at him from beneath her lashes.

She listened to his rich voice as he read the Christmas story, rejoicing that his gaze was fixed on the page, enabling her to study him without his knowledge. How a man could grow even more handsome than he'd been the day before was a mystery, but James had done just that.

The instant he finished reading and set the Bible on the side table, Lottie leaped from her father's lap. "Can we open them now, Mama?"

Kate grinned. "Yes, darling."

A mound of presents hidden beneath brightly colored tissue paper had appeared under the Christmas tree that morning. From the look of it, most were for Lottie. The adults watched as she ripped and tore her way through the wrappings, revealing a vast array of toys, along with more dresses than Becky owned, two hats and a new pair of boots. Never in her life had she seen such a lavish display.

Kate, Artie and James exchanged gifts. Becky watched and waited, her anticipation mounting. She might not have much to give, but she'd put a great deal of thought into her choices.

"Is that all?" Lottie asked.

Artie pulled her to his side and lifted her drooping chin with a finger. "Sweetheart, you got a lot of things. What do you say?"

She dipped her chin and mumbled dutifully, "Thank you, everybody."

James leaned forward. "You have one more gift, and it's a special one from Becky."

She handed Lottie the package. The little girl pulled off the wrapping and squealed. "Look-ee! They're mittens, and they're red, just like my sled."

Her childish glee surpassed Becky's expectations. Now to see what James and Kate thought of their gifts. They took the identical packages Becky handed them and opened them simultaneously.

Kate inhaled sharply and pressed a hand to her throat. "Oh, Becky! This is wonderful." She stared at the small cardboard-mounted photograph, her chin trembling.

"I'm glad you like it."

"Like it? I love it. Don't you, Jimmy?"

James tore his gaze from the *carte de visite*. "No one's ever given me anything that means as much as this. To be able to look at *Mutti* again whenever I want…" He traced the image of his mother's face with a fingertip. "When did you do this? *How* did you do this?"

"Back in September. I was in town when a traveling photographer arrived. When I heard him talking about how nice it would be to have a memento of a loved one, I asked if he could come to the house and have *Mutti* pose for him. He did. She was so happy with my idea that she insisted on getting dressed and sitting in her chair. *This* chair." Becky ran her hands over the smooth arms of *Mutti*'s rocker.

"September, you say? I see." James glanced toward the pantry where he kept the cocoa tin that contained the household money, from which she'd borrowed the two dollars, and nodded. "You've kept your secret a long time. And what a secret. Thank you, Becky. I will treasure this for the rest of my life." He cradled the photograph in his hands and continued to study it.

"As will I." Kate handed Becky a small package. "Artie and I got you a little something from San Francisco. They're Ghirardelli chocolates. I think you'll like them."

"Oh, I'm sure I will. Here, I'll open them, so we can all share."

Artie chuckled. "Better not do that, or James will devour them. He has a fondness for sweets."

James grinned. "Becky knows that. She keeps my sweet tooth happy. And now it's my turn to give her a gift. I'll be right back." He went to his room and returned moments later. "Here you go."

He handed her a package the same size, shape and weight as the dictionary he'd given her. Anticipation swirled in her chest. It had to be another book. She itched to rip off the brown paper as Lottie had the tissue paper on her presents earlier, but forced herself to behave like a sensible adult instead.

Pulling back the paper, she spied a light brown cover. She read the spine to herself, unsure how to pronounce the two words in the title: *Roget's* must be a name, but what was a *thesaurus*?

"Your face is scrunched. Don't you like it?" James sounded crestfallen.

Kate responded before Becky could think of anything to say. "Jimmy, dear, I think if you'll explain what it is, she'll like it just fine."

"Of course. I didn't realize… It's *Roget's Thesaurus*, a book of synonyms. You look up a word in the index, note the number next to it and go to that entry, where you'll find a list of words like it."

She followed his directions, choosing the first word to come to mind—*overwhelmed*—flipped to entry 824 and found half a page of words with similar meanings.

She covered her gaping mouth and leaned forward and back several times, setting *Mutti*'s chair to rocking. After drawing in a series of calming breaths, she was able to speak.

"I had no idea anything like this existed. It's amazing, and I'm—" she scanned the list of words "—*shocked, stunned, astounded, enraptured, excited* and very, very grateful. I thought the dictionary you gave me was incredible, but this… I don't know quite what to say."

Lottie chimed in. "You're happy."

Becky laughed along with the others. "That I am. Oh, James, I don't know how to thank you."

"Seeing your joy is all the thanks I need."

"There's another present hiding in the back." Lottie hopped off Artie's lap and belly-crawled under the tree, pulling out a flat, floppy package. "Is it mine, Mama?"

"No, dear." Kate took the parcel from her daughter. "I'd forgotten all about this. A delivery boy dropped it by soon after we got here. He said it's for Becky, but he had no idea who had sent it. Apparently the giver wanted to remain anonymous."

"More? For me? How can that be?"

"Open it and see." Kate handed her the package.

All eyes were on Becky. She set the mysterious gift on top of the thesaurus and wound the loose ends of the twine around her finger. "Maybe I should open this later…alone."

Kate assumed the commanding air Becky had seen her use on James. "And leave us wondering what it is and who planned this surprise? I think not."

"All right, then." She willed her fingers not to tremble as she removed the twine and pulled back the paper. "Oh! It's a piece of silk and all the notions needed to make a very fancy gown." She held up the beautiful royal blue fabric for all to see. A slip of paper fell to the floor, landing at Kate's feet. She grabbed it and held it out to Becky. "Here."

"Would you please read it aloud?"

Kate obliged. "'Enjoy the concert.' That's all it says. So that would mean...?"

Becky smiled. "That it's from Matthew—um, Dr. Wright. What a sweet thing for him to do. He told me I didn't need a special dress, and then he sends me this. I can't wait to make the gown. I'll have plenty of time to get it finished before the concert next month." She patted the thesaurus. "Thanks to you, James, I'll be able to find the perfect words to express my gratitude when he picks me up."

He didn't say anything, just grunted and scowled the way he used to. Well, she wouldn't let his swift change of mood affect hers. This was the most joyous Christmas she'd ever had, and she was going to enjoy every minute of it.

Chapter Nineteen

At long last Becky had time in her busy schedule for her first grafting lesson. James couldn't wait for it to begin. What with baking, sewing and preparing his meals, she'd been occupied from sunup until well past sundown, while he'd waited impatiently for this lesson. But at least he got to see her every day. The doctor hadn't had the pleasure of her company since before Christmas, a fact that made James happier than it should.

The squeak of the barn door's rollers signaled her arrival. She rushed over to his workbench. "I can only work a couple of hours. I need to serve supper early so I have time to get ready for the concert before Matthew arrives. Lizzie's coming to help me with my hair. And then I get to put on my beautiful new dress."

"I'm sure Dr. Wright will enjoy seeing you in it." He certainly would.

Becky deserved nice things. If she didn't balk, he would see to it that she had more of them. For the time being he would have to be content watching her gush about the *mysterious* gift. Wait until she learned who it was from.

"It was so thoughtful of him to give me the fabric and findings. I'm eager to thank him for his generosity."

He really should set the record straight, but he couldn't bring himself to spoil her fun—or his. She would have a better time at the concert if she wasn't concerned about her appearance. "I take it you aren't going to offer to repay him."

She laughed. "Of course not. It was a gift, just like that incredible, fascinating, stupendous thesaurus you gave me."

Her delight in the thesaurus couldn't be more evident. She often used multiple words to describe something now, when one would suffice. "You've been reading it, I see."

"As often as I can, although I've only been able to squeeze in a few minutes here and there. Ever since the holiday functions at the hotels, word has been spreading about my business. I have so many special orders right now that I'm scrambling to keep up. At this rate, I won't be indebted to you much longer."

He was well aware of that and had yet to figure out what to do about it. All he knew was that he had to do something to eliminate the threat of her brother discovering her whereabouts, or she would leave.

She raised one of her delicately arched eyebrows. "Are you going to show me how you prepare the new trees, or are you going to stand there staring at me?"

"I wasn't st—" Yes, he probably had been. He couldn't take his eyes off her lately. "Fine. I was. You've got some flour on your face." He brushed her cheek to remove the powdery white streak, and she shuddered.

An aching hollowness filled his chest. After all this time, she was still repulsed by his touch. No matter what he did, he couldn't seem to break through her defenses.

Well, she'd just have to endure being close to him, because it was nearly impossible to teach someone how to graft without making contact. She'd need help making the cuts and fitting the two pieces of wood together correctly.

She picked up a grafted whip and studied it, her back to him. "So is this what a baby tree looks like when you finish?"

Her reluctance to look at him was understandable, but the catch in her voice was puzzling. "Here's how it works." He grabbed the two pieces he'd prepared ahead of time.

"I've read about it. This piece, the rootstock—" she pointed to the section in his left hand "—is from the crab apple trees you started from seed two years ago. You use them because they produce the strongest trunk possible. The other piece is from the new variety you want to grow. Is that right?"

"Correct. First, I remove the excess portion of a twig from my producing trees, or what we orchardists call a scion." He sliced the top off a slender branch. "Next, I make an angled cut across the bottom end of the scion and another at the top end of the rootstock. This part can be tricky because the two pieces of wood must have the exact same diameter. It takes a steady hand." With her watching him so intently, he had to work to keep his hands from shaking.

He made clean cuts with the sharpened knife blade and held the two pieces of wood together. "That's what I like to see. A perfect fit. Now I make small cuts in each of the two ends and fit the pieces together somewhat like the cogs on a gear." He demonstrated. "This makes a stronger bond than a simple splice."

"A strong bond is important. I understand that."

She glanced up at him through her lashes with her

chin dipped in a coquettish fashion. He almost dropped his knife. Swallowing, he set the tool on his workbench and continued.

"And now to keep the two pieces together." He dipped a length of cotton twine in melted grafting wax, let it cool slightly and wrapped it around the two pieces. "I have to be careful that I don't tie the string too tightly. I can't remove any bark and give those pests a chance."

One side of her mouth quirked. "Like a codling moth. I've heard they can come from the most unlikely sources."

Becky was teasing him. That had to be a good sign. "Yes. An unlikely source that has, on occasion, been discovered by a clever person, humbling the haughty orchardist."

"Why, James, I believe you just paid me a compliment." She flashed him another of those wide-eyed glances that made concentration virtually impossible. "What happens next?" She returned her attention to the workbench.

"Um, yes. The wax. I brush some of it on the upper end of the scion that I cut off earlier to protect it, too." He did so. "And that's how I graft. What do you think?"

"It's fascinating. I can't wait to do it myself."

"I'll have you practice on twigs before you cut into an actual seedling."

"What? You don't trust me?" Her playful pout drew his attention to her pretty pink lips. Lips he would like to feel against his again.

He couldn't, of course, but he did have a valid excuse for being close to her. He stood behind her, reached around and guided her hands as she made her first cuts.

Becky tensed. She was clearly not enjoying this as much as he was. His decision to have her begin by working on excess bud wood was a wise one. Her cuts were as jagged as the peaks of the Sierras. She twisted around, tilting her head until her tempting mouth was just inches from his. "How am I doing?"

He cleared his throat. "Better. It takes time to get the feel of the knife."

Her face fell. She turned back to the bench. "It's not exactly like slicing bread, is it? Would you help me one more time? I want to get it right before I try it on my own."

Gladly. Her small hands felt wonderful in his.

When he was with Becky, he felt whole again. He could almost forget about the scar that had turned him from a man women admired into a freak adults pitied and children pointed fingers at.

Her second attempt was an improvement over the first. By the time he'd guided her through a third, his heart was thudding against his rib cage, but she'd done a passable job. "I think you're ready to try it on your own."

She performed a faultless graft and grinned. After three more successes, he left her to work on her own while he cleaned the tack.

He returned to check on her an hour later. "You're a champion grafter, Becky. I couldn't have done any better myself."

"I find every aspect of caring for the trees fascinating." Tilting her head, she studied him, that hint of a smile on her lips wreaking havoc with his control. "I understand why you returned to Diamond Springs, but if your dream is working as an engineer, why are you still here? There's nothing holding you back now. You could sell the orchard."

"I couldn't do that. It's my legacy."

"I think it's become your hiding place. You have so much to offer and can't let this stop you." She trailed a fingertip along his scar, her featherlight touch sending a shudder down his spine.

"Who says I'm hiding? I'm simply repaying a debt, the same as you."

"How's that?"

He rubbed a hand over his cheek to stop the tingling that made it impossible to focus. "Papa and *Mutti* sacrificed for me. He worked hard establishing the orchard and did odd jobs for others to bring in extra income. *Mutti* took in sewing projects and worked far into the night, never once complaining about her aching back or throbbing headaches. I can't walk away from their dream when they sacrificed for mine."

"You're a good man and a loyal son. I admire that." A series of emotions flitted through her beautiful blue eyes. Understanding, compassion and…attraction? That had to be what he'd seen earlier when she'd looked at him through her lashes because there it was again.

Her lips parted, an invitation if ever he'd seen one. He leaned toward her, slowly, cautiously.

Before he could be certain of her response, the rollers on the barn door squeaked, and the two of them jumped apart.

Quon slipped inside. "Boss, you wanted me to say when it five o'clock."

She gasped. "I—I didn't realize it was so late. I need to go, or I won't have time to get everything done before Matthew picks me up."

Reason returned, and James shrugged away his disappointment. He'd come dangerously close to jeopardizing his carefully laid plan to regain her trust. Thanks to the interruption, he hadn't repeated his mistake and kissed her again.

Quon couldn't have shown up at a better time.

* * *

Quon couldn't have shown up at a worse time.

Working with James and feeling his hands on hers had been wonderful. Even though he'd scrubbed away her touch after she'd run her finger over his scar, Becky had been certain she'd seen interest on his part and that she'd been about to receive a real kiss, not one brought on by grief and the need for comfort. If only they hadn't been interrupted...

"I'll ring the bell when supper's ready." She flitted out of the barn, grateful for an excuse to escape and regain a measure of self-control before facing him again. If the table in her cabin wasn't covered with the items she'd be wearing, she would take her plate there. It was, though, so she had no choice but to dine with him.

Supper was a rushed affair, but that didn't seem to bother James. He kept his attention on his plate and wolfed down his chicken potpie. The minute he finished, he grabbed a handful of gingersnaps, excused himself and headed to the barn to see to the animals.

The following hour passed in a flurry of activity. Lizzie showed up promptly at six, basket in hand. While Becky had assured her friend a simple chignon would suffice, Lizzie had pooh-poohed the idea, appointing herself Becky's personal hairdresser and planning something she promised would turn the heads of the gentlemen present, including her escort.

Not that Becky had any designs on the doctor. Even so, she couldn't bring herself to turn down his invitations. Escorts willing to take her to concerts and other such delightful events didn't come around every day. Besides, it wouldn't hurt James to think that another man was interested in her, would it? A woman did enjoy feeling sought after, especially a plain one like her.

Lizzie admired her handiwork. "I daresay I've outdone myself. You're gorgeous. Take a look." She held up the hand mirror.

Becky peeked at her reflection, unsure what to expect, aside from some curls. Lizzie had kept her curling irons busy, heating and reheating them on the cabin's tiny stove. "Oh, my. Is that really me?"

The woman in the mirror looked...lovely. Lizzie had swept a portion of Becky's hair up into something that resembled a fluffy bow, with the "ties" swooping across either side of her forehead. A curtain of ringlets hung to her shoulders. The style seemed to change the shape of her face, drawing the eye away from her dreadfully round cheeks.

"Thank you, Lizzie. You've worked wonders. Matthew will be surprised to see me looking like this."

"He's not the only one. Every man in that room will take notice of you. Your hair does look nice, if I say so myself. That gown you designed is stunning. I love the ruffles at the bottom of your sleeves and skirt. The sweep of the overskirt inspired the hairstyle I chose. See how I mimicked the line?" She traced one side of the "bow" with the back of a hand.

Becky tugged the bodice of the royal blue silk into place. "I'm not out to garner the attention of the gentlemen."

Lizzie chuckled. "I know that. No other man can measure up to James O'Brien in your eyes. I had my doubts about his worthiness, but recent events have led me to revise my opinion."

Becky chose not to refute Lizzie's misconception. Her friend would just dismiss the protests. "Really? What has he done to change your mind?"

Lizzie busied herself packing up her combs, brushes

and hairpins. "I ran into him in town one day, and we had a nice chat. He didn't mean for me to find out, but I caught him in the act of being kind to someone I care about."

"He is kind. And generous. He's making more furniture for the cabin. I'm to have a wardrobe, washstand and bureau. He's even going to add a sink and running water for my cabin as well as the Lees', like he did in the main house."

Lizzie bristled. "If he's increased your debt—"

"No. He said it's his duty as a landlord and apologized for not having seen to it sooner. He hadn't been inside the cabin in years, so he didn't realize how little furniture it had."

"I'm glad to hear that. Now, if he'll just return to the fold, I'd think him worthy of you. Dr. Wright is a wonderful fellow, to be sure, but he doesn't make your eyes sparkle the way a certain apple grower does."

She should have known her outspoken friend wouldn't let the matter drop. "Please, Lizzie. I wish you wouldn't go on about that. There's nothing between us. James and I are just friends. It's the same with Matthew and me." And that was the way it had to be.

"Friends? Nonsense. Do you think me daft? It's as clear as the clock on my hat that those two men are vying for your affection."

"No! That can't be. I'm not in a class with either one of them."

Lizzie's face pinched into a scowl, and she spoke in a firm tone that reminded Becky of her fiercest schoolmaster. "Don't ever let me hear you belittle yourself like that again. You are bright and beautiful and you have a heart of gold."

Becky gave a dry laugh. "Bright? No. I'm woefully uneducated."

"Education doesn't make a person bright. Knowledgeable, perhaps, but not bright."

"How can you say that? Education is essential. It's what I've always longed for, but I wasn't allowed to—" She clamped her lips together. Matthew was to come for her soon. If she allowed herself to dwell on past disappointments, she wouldn't be fit company for the learned doctor.

"What weren't you allowed?"

Lizzie's softly spoken question and compassion-filled eyes overcame Becky's resistance. "When I was six, Chicago opened its first public high school. I dreamed of going there, even though the few spots were highly sought after. Students came from all over the East and even from other countries. Applicants had to pass an entrance examination with questions in mathematics, history, geography and grammar. I studied hard in school so I'd be deemed a worthy candidate, but before I was chosen, my mother's consumption got worse."

"And you set aside your dream to care for her?"

"I was happy to do it. After she was gone, I thought perhaps my time had come. I went to Papa, and…" She tamped down the flood of memories. "He'd always been good to me. He was so lavish with his praise at times that it drove a wedge between my brother and me. Dillon didn't put forth much effort, but I did. My parents had come to America for the opportunities, and I wanted to embrace them. We were living in the city with the first high school to admit girls. *Mutter* had encouraged my dream of going there, but Papa laughed at me when I told him I wanted to apply again."

Lizzie patted Becky's cheek. "I'm sorry your father

didn't support you, but I'm afraid you've elevated education to such a level that you've forgotten an important truth. Being educated doesn't make us any smarter. Intelligence is something we're endowed with by our Creator. In your case, He was generous with His gift." Lizzie gave a decisive nod, dropped her hand and stepped back, effectively ending the conversation. "Now, dear girl, spin around and let me see you."

Becky turned in a circle and came to a stop facing Lizzie, who was beaming. "You're a vision. A certain gentleman is going to be quite pleased." She rested a hand on her hip and narrowed her eyes, her smile undermining the serious stance. "Let an old woman give you a word of advice. Don't be too quick with your thanks. Allow things to unfold a bit first."

"Why? I wouldn't want Matthew to think I'm ungrateful."

"I'm not at liberty to say, but things aren't always as they appear."

Lizzie's cryptic response came as a surprise. She was usually so forthright. "Is there something I should know?"

"You will, when the time's right. And now, I must be off." Lizzie dropped her cooled curling irons into her basket and flew out of the cabin.

Becky closed the door and leaned against it, pondering her friend's odd behavior. Could it be that the fabric hadn't come from Matthew, after all, but from someone else? James, perhaps? He *was* generous. But surely he would have said something if he was the giver. She would have to gauge Matthew's reaction to her gown before gushing her thanks.

Minutes later Matthew knocked. Becky greeted him,

the mystery of the gift giver holding her captive. She must solve it or go mad.

He gave her an apologetic smile. "I'm sorry I'm late. My last case was more complicated than I expected, and I didn't get away as early as I'd intended."

"It's not a problem." She'd been so absorbed in her thoughts that she hadn't noticed his slight tardiness. Standing in the light from the lantern, she held her breath.

He took his time studying her, his gaze moving from her head to her hem and back again. "You look lovely. After our conversation, I wasn't expecting you to wear something so fancy. My sisters would approve."

His sisters' approval didn't matter. They'd returned to Chicago anyhow. His thoughts were the ones she cared about, and he wasn't being forthcoming. A more direct approach was required. "I received this lovely fabric as a gift, an anonymous one, and was delighted to create a pattern for the dress."

She rested a hand at her throat, drawing attention to the ruffled edges of the pagoda sleeves. Since her benefactor had been so generous with the yardage, she'd opted for the funnel-shaped design with inner sleeves and lining. "I'm happy with the outcome."

"Indeed. The gown is gorgeous, and you wear it well." He consulted his pocket watch. "Shall we be going?"

Curiosity overrode caution. "I'm wondering. Are you the one behind the surprise?"

"You thought I—" He shook his head. "It wasn't me. Although had I known how much such a gift would mean to you, I would have gladly given it." His admiring gaze held a hint of attraction. Could Lizzie have been right? Did Matthew view her as more than a friend?

The idea disturbed her. She'd done nothing to encourage him, aside from accepting his invitations. Perhaps she'd be wise to decline them in the future. She had no desire to mislead him.

"It wasn't you? I mean I know now it wasn't." She smiled. "I'm just trying to figure out whom I have to thank for it."

Becky turned down the lamp, donned her cloak and was soon seated beside Matthew in his buggy. The moon, just slightly past full that late January evening, illuminated his profile. Normally pleasant company, his furrowed brow evidenced his concern.

"You seem troubled. Are you thinking about a patient?"

"I'm sorry I'm preoccupied. I conferred with a patient this afternoon, a former soldier wounded in the war and left with a limp. I believe he could be helped if he'd undergo surgery, but he's unwilling. I know there are risks involved, but I felt it was my duty to present all the options."

She pulled the sides of her cloak together to fend off the chill. "It sounds to me like you did the right thing. Perhaps the gentleman will change his mind."

"Perhaps. Now I'd best stop dwelling on such things, or you'll think me a poor companion. I have something sure to lift your spirits. This came for you." He slipped a hand into his inside jacket pocket, pulled out a letter and handed it to her.

She squinted as she attempted to read the sender's name but was unable to make it out in the moonlight. This letter must be from Reverend Hastings's wife, as the earlier one had been, but she'd like to know for sure.

As though he'd read her mind, the doctor supplied the answer. "It's nice of Mrs. Hastings to keep you informed. Perhaps you'll let me know how she and the reverend are doing."

"Of course." She would read the letter at her earliest opportunity, but for now she'd enjoy the anticipated outing.

Conversation flowed freely, punctuated by the raspy call of a raven and the throaty crow of a rooster, whose clock was off. Becky did her best to relax, but no matter how hard she tried to deny the truth, she couldn't. Matthew did indeed appear to have taken a shine to her, as inconceivable as that was.

What harm would it do if for one glorious night she pretended that she, an uneducated immigrant's daughter, was worthy of being escorted by such a man? She had, after all, expanded her vocabulary greatly over the past few months, due in large part to her conversations with James and the wonderful books he'd given her. Perhaps by choosing her words carefully, she could make it through the evening without saying something that would showcase her ignorance.

Matthew turned onto the main road in Diamond Springs. Becky spotted a lone figure strolling down the street, wearing an unmistakable top hat. "Would you please stop for a minute? I'd like to have a word with Lizzie."

"Certainly." He drew the buggy alongside the walkway, parked and helped Becky disembark.

She caught up to her friend. "Lizzie."

"Becky! What is it?"

"The fabric wasn't from Matthew. Tell me the truth. Was it from you?"

Lizzie shook her head, the oversize pocket watch on her hat going along for the ride. "As much as I'd love to shower you with gifts, I haven't the resources."

"If it wasn't you or Matthew, then whom? You're the

only ones who knew I was attending the concert. Other
than…"

"I gave my word I wouldn't say a thing—" Lizzie
chuckled "—but it appears I don't have to."

Becky smiled. She'd been right, after all. "James."

Chapter Twenty

The last time James had worn his black swallowtail jacket was at one of the many parties he'd attended with Sophie. He hadn't enjoyed them half as much as she, although, as she'd been wont to remind him, they'd provided opportunities to meet men who could help further his career.

But tonight was different. He aimed to give the doctor some serious competition. The man had become more trouble than a codling moth, whisking Becky off hither and yon whenever it suited his fancy. She said she appreciated being escorted by a fine gentleman. Well, she'd soon see that there was more to James O'Brien than she thought. He might be an apple grower now, but he'd held his own among Sacramento City's elite back in his engineer days.

In order to look his best, he'd shaved twice to make sure his face was as smooth as possible, snipped some wayward hairs that dared hang over his collar and used copious amounts of tooth polish to scrub his teeth. He'd gone so far as to rub some of that oil Lizzie had given him on his jaw. She'd assured him it could help reduce the scar tissue. He couldn't tell any difference, but the spicy scent wasn't unpleasant.

Having reached El Dorado, he jumped from the wagon, tied his team to one of the hitching posts along the wide main street and tugged at his cravat, which had him in a stranglehold. Fancy clothes didn't suit him, but Becky was worth the sacrifice.

A quick scan of the area revealed Dr. Wright's buggy, empty, just as James had planned. Several latecomers rushed toward Rutledge Mercantile, disappearing behind the large building. He checked his pocket watch. Three minutes to seven. If he hurried, he'd be able to slip into Rutledge Hall and find a seat without being noticed.

His long strides took him up Church Street and down the alley behind the mercantile. He climbed the stairs leading to the large room over the shop and slipped inside. The lamps had been dimmed, aiding him in his stealth.

It took him a few moments to locate Becky, seated in the second row, beside the doctor. Close, but not overly so. James tamped down the spurt of jealousy that surged through him at the sight of her smiling at her escort.

If he hadn't known what she would be wearing, he might have overlooked her, thinking those springy curls hanging down her back belonged to another. But the striking woman with the captivating glow on her face was Becky. She'd never looked more beautiful.

He sidestepped his way down the third row of benches to a vacant spot that afforded him a good view of her. Since she was unaware of his presence, he could drink his fill.

No sooner was he seated than the curtains hiding the stage parted and a tall, mustached gentleman greeted them. "Good evening. I'm Miles Rutledge. My wife,

Ellie, and I would like to welcome you to the Mud Springs Musical Society's winter concert." He held out a hand to the only female member of the orchestra, who stood and dipped a curtsy.

"Our esteemed conductor, Mr. Morton, has chosen selections you're sure to enjoy. For those of you who wondered if Ellie would perform so soon after our son's arrival, the answer is obviously yes. I tried to dissuade her, but she's as determined as ever. I've learned to pick my battles."

Mr. Rutledge paused to let the ensuing laughter die down. "We have a treat for you at the end of the concert. Our daughter will make her debut as a pianist. If all goes well, her brother won't disrupt the proceedings." He indicated a baby in the arms of an older woman in the front row, who bore a striking resemblance to Mr. Rutledge. His mother, no doubt.

A sharp pain pierced James's heart. He missed *Mutti* something fierce.

Becky craned her neck to see the infant and smiled. She would make a wonderful mother one day.

The orchestra began playing the first number. As had been the case at the Chicago Benefit when Placerville's Philharmonic Society had performed, Becky was enraptured. She kept her gaze riveted on the musicians, whereas the doctor's strayed from time to time. He spied James, leaned toward Becky and whispered in her ear.

She cast James a sidelong glance and quickly faced front again. Her adorable round cheeks turned as red as the blossoms in the flowery wallpaper.

When the number ended, she flashed him a smile. She might be sitting beside Dr. Wright, but if James wasn't mistaken, her escort wasn't the one on her mind.

Her focus still on James, she ran a hand down the

sleeve of her new dress, pinched the blue silk between her fingers and mouthed, *Sorry.*

Apparently, she'd figured out who had given her the mysterious package. No doubt she'd soon be protesting, but he wouldn't back down this time. A gift was a gift. If she insulted him by offering repayment, he would stand his ground.

The conductor faced the audience. "Ladies and gentlemen, it's my pleasure to introduce the final number the Society will be performing. Miles and his lovely wife will be the featured musicians." The couple stood and took their places. "We hope you enjoy our rendition of Vivaldi's Concerto for Two Violins and Strings in A Minor." Mr. Morton bowed, returned to his podium and lifted his baton.

The music swelled once more, filling Becky with awe. Mr. and Mrs. Rutledge were talented musicians. Having memorized the piece, their gazes drifted between their violins and the conductor, but every so often they came to rest on one another.

Someday she wanted a man to look at her the way Mr. Rutledge was looking at his wife. His eyes shone with obvious pride, hers with joy. To love and be loved like that would be bliss.

When the concerto ended, Becky peeked over her shoulder at James and started. He was looking right at her, a broad smile lifting his lips and crinkling his scar, although he seemed delightfully unaware of the latter. A sense of wonder filled her.

James was here, in public, wearing clothes far finer than anything she'd seen him in before. If she wasn't mistaken, he'd come for her benefit. She recalled their conversation outside the shops the day he'd asked her if she planned to attend. At the time she'd found his question odd. Now, given the gift, it made perfect sense.

He'd intended to ask her, which accounted for his stony face when she'd told him she'd already received an invitation. And yet he'd given her the fabric and hadn't said a word when she'd assumed it was from Matthew. She'd have to correct her mistake forthwith.

The conductor informed them that there would be a brief intermission while the piano was moved to the front of the stage. The curtains closed, and Becky used the time to read the letter from her minister's wife.

January 18, 1872
Dearest Becky,
The reverend and I are doing well. Members of the congregation have already pledged funds for a new church building, and construction will begin once the weather has improved. We feel blessed to have such support.

I do have disturbing news for you, though. Apparently, your brother located false witnesses willing to testify that they'd seen you enter the factory carrying a can of kerosene and leave moments later, just as the fire broke out. The police aim to arrest you, my dear. The factory owner has offered a sizable reward.

You can never come back here. It pains me deeply, but this must be my last communication with you. Although I have no idea how he did it, your brother located us a few weeks back. I can't risk having him bribe our postal workers to get information on your whereabouts. It's with a heavy heart that I entrust you to the Lord and pray all goes well with you.

Your devoted friend,
Hortense Hastings

Matthew leaned close and whispered, "You're shaking. Is everything all right?"

She willed her trembling hands to be still, folded the letter and tucked it into her reticule. Pasting on a smile, she attempted to sound cheery. "They'll be building a new church soon."

"That's wonderful. Look." He inclined his head toward the stage, where the curtains had swished open.

Mr. Rutledge stepped to the front. "And now the final performer of the evening—our delightful daughter, Tildy Rutledge. She'll begin with Bach's Minuet in G, which her classically oriented mama insisted she play, and finish with 'Oh! Susanna,' which she talked her indulgent nana into teaching her. Come on up, Tildy girl."

A thin girl around ten bounded up the stairs, braids bouncing, and joined her father on stage. He gave her an encouraging chuck under the chin. She sat at the piano, tossed a mile-wide smile at the audience and began. Becky hadn't heard the first piece, but she knew the second. Her mother had often hummed the Stephen Foster tune, believing that doing so made her sound more like an American.

Becky sighed. If her mother could see her now, sitting in a silk dress beside one dignified gentleman with another practically making eyes at her, she'd be proud. Her words came back to Becky: *You deserve good things, Rebecca. Don't let what others might say about you hold you back. You're a daughter of the King, so hold your head high.*

If only her mother hadn't contracted consumption. A teacher herself, she would have done her best to persuade her husband to grant their only daughter permission to take the high school entrance exam once more.

As a German immigrant with a thick accent, Becky's mother had understood what it was like to have others assume you lacked the intelligence attributed to the privileged few perceived as true Americans simply because English was their native tongue. Yes, her mother had been her ally.

But an advanced education was not to be. No matter how many times Becky had tried to accept her father's decision, the smoldering embers of her lifelong dream had ignited. They'd grown until her desire of achieving the highest level of education possible burned with such intensity that at times it had threatened to consume her, just as the Great Conflagration had Chicago.

The sound of feet hitting the floor brought Becky back to the present. The spirited girl had completed her enthusiastic rendition of the famous tune, and the audience had risen en masse, clapping loudly. Tildy took the attention in stride, dipping one curtsy after another and beaming all the while.

A short time later Becky stood beside Matthew, who grimaced guiltily when she caught him checking his pocket watch. "I'm sorry, but I was thinking about another of my patients—a young girl Tildy's age with scarlet fever, who has yet to show any signs of improvement."

Becky grabbed hold of the excuse to end the evening early. She needed time to think. The letter had made it clear she wasn't safe. "Do you need to go? If so, we could leave now."

"And deprive myself of the pleasure of your company? Definitely not." The attraction in his eyes was unmistakable. "Another hour won't make much difference, although I do plan to check on her as soon as I get back to Placerville. For now, let's enjoy ourselves, shall we? I see they have refreshments." He headed toward a table at the side of the spacious room.

She had no choice but to take the arm he'd offered and accompany him. "The concert was magnificent. I particularly enjoyed Mr. and Mrs. Rutledge's duet at the end."

He patted her gloved hand. "I'm glad to hear that. The Placerville Philharmonic Society will be presenting a concert next month. You were so moved by their music at the benefit last October that I thought of you immediately. I'd love to have you join me. Do say you will."

Although his invitation didn't come as a surprise, she couldn't commit to anything. Not when she could be leaving town before then. "I'm not sure. What day does it take place?"

"The fourteenth." He flashed her a beguiling smile.

February fourteenth? "But that's—"

"Valentine's Day. Yes. I know." His eyes held a twinkle she'd never seen before.

As much as she would enjoy watching the orchestra perform, she couldn't give way to temptation. "I'm not sure. I expect to have several orders for that day." Large ones, if she could convince certain hoteliers to serve her baked goods at their festivities. In addition, three women from church had asked about the possibility of supplying them with desserts for Valentine suppers they were hosting in their homes.

If all the orders came through, she would earn enough to give James the last of what she owed him, with enough left over to cover the cost of a stagecoach ride and a week's lodging in a new location. One she wouldn't reveal to anyone. Even James.

An animated conversation at the door to Rutledge Hall drew their attention. A messenger with an envelope in hand spoke to one of the guests. The gentleman motioned for the boy to follow him. They headed straight for Matthew.

"I'm sorry to interrupt, Doctor," the man said, "but this lad has an urgent message for you."

"Thanks." All business again, Matthew took the telegram and dropped a coin into the boy's outstretched hand. He and the older man left.

Matthew scanned the few lines. His brow creased with concern. "The young girl's situation has deteriorated, and I'm needed right away. That leaves me with a dilemma. How am I to get you home?"

James approached, looking and acting the part of the quintessential gentleman, all graciousness and charm. "I couldn't help but overhear. If you'd like, Doctor, I could take Becky back with me."

Warring emotions played across Matthew's face. He glanced from Becky to James and back again, heaved a sigh of resignation and gave a single crisp nod. "If she's agreeable, that would be a help. I don't know what else I can do for the poor child, but I have to try."

Becky hastened to assure him. "It's fine. Go."

"Thank you both." Matthew took her hands in his. She couldn't resist peeking at James, whose eyes narrowed briefly. "I'm sorry we didn't get to finish our conversation, Becky. I'll contact you soon. Good night." Matthew gave her hands a squeeze, tore his gaze from her and slipped out.

James watched the doctor's retreating form. "I feel for him. Caring for an ailing child must be difficult. I'm sorry he had to leave so suddenly." Despite the well-modulated, parlor-perfect delivery of his final statement, the light in his eyes told a different story. He held out a hand toward the refreshment table. "Would you like me to get something for you? It appears they have warm beverages and desserts."

"No, thank you. I've already sampled the sweets."

"They're yours?"

She nodded.

"I should have known. Your business is certainly doing well."

"This order was all Lizzie's doing. Since her patient lives here in El Dorado, she frequents the mercantile and spoke with Mrs. Rutledge on my behalf."

An awkward silence followed, broken when Becky and James spoke at the same time.

"James, I—"

"Did you—"

They laughed, and he held out a hand. "You first."

She looked into his eyes, the admiration in them warming her. "I owe you an apology. It wasn't until tonight that I learned that the fabric and notions had come from you. I'm sorry I jumped to conclusions when I opened the package, but you didn't correct me. Why is that?"

"Why do you think?"

"Because you wanted it to be a gift and were afraid I'd insist on repaying you."

A lopsided smile was her reward. "The thought had occurred to me."

"I said I didn't need a fancy gown, but I had no idea the people in a small town such as this would don their finest for a concert. I would have felt out of place in one of my work dresses. Because of your generosity, I fit right in."

"No, you didn't. You stood out. You look—" his appreciative gaze traveled from her head to her feet and back again "—nice."

Nice? She'd hoped for something more descriptive. "I'm glad you approve."

"The dress is stunning, and I love what Lizzie did with your hair."

That was more like it. "Thank you."

James's compliments warmed her clear through. He looked more handsome than any other man in the room. And the way he was regarding her with his expressive eyes, the deepest, darkest shade of brown she'd seen yet, was exhilarating. A woman could get used to such treatment. If only she didn't have to leave.

The room that had seemed so spacious before closed in around her. She needed fresh air. "You offered me a ride. Might I take you up on it now?"

"Certainly."

They made their way toward the exit. Clusters of people milling about forced him to wrap his arm around her waist and pull her to his side in order to pass. Not that she minded. This would be her only time to see him like this, and she would savor every second. When she returned to her cabin, reality would resurface, and she would have to face the fact that her remaining days here were few.

When they reached the street below, she wrapped her hand around the arm he offered. Inhaling deeply, she sought to identify the source of his woody, slightly spicy and refreshingly masculine scent. When she did, the realization struck her with such force she stumbled on the wooden walkway.

He caught her, holding her shoulders and studying her face. "Are you all right?"

She couldn't keep the surprise out of her voice. "You're wearing the cypress oil Lizzie gave you. And you didn't sit in the back of the room. What's changed?"

"A wise woman told me not to hide out at the orchard

and not to let this—" he brushed his scarred jaw "—keep me from living. You were right. On both counts. I was hiding, but thanks to you, I feel more alive than I have in a long time."

Happiness bubbled inside Becky. "You look rugged and heroic. And you were my hero tonight. Thank you for the fabric, your support and encouragement and your friendship."

"So we're friends again? That's good to know. This evening has turned out well. I got to attend a concert and now I'm to escort the loveliest lady in the hall back to her place."

She chuckled. "Careful, James, or you'll turn my head with your flattery."

"It's not flattery. I mean it."

Unsure how to respond, she took his arm once again, and they resumed their walk to the wagon in companionable silence.

En route to the orchard minutes later, they sat side by side on the wagon seat and chatted about his orchard, her business, the weather. As though they'd made an agreement, both avoided the subjects they'd discussed after the concert. The air between them was so charged it practically crackled.

James pulled up to the barn, hopped down and came around to help Becky. His strong hands spanned her waist, and he lifted her to the ground, his hands lingering longer than necessary. As much as she'd enjoyed his company, she couldn't indulge in her flight of fancy any longer. Like Cinderella, she must leave before the lovely illusion was shattered. "Good night. I'll see you tomorrow." She turned to go.

"Becky, wait."

She paused, willed herself to remain strong and slowly turned toward him. "Yes?"

"The Placerville Philharmonic Society is performing on February fourteenth. I'd like to take you."

Two invitations to the same event by two dashing gentlemen in one evening? The fairy-tale aspect of the evening continued. "I don't know what to say. Matthew asked me to the same event."

"You're going with me."

"I beg your pardon."

James groaned. "Forgive me. That didn't come out the way I intended. What I meant to say was I'd be honored if you would accept my invitation."

"I wish I could, but I can't."

"Because Dr. Wright asked you first?"

"Yes and no. He delivered a letter from my minister's wife back East." She swallowed in an attempt to dislodge the lump in her throat. "The situation is worse than I thought. I'm wanted for more than questioning now. There's a reward for information leading to my arrest."

James smacked a fist into his cupped hand. "What? No! You're innocent."

His staunch support warmed her heart, but the facts remained. "My brother has apparently paid off some people to pose as witnesses. They're saying they saw me set the fire."

"How could he do that? Your own brother? Kate and I didn't always get along, but we stood up for one another. That's what families do."

"Dillon harbors a great deal of resentment toward me. He believes our father loved me more than him. It wasn't true, of course, but there was no convincing him. I shudder to think what he might do next. I'm afraid he'll come after me just to get the reward. I can't stay here any longer than absolutely necessary."

"He can't find you. You used a different name and didn't tell anyone where you were going. Besides, you said the rail station you left from was destroyed in the fire. The records were, too. They had to be."

"He found the reverend and his wife in their new location. If he could find them, I'm sure he could find me."

James grasped the side of the wagon and stared at the crown of the massive oak overhead. His shoulders rose and fell as he drew in a deep breath. He returned his attention to her, his voice level once again. "I understand your concerns, but your friends wouldn't give him any information, would they?"

"Well, no."

"Then you're safe here."

She shook her head. "I wish that were true, but you don't know Dillon. He'll go to any lengths to get what he wants."

"It's highly unlikely, but suppose he were to come to Placerville. If you were at a concert, he'd have a hard time locating you in the crowd. And if he did, he wouldn't be able to do anything, not with me by your side protecting you."

An owl hooted. If only she had the creature's supposed wisdom. All she had to rely on was her knowledge of her brother and his past actions. The memory of that horrid evening when he'd struck her resurfaced, and she shuddered.

"You're cold. I should get you inside." James took her arm and guided her toward her cabin.

She wasn't aware of the temperature, but she allowed him to lead her, grateful for the break in the conversation. As much as she wanted to accept James's invitation, she couldn't. To do so would be foolhardy. She couldn't afford to flirt with danger. If Dillon were to find her, there was no telling what he'd do to her. Leaving was her only option.

Chapter Twenty-One

James unlocked the door of Becky's cabin and followed her inside. "I'll get a fire going for you."

"You don't need to trouble yourself. I can take care of it."

"It's no trouble. I'm happy to help." He'd gladly do whatever he could for her.

"All right, then. Thank you."

"Two thank-yous in one night? Are you feeling all right?" His attempt at levity elicited a feeble smile.

She pulled out one of the new bentwood chairs he'd added to her furnishings, sat and watched him work. No. *Watched* wasn't accurate. Although she looked his way, her gaze was distant, vacant.

The letter had upset her more than he would have expected. If he didn't figure out a way to reassure her that her fears were unfounded, she would leave. He couldn't allow that. Wouldn't allow that. An idea began to take shape.

He crouched in front of her tiny stove with the door open, making sure the fire caught. Satisfied that it had, he rose, dusted off his hands and sat in the chair on the opposite side of the table. "When I was reading the *Mountain Democrat* this morning, I noticed an advertisement for a confectionery demonstration over in Placerville the afternoon of the eighth."

She gave him her full attention, but wariness clouded her eyes. "Really?"

"Yes. A French chef is going to— How did they say it? Ah, yes, I remember." He formed quotation marks in the air. "'Elucidate the intricacies of the éclair and other French pastries.'"

"That's wonderful! I've tried to master the éclair, but my results so far have been disappointing. To learn from a master would be incredible."

"An opportunity too good to pass up, eh?"

Her face fell. "I was so overcome I forgot. As much as I'd like to attend, I dare not."

He was prepared for her objections. "I doubt your brother would search for you at such an event." The likelihood of Dillon showing up at all was so slim as to be inconsequential. All James had to do was convince Becky of that fact. "I'm so certain he won't be there that I'll include supper at the Cary House after the demonstration as further enticement. What do you say? Will you allow me the pleasure of your company?"

She rested her chin on her thumb and ran the knuckle of her index finger along her lower lip. The gesture drew attention to her lovely mouth, making it hard for him to concentrate.

A good fifteen seconds passed before she answered. "All right. I'll do it. But if there's any sign of trouble—"

"I'll get you to safety immediately."

"Very well, then. I'm looking forward to the outing." So was he. More than she knew.

The next few days were some of Becky's busiest ever. James was hard at work pruning the trees from sunrise to sunset, assisted by the Lees, which suited her purposes. She was able to avail herself of his kitchen for hours on end, testing one recipe after another in preparation for fulfilling her Valentine's Day orders. To her surprise, two hotels in Placerville and one in El Dorado had contacted her, asking if she could supply them with desserts for the special day.

Although the increase in the number of orders would mean working full tilt from the twelfth through the thirteenth, stopping only for a brief night's sleep, she couldn't turn away the business. Not when she needed every cent she could get for coach fare to her new location plus room and board once she arrived.

Her goal would be to locate a housekeeping position with kitchen privileges such as she had now. Once she could get her business up and running again, she could start saving. She'd need to amass a tidy sum if she was to spend her life moving from town to town, forever starting over. Not that she had any choice. If Dillon—or anyone, for that matter—found her, she could end up spending the rest of her days in jail.

She heaved a sigh and set James's dessert in front of him. He made short work of the caramel pudding and dropped the spoon in his bowl with a clink. "I got news today about a meeting of fruit growers the evening of the eighth. They're going to be discussing the feasibility of shipping a portion of our crops to the East. I know we have our plans, but if you wouldn't mind staying in town a bit longer, I'd like to be there. Unfortunately, you would have to wait around for me. Either that, or go with me. It would also mean we'd get back quite late."

"That's fine. I'd love to learn more about marketing your apples." She had no idea when she'd have such an opportunity again, and she intended to avail herself of it. Although Dillon might attend a confectionery demonstration if he heard it involved sampling the pastries, she couldn't imagine him at a meeting of fruit growers.

"Good. It's settled, then. I'd better get back to work. Those trees aren't going to prune themselves."

"How are things coming?"

"We've made it through ten acres so far, but there's plenty of work ahead of us. It's a good thing I have you filling me with tasty food to keep up my energy." He patted his trim waist. "I'll see you at supper."

He strode to the lean-to door and paused. "You don't have to walk to church tomorrow. I'm going, too, so you can ride in the wagon with me."

Excitement danced a jig down her spine. "I'd appreciate that."

In no time, she had the dinner dishes done and opened the cupboard that housed her baking supplies, ready to complete her regular orders due at the hotels Monday morning. The cheesecakes seemed to make themselves as she reflected on James's surprising announcement. Perhaps he'd finally made his peace with God. If not, he was on the right path.

Leaving would be difficult, but at least she would have the satisfaction of knowing she'd honored her promise to *Mutti* and had stayed long enough to witness James's reconciliation with the Lord.

The last time James had set foot in the white clapboard church, he'd said his final farewell to *Mutti*. That day sorrow had tied his gut in knots. Today anticipation coupled with apprehension and set his stomach to roiling. If only he could recapture the peace he'd felt when he'd occupied the pew beside his parents all those years ago, but it had fled when he had.

He'd left Diamond Springs far behind, along with his faith. Pursuing his education and advancing his career had consumed him.

Then had come the explosion, months spent fighting for his life and his decision to put an end to things with Sophie. She'd agreed without a fuss. Not that he could blame her. No woman should have to endure the agony of watching, waiting and wondering if her beau was going to live or die.

His prognosis had been grim. If it hadn't been for *Mutti*'s diligent care and her earnest prayers, he wouldn't be here. God must have had a plan for him, though, because he'd survived, despite the dire predictions. It was high time he stopped hiding from the Lord and started seeking His will—after some serious repenting.

Becky's voice roused James from his reverie. "We'd best get inside, or we'll be late."

She stepped into the foyer moments later and hesitated. "I usually sit in the fourth pew."

"I'll join you, if you don't mind." He could use her comforting presence.

They sat side by side. He kept plenty of room between them so no tongues had reason to wag.

Since Mr. Parks was preaching in Georgetown that Sunday, one of the elders filled the pulpit. The bespectacled man delivered a message about Zacchaeus, who, because he was short, climbed a tree to see Jesus pass by. Even though Zacchaeus was a reviled member of society, the Lord chose to dine with him. The corrupt tax collector admitted his wrongs, did his best to right them and was welcomed into the family of God.

James closed his eyes and imagined sitting in one of the massive oaks lining the road to his orchard. If he were to see the Lord walk by, what would he do?

The answer came with remarkable clarity. His heart seemed to stop, and then it resumed its beating, thumping wildly. All this time he'd been running *away* from the Lord, when what he'd needed to do was run *to* Him.

Something jabbed him in the side, and his eyes flew open. Fan in hand, Becky cast him a sidelong glance filled with mild rebuke. She mouthed the words, *Were you sleeping?*

He shook his head and pressed his palms together in the classic prayer pose.

Her face lit with a smile so bright it rivaled the shaft of light streaming in the window. She lifted her gaze to the ceiling, the smooth planes of her throat drawing his eye. An elderly woman across the aisle shook a finger at him. Heat crept up his neck, and he snapped his attention to the front of the small sanctuary.

The service ended, and James followed Becky down the aisle and out into the sunshine. The crisp February air had a bite to it. He raised the collar of his overcoat and offered her his arm.

She took it without hesitation. "I'm glad you came today."

"I am, too. It's time to move on."

He didn't know what the future held, but, Lord willing, Becky would be part of his. He couldn't imagine life without her. He just had to prove she was safe here in Diamond Springs so she'd quit insisting she must leave.

An idea occurred to him. It would require seeking Dr. Wright's help, but so be it. He'd do whatever it took to give Becky peace of mind.

Chapter Twenty-Two

"I don't know how you could possibly eat another bite after all the desserts you put away." James's appetite never ceased to amaze Becky. Despite having sampled every delectable item at the confectionery demonstration, he rubbed his hands when the waiter set a large steak in front of him. The rich, meaty scent filled the air.

He grinned. "A man needs to keep his strength up. Shall I ask the blessing so I can set to work on this?"

"By all means." Ever since the service the past Sunday, James had said grace without hesitation, offering heartfelt prayers that showed his openness to the Lord. *Mutti* would be so happy. Becky certainly was.

As soon as he said "Amen," James stuffed a bite of steak into his mouth. "Mmm."

Too excited to eat, Becky looked around the restaurant. The Cary House, with its gleaming mahogany-and-cherrywood interior, was the height of luxury. From the linen tablecloths to the sparkling crystal goblets, everything in the hotel's restaurant bespoke elegance.

He paused. "Aren't you going to eat?"

"I was just savoring the moment. I've never been to a place as fine as this." She doubted she'd be able to indulge in such a treat for a long time to come. Life for a woman on the run would be challenging.

"You've never told me much about your life back in Chicago. What was it like?"

She squeezed lemon on her salmon. The spray from the zest reminded her of the tangy filling for the éclairs the chef at the demonstration had made—and the way James had wiped an errant bit of it off her lips after she'd sampled it. Try as she might, she hadn't been able to stop the shiver that shimmied down her spine at his tender touch.

"It's not a very interesting story. What do you want to know?"

He dove his fork into his baked potato. "What type of a girl were you?"

"Curious. I wanted to learn as much as I could about the world around me—how things work, what life was like before I was born. Anything and everything."

"Your thirst for knowledge seems to be unquenchable. I can understand why. A bright young woman like you…"

Bright? There it was again. Lizzie had said much the same thing. "I appreciate the compliment, but I'm not educated like you and Matthew. You're both college men."

"Tell me. What did we do while we were at school?"

"What do you mean? I don't understand."

He rested his fork on his plate. "It's a simple question. Please answer it."

"All right. You went to classes and listened to lectures. You read books. You completed assignments. You probably practiced what you were learning, too."

"And how have you learned about apple growing?"

"That's easy. I've listened to you, Quon and Chung tell me what you know. I've read all the pomology books you own. I've worked alongside you on the many tasks involved."

He said nothing, just watched her expectantly.

Was she missing something? She went back over the conversation. Realization sent tingles racing over her. "It's not that much different, is it? I didn't do my learning in a classroom, but I've still learned a great deal. For instance, today I learned that you can consume more French pastries than anyone I've ever known."

"Indeed. You crave knowledge the way some of us crave sweets." He grinned.

How silly she'd been. All this time she'd looked at what she'd been denied rather than what she'd been given. But no more. She would embrace the educational opportunities around her, no matter their form.

James cut a bite of steak. "I saw you talking with Dr. Wright earlier. Did you find out about the little girl with scarlet fever?"

He remembered. How nice. "She recovered."

"That's good."

She took a sip of water from her goblet. "I told him I won't be accepting his invitation to the Philharmonic Society's performance next week."

"How did he take the news?"

"He's disappointed, of course, but when I told him the reason, he understood."

"Did you tell him everything?" James grimaced. "I'm sorry. I didn't mean to pry."

"It's all right. I told him only as much as he needed to know. Certain things are too humiliating. He saw the condition I was in when I arrived and knows who's responsible. I'm certain that if Dillon was to show up, he wouldn't find Matthew forthcoming."

The less people knew, the safer she would be. No

one must know where she went after she left Diamond Springs. Or when she was leaving. Not even James.

A swish of skirts drew James's attention. Becky had returned from the ladies' lounge and joined him in the elegant lobby of the Cary House. She looked beautiful in her blue silk. Her eyes shone, and her radiant smile warmed him clear through. "I'm ready."

"Are you sure you want to go? Ralph and his older boys will be at the meeting. I could get the information from them later." As much as finding new markets back East could help his business, James would have a hard time concentrating on the discussion. All he could think about was how intent Becky was on leaving town.

His own discussion with Dr. Wright awaited him. It could prove to be awkward, especially since Becky had declined the doctor's invitation to the concert the following week. But awkward or not, the conversation must take place. Having lived in Chicago, he might be able to direct James to a private investigator who could learn the details of the case against Becky—discreetly. She would never feel free as long as there was a warrant for her arrest.

"Is something wrong, James? You're going to cause your collar to come undone if you keep tugging on it like that."

He lowered his hand to his side. "I'm fine." He wasn't, and he wouldn't be until he'd righted the wrong that had left Becky facing a life on the run.

"If you're sure. I know it could be awkward having me at the meeting since the men aren't used to having a woman present."

"I want you there. We all do. The apple growers from Diamond Springs, anyhow. You earned their respect and mine when you discovered the source of the codling moth and again when you took over for me during the harvest and streamlined procedures." She still didn't seem to understand how much he valued her input.

"Then let's go, shall we?" She slipped both hands around his elbow. Her willingness to reach out to him showed how far he'd come in regaining her trust. But would she trust him when she learned about his plan to clear her name?

He led her out of the Cary House onto the walkway in front, where the flickering gaslights cast shadows on the street. They headed west toward the Ohio House hotel at the corner of Main and Sacramento Streets. They'd made it halfway across Quartz Street when a stout man with shaggy muttonchops like those worn by the late President VanBuren burst out of the Arch Saloon next door to the Cary House and staggered toward them.

The drunken sot shook his head and rubbed his eyes. He addressed them with slurred speech. "It's you! Don't that beat all? Almost didn't recognize ye all gussied up like that."

Becky froze, and her grasp on James's arm became viselike. She dipped her head and whirled around, taking him with her.

He leaned close. "What is it?"

"He's Fergus Kane, my brother's friend. We have to go."

"Oh, no, you don't!" the man hollered. "Dillon ain't of a mind to let you go after we come all this way. Yer comin' with us, Rebecca Donnelly."

Anger surged through James. Her brother had found her!

Before James had a chance to react, Becky released his arm and took off running down the narrow street, away from the saloon.

He spun around to deal with the drunk, but the bald-headed fellow had disappeared inside the saloon, presumably to get Becky's brother.

Her boot heels pounded the bricked surface.

James took off after her.

She didn't slow.

He caught up to her just as she rounded the back corner of the hotel and headed east on Reservoir Street. With the businesses closed, an eerie silence had enveloped the street.

"It's me. James. Here. Take my hand." He held it out, but she sped up.

He matched her pace. "Becky, please. I'm here to help."

She stopped halfway down the deserted street and leaned over with her hands on her knees. Her words puffed out between labored breaths. "He…found…me."

"I know. But we can get away."

"How?" She straightened and peered into the darkness behind him, wary and watchful. Terror had her wound tighter than any spring.

"We'll cross Main, get my wagon and hightail it home. Can you walk?"

"No!" She spoke rapid-fire, despite her winded condition. "We have to run. That was Fergus, one of Dillon's cardsharp cronies. They'll be coming after me."

"Fine. We'll run, then. Hold on." He offered his hand once again, and she took it.

They reached the end of the narrow street in no time. She started around the corner, but he pulled her back. "We can't draw attention to ourselves. Couples are out promenading. If we blend in with them, we can get across the street without being noticed."

"I understand. And then what?" She sounded more like herself. A good sign.

"We'll slip behind the courthouse and follow Hangtown Creek until we reach my wagon. As soon as we've put some distance between us, I'll give my team free rein. They'll get us out of here in a hurry."

Her voice held a note of desperation. "Do you think your plan will work?"

"Yes." It had to.

Chapter Twenty-Three

Lord, please protect me from Dillon.

Becky wrapped both hands around James's elbow, leaned in to his side and sashayed into the street. With the number of couples strolling on a Friday evening, they blended right in.

If their situation hadn't been so perilous, she would have enjoyed acting the part of a smitten maiden. As it was, she had to force herself to look straight ahead and not scan Main Street in search of her brother or Fergus.

They made it across the wide street without incident, disappeared behind the courthouse and slunk along the creek, keeping to the shadows. She kept a fierce grip on James's hand as he led the way but said nothing.

Memories of their first meeting returned. He'd rescued her that day, and here he was helping her once again. She'd imagined him to be a bit of a rogue, but she knew better now. He was a gentleman through and through. How she'd miss him when she left, which she must do very soon. If Dillon was to find her—

No! She mustn't think about that. She would busy herself with her final orders and not allow herself to dwell on the danger awaiting her if he figured out where she lived.

They reached the wagon. James grabbed a tarpaulin from under the seat. "I want you to lie in the bed. I'll put this over you."

"Certainly. What will you do?"

"Keep a cool head—and pray."

He helped her up. She flattened herself on the wooden surface, her face to the stars. James shook out the thick canvas covering and placed it over her. She tried not to imagine what Dillon would do if he caught up to them.

A tense half mile later, James stopped the wagon and helped Becky out of her hiding place. She sat up and looked around. He'd shed his frock coat and hat, rolled up his shirtsleeves and loosened one side of his collar. She clambered out of the wagon and reached up to smooth his mussed hair. "What happened to you?"

"I thought disguising myself as an unkempt saloon patron would be a good idea."

"I'm afraid you're not very convincing, but I admire your quick thinking." She hung her head. "I'm sorry I lost my nerve back there."

He lifted her chin with his forefinger until she was forced to meet his gaze. "You did just fine. We got away, didn't we?"

"Are you sure no one followed us?"

"Not that I can tell. Since you came to Placerville initially, I figure your brother will be looking for you there."

"For now. But the town isn't all that big. It won't take Dillon long to figure out I'm not there. When he does, he'll widen his search. It's only a matter of time before he finds me. I can't let that happen. I have to fill my orders so I can finish repaying you."

James sliced the air with a hand. "I don't care about that."

"I do." She had to make him understand. "It's more

than just the money. I'll need the recommendations from my customers. If I were to let them down on such an important order…"

"My only concern is keeping you safe. You can't be seen again."

She grudgingly agreed. "I suppose I'll have to hire someone to make the deliveries for me, then. Perhaps Mr. Stratton's sons would like the job."

"I'll do it."

When James used that firm tone, there was no arguing with him. "Thank you."

He grinned, his teeth flashing white in the moonlight. "Well, would you look at that? You've finally learned to accept a gift without protesting."

She attempted an answering smile, but it faded quickly. "I was right, you know. I told you he'd come after me."

James sobered. "I'm sorry, Becky. I don't know how he could have found you. I was so sure you were safe."

She gave a dry laugh. "When Dillon wants something, he'll do whatever it takes to get it. I'm guessing he aims to turn me in and collect the reward."

"For a crime he committed? That's reprehensible."

"I agree. His actions are abominable, contemptible, despicable. If I had my thesaurus I could come up with more, but what good would that do? He is what he is. All I can do is pray that the Lord will protect me from Dillon and that maybe one day he'll see that there's another way to live. A far better way."

"I'm too angry to pray. If your brother dares set foot on my property, he'll be sorry. I'll—"

"Please. Don't say it. He deserves to be punished for what he's done, but it's not our place. The Lord and the law will see to that."

Her next steps had become clear. She needed to leave

the moment her obligations had been fulfilled. That left her four days to figure out how to say goodbye.

"I can't believe it. What kind of man would treat his own sister that way?"

Dr. Wright's shock mirrored James's. He could understand the doctor's reaction. When he'd first learned about Dillon Donnelly's crime and his attempt to frame Becky for it, white-hot anger had surged through him. It had taken considerable restraint not to smash something. "So you'll help me?"

"By all means. I've never had need of a private investigator myself, but I'm sure some of my fellow students can help you locate a reputable one. I've kept in touch with three who have practices in Chicago. I'll send a telegram to each of them right away. I'll draft one now."

The doctor opened a desk drawer and pulled out a piece of paper. He dipped his pen in the inkwell and wrote a message.

Guilt squeezed James so hard that he had a difficult time drawing a breath. If Becky knew what he was doing, she would be mighty unhappy. She'd probably say he was making things worse, but what could be worse than living in fear? He'd discounted her fears, but they were real. Her brother had followed her.

If he found her, there was no telling what he would do. The man was beyond wicked.

Dr. Wright blotted the ink and handed the sheet to James. "Do I have the facts straight?"

"Yes. That should work."

"Very well." The doctor stood. "If there's anything else I can do, please let me know. I care a great deal about Becky."

"I know. So do I."

"I see. Well, I'm happy to know that if I've lost her, it's to a man deserving of her."

Was he? James doubted that, but he would work hard to be such a man. "Thank you, Doctor, for your understanding—and your help." He held out his hand, and Dr. Wright shook it.

"I'll keep you informed. As soon as I hear something, I'll get a telegram off to you."

James left the doctor's office and headed for his wagon. His step was lighter than it had been since the encounter with that Fergus fellow outside the saloon.

He'd enacted his plan. Now all he had to do was tell Becky. That would be hard, but handing over the payment he'd collected from the Placerville hoteliers would be harder yet. She'd have no reason to stay.

Although he wanted her to remain in Diamond Springs, he had to let her go, trusting that his plan would work. If it did, he'd be able to free Becky from the need to run—and give her a reason to return.

Chapter Twenty-Four

The nutmeg-like aroma of the mace lingered in the air. Becky had used the fragrant spice in the Love Cakes she'd made. When the owner of Placerville's Ohio House hotel had insisted on something with a romantic name, nothing had come to mind. And then she'd found a recipe for the dessert she needed in *Mutti*'s copy of *The Godey's Book of Receipts and Household Hints*.

Becky sat at the kitchen table opposite Lizzie.

Her friend placed her empty teacup on its saucer. "You must be happy that the baking is behind you. James said he's tried more sweets in the past two weeks than he knew existed."

"I love trying new things, but the past two days were a bit much. I'm not sure I'll take on that many orders at one time again. I wouldn't have done it this time if it hadn't been necessary. I've fulfilled my obligations and can leave with a clear conscience."

"Must you go? I'll miss you something fierce, and I know a certain man who will be lost without you."

Saying goodbye wouldn't be easy, but Becky refused to cry. Giving way to her feelings would make the parting that much harder. "I can't stay here. Not with Dillon on my trail."

"Well, I don't envy you your task. Saying goodbye to the man you love won't be easy."

"I don't love him." She couldn't, even if she wanted to. The trouble was she'd allowed herself to care for him. To spare them both the pain of an emotional parting, she would leave quickly and quietly.

"Deny it all you want, but I've seen the way you look at him. If only this ugly business with your brother could be put to rest…" Lizzie stood. "I must be on my way. I won't make this any harder on you—or me. Just a brief hug. Goodbye and Godspeed, dear girl." She embraced Becky tightly, patted her cheek and was gone.

Becky finished putting the kitchen to rights. She pulled the note she'd written out of her pocket and unfolded it. The words were few, but she couldn't say everything in her heart. If James knew how much he'd come to mean to her, he might search for her. She refused to put him in danger again.

James,
Thank you for allowing me the privilege of serving *Mutti* during her last days on earth, for the many wonderful gifts you bestowed upon me, for investing in my business and for teaching me all about your beautiful apple trees. I will treasure the memories I've made here for the rest of my life.

I'm sorry to leave without a formal farewell, but it's for the best. If Dillon should find you and ask where I've gone, you'll be able to tell him that you know nothing, thus protecting both you and me.

I'll miss you. Please tell Quon and Chung I'll miss them, too.
Becky

She'd given a lot of thought to the final paragraph. She couldn't very well say she would miss the Lees without telling James she would miss him, too. Which she would. Greatly.

Satisfied that she'd said things as well as she could, she folded the note, entered his room and propped the note against his shaving mug, where James would find it later—after she was long gone.

She'd left a full accounting of her loan in the pantry with the ledger, along with the remaining balance owed him—minus the payments he would receive on the orders he was currently delivering. It had taken her several months, but she'd paid her debt in full.

With a heavy heart, she returned to the great room and donned her cloak. Memories lingered everywhere she looked. She stepped onto the porch and closed the door on some of the best days of her life.

The apple trees, their branches bare, shivered in the icy breeze. It had been snowing in the Sierras, although they had yet to see a drop of rain in the Foothills. Just wind and plenty of it.

Her final goodbye couldn't be conveyed in writing. She slipped into the barn hoping to find Spitz inside, but he was nowhere to be seen. He must be far afield with Quon and Chung, who were pruning the Baldwins on the eastern edge of the orchard.

Although she longed to see the loyal dog one last time, she didn't dare call him. One of the Lees might think she needed something and come to check on her. She knelt by the blanket the beautiful Irish setter slept on and patted it. "So long, Spitz. You were the first friend I made here. I'll remember you fondly."

She left the barn and trudged toward her cabin. How she'd make it through the next hour she didn't know, but she would. All she had left to do was pack her bag and catch the stage heading south. She had enough money to get her to Angels Camp and pay for a week in a boarding-house. She'd chosen the town down in Calaveras County because of its name. She liked to think the Lord would have His angels watching over her.

A good five minutes passed while she contemplated what to take. Her dilapidated carpetbag couldn't hold everything she owned now. The hardest things to leave behind would be her new dictionary and thesaurus, but she didn't have any way of transporting them. Unless... Surely James wouldn't mind if she took a single crate. It would be heavy, but she was strong enough to cart it the half mile to town.

Her decision made, she pulled her brown wool dress from the wardrobe. She folded it and reached for the next garment.

Footfalls on the small porch startled her. James couldn't be back yet, could he?

The door flew open with such force that it banged against the wall. She spun around and gasped.

"Dillon!"

He marched into her cabin. "It's me, all right. Thought you could hide, did you, sis? Well, I done found you." He took a step forward. "And you're comin' with me."

She resisted the urge to back up. "What makes you think I'd go with you?"

"Way I see it, you ain't got a choice. Not if you care about James O'Brien."

"Leave him out of it."

Dillon's lips twisted into a cruel smile. "I heard you'd gone and fallen for the feller. That makes things easy."

Dread snaked its way down her spine. "What do you mean?"

"Since you're slow, I'll make it nice and clear for you." He enunciated each word and spoke loudly, as though she were hard of hearing. "If you don't come with me, your precious James will pay the price."

She wasn't going anywhere with her bully of a brother, not if she could help it. She looked around for something to use as a weapon.

Dillon let out with an evil laugh. "I know what you're thinkin', but there ain't no coal scuttle handy this time. But to be on the safe side..." He turned to the open door and hollered. "Fergus, git in here."

The bald-headed man appeared, reeking of alcohol but appearing steadier on his feet than when she'd seen him outside the saloon. Her hope of escape evaporated. She might have been able to get away from Dillon, but she couldn't take on two men at once. *Lord, help me.*

Her high-handed brother barked an order at Fergus. "Hold on to her while I pack her bag."

"Sure thing, boss." The lout grabbed her arms and pinned them behind her back.

Dillon shoved her purple poplin into her carpetbag. Her brown wool followed. With a swipe of his arm across the top of her bureau, her hairbrush and reticule joined her dresses. He upturned the two drawers that held her nightwear and undergarments, dumping the contents into the bag. Showing no consideration for her things, he mashed them down and snapped the bag shut.

"My dictionary." The words had escaped before she could stop them.

"That old thing? You won't have no need of it where you're goin'."

How could he talk about their mother's dictionary that way? "It wouldn't take much room."

He raised a hand. "Say another word, and you'll regret it."

She was at his mercy, so she kept quiet.

"I see you learned your lesson. That's good. Now we'll be going. We got us a stage to catch."

Her mind raced. James wasn't here, so Dillon couldn't do anything to him. All she had to do was get outside. Once there, she could call for help. Quon and Chung would round up the neighbors, and Dillon and Fergus would be captured before they reached Diamond Springs.

Dillon stepped in front of her and shoved his face forward until it was inches from hers. To her surprise, his breath smelled of licorice, not liquor. "Don't even think of screamin', or my man will take care of O'Brien."

"Fergus?"

"Naw. Not Fergus. I found a local chap eager to do the deed for the price of a keg. He's outside keepin' a lookout."

Fergus shoved her through the door, where a brawny man waited. He had a bushy black beard and the biggest hands she'd ever seen. One punch from his fist could be fatal.

Dillon made a mockery of the introductions, speaking in a sickeningly sweet voice. "Sis, this here's Buck. Buck, meet my spoiled little sister, Rebecca, the apple of our father's eye." He pinched her cheek. Hard.

"Let's go." Dillon cut through the orchard, not venturing onto the road until they neared the edge of the Strattons' property. Fergus kept a firm grip on her wrist and followed Dillon. Buck brought up the rear.

Becky's mind raced. All she had to do was get on the stagecoach without protest. Since the threat to James would no longer exist once they'd left town, she could find a way to let someone know she was being taken against her will. Surely an opportunity would present itself when they transferred from the stage to the train down in Shingle Springs. A trip to the ladies' lounge, perhaps? Why, James might come after her himself when he realized she was gone.

No. He wouldn't. He would read her note that evening or the following morning and think she'd taken off on her own. She must rely on the Lord—and her wits—to get out of this predicament.

When they neared the main street of Diamond Springs, Dillon motioned for everyone to join him behind the nearest business. "Here's how things are goin' to play out, sis. You're gonna get on the coach with Fergus and me. You won't say or do nothin' that will cause a stir, or O'Brien will suffer the consequences. Buck will be staying here to see to things on this end."

She inhaled sharply. "What things? You said that if I would go along willingly no harm would come to James. I've done that."

Dillon gave a derisive laugh. "You're even slower than I thought, girl. Our trip ain't even begun. Fergus and me are gonna take you all the way to Chicago, where we'll be collectin' the reward for turnin' you in. And to make sure we get it, you'll do everything I say. If Buck don't get a telegram from Promontory, Utah, he'll torch O'Brien's orchard. If he don't get one from Omaha sayin' I got the dough in hand, Buck will put an end to your sweetheart. Right, Buck?"

"Gladly." The brute grunted and patted the pistol slung at his side.

She wouldn't let any harm come to James on her account. Lifting her chin, she looked her brother in the eye. "I understand. I'll do it."

Going with Dillon meant she'd have to stand trial for the very crime he'd committed, but she would pray that somehow, someway, the truth would come out.

Chapter Twenty-Five

"Thanks for getting me home before the storm, fellows. You've earned your rest." James patted his horses, buttoned his overcoat to fend off the chill and left the barn.

Despite predictions of rainfall in the Foothills, all they'd seen was wind. The dark clouds had dumped their load over the Sierras instead. He looked forward to a warm house and the cup of hot cocoa Becky was sure to have waiting for him.

Entering through the lean-to, he was met with silence. While welcome after the rattling windows and whistling chimney he'd endured the past two days, there were no reassuring sounds of a meal underway. No humming as Becky bustled about the kitchen.

She should be here, provided she hadn't gone to Lizzie's. If she had, she would have told him or left a note on the table like she'd done in the past, but there was none. Perhaps she'd cracked open her thesaurus and lost track of the time, as she'd done a time or two. He smiled. She did love her words.

James dashed to her cabin, rapped on the door and waited for her cheery call.

Silence greeted him once again. Eerie, ominous silence. His hands fisted. If her brother had found her...

"Becky, I'm coming in."

Throwing open the door, James entered the small room. She wasn't there. Considering the images that had flashed through his mind of her lying wounded on the floor—or worse—he was relieved.

The place was clean and tidy, with the bed made and her beloved books on the table, opened to the pages she'd been studying. A glance at her thesaurus evidenced her state of mind the past few days. The heading read Courage—Cowardice.

He left her cabin and headed for the house to await her return.

"James!"

He recognized Lizzie's voice and stopped. If she was here, Becky wasn't at her place. "What is it?"

"I was in town and saw Becky leaving town on the stagecoach. She asked me to deliver a message, so I came out as soon as I could."

He rubbed his forehead. "What are you saying? She hasn't left. Her things are still in her cabin."

"She was leaving, all right. She'd said goodbye to me earlier, but I couldn't resist a final farewell."

That didn't make sense. Becky wouldn't leave her beloved books behind. And she wouldn't leave without saying goodbye to him. Would she?

"I gave her a quick hug. That's when she asked me to tell you she's sorry she won't be here to see the pretty pink Rome Beauty blossoms this spring."

"No!"

"What is it?"

James forced himself to remain calm. "I'm afraid Becky's in trouble."

Lizzie's eyes widened. "What makes you think that?"

"Rome Beauty blossoms are white. She knows that."

He gripped Lizzie's upper arm. "Tell me everything she said, everything you saw."

"Let me think." Her brow furrowed. "That was all she said. She boarded the coach after a man with brown hair the same color as hers. A different man tossed her satchel to the driver, got in and then they left."

"What did that man look like?"

"He was a stocky fellow with muttonchops."

Dread soured his stomach. "Fergus—her brother's henchman. Was she all right?"

"She looked sad, but that makes sense. She didn't want to leave."

James fisted his hands. "Her scoundrel of a brother must have come here while I was away and forced her to go with him. Did you see a gun?"

"I believe the Fergus fellow had one, but it was holstered." Lizzie's face crumpled. "Oh, James. I feel terrible. I had no idea she was in danger. If I had known, I'd have gotten help in town."

"Don't worry. It will be all right." It had to be. "I just have to catch them."

A shout rang out. "Boss!"

What now? James raced toward the apple trees with Lizzie on his heels. A dog barked in the distance. "What's going on, Chung?"

His friend stood open-mouthed, pointing at the far corner of the orchard where the Esopus Spitzenburg trees grew. A plume of smoke rose into the gray sky.

The barking grew louder. "Tell me Quon's out there and that he decided to burn the slag today."

Chung shook his head. "No burn. I come cook. He stay. Prune tree." He mimicked the motion of the shears.

Spitz raced through the trees with young Bobby Stratton right behind. The boy came to a stop in front of James, his eyes wide. "Pa sent me to get you."

"What happened?"

"A man piled wood under your trees, poured kerosene on it and set the wood on fire. Pa snuck up behind him and bonked him on the noggin. He fell over, and Pa tied him up. Pa and my brothers are trying to put out the fire, but they need help."

So did Becky.

James watched the smoke now billowing from multiple sources. The man who'd started the fires knew what he was doing. Apparently, he'd moved the woodpiles kept in readiness for frosty nights under the only trees that were not yet pruned. "Bobby, I need you to tell your pa and the others to do what they can to stop the fire from spreading to anyone else's place." He might lose everything, but no one else should suffer.

"Yes, sir, Mr. O'Brien. You can count on me." The boy took off running as fast as his legs could carry him.

"What are you going to do?" Panic added an edge to Lizzie's voice.

"My guess is her brother aims to catch the last train to Sacramento City and head east tomorrow. I'll ride north to Auburn and try to get to the rail station there before they do." It would mean riding all night through rugged terrain, but he wasn't about to let that stop him.

"Sounds good to me. I'll pack some things for you."

He dashed into the barn, saddled his gelding and led him into the yard.

Lizzie met him, her hands full. "Here." She held out a small bundle. "There's some food and a change of clothes."

"Thanks." He stuffed the items into his saddlebag and mounted his horse. "Say a prayer for us, Lizzie."

"Of course. Now off with you. Get our girl, and bring her home."

He planned to.

Chapter Twenty-Six

As unnerving as the trip out West had been, the one heading East with Dillon made Becky's first train ride seem like a party by comparison. If he wasn't watching her, his crony was. The way Fergus kept leering at her made her skin crawl.

The thug had guarded her while Dillon slept, sitting outside her room in that poor excuse for a hotel. Not even the nights she'd spent lying in her bed across from *Mutti*'s, drifting in and out of sleep as she listened for any changes in her beloved patient's breathing, could compare to the restless night Becky had just endured.

They were traveling on the slower train with a mix of passenger and freight cars, which meant longer stops as cargo was loaded and unloaded. Not that the extended travel time made much difference to her. Her arrival in Chicago wasn't something she anticipated. Dillon would deliver her to the police and collect his reward. She'd find out what it felt like to be in jail awaiting trial for a crime she hadn't committed.

Not that she would do things differently. If ensuring James's safety meant sacrificing her freedom, she would bear the confinement as best she could. The Lord had been with her when she'd faced trials before. Prison walls couldn't keep Him out. With His help, she could work to prove her innocence.

The hours dragged by. Unable to concentrate on the newspaper a previous traveler had left behind, she stared out the window. Her melancholy deepened as they passed through Newcastle, Auburn and Colfax. The slanting sun as the day drew to a close caused the snow to sparkle like diamonds, but even that beautiful sight failed to lift her mood.

They reached Cisco after seven, their supper stop. Becky disembarked and strode to the way station with Dillon her ever-present shadow. They were seated promptly.

Her brother plopped down on the chair opposite her. "I hope the grub's good."

The Chinese waiter took their order and hustled off, reminding her of the first time she'd met Chung and he'd rushed to help her with the horses. Sadness had settled in her stomach, robbing her of her appetite.

Becky smoothed a napkin in her lap and pinned her brother with a piercing gaze. "Why are you doing this?"

"For the money. Why else?"

"That's not what I mean. Why are you bent on framing me? Do you hate me that much?"

He grabbed a toothpick from the holder in the middle of the table. "All my life I watched Pa heap praises on you, but he had nothin' good to say about me. It ain't fair. I'm just makin' you pay. Your arrest is money in my pocket."

"And what if I tell the police that you set the fire?"

"You won't."

"How can you be so sure?"

Dillon let loose with a raucous laugh that caused several heads to turn. "Because you don't want me to do nothin' more to O'Brien than I already have."

Her stomach churned. "What have you done?"

"Lower your voice, girl."

His patronizing tone infuriated her. "Tell me, or I'll—"

"You won't do a thing, and here's how I know." He twirled the toothpick between his fingers. "Right about now O'Brien is walkin' around his property moanin' about the loss of his precious trees that have burned to the ground."

"No! That can't be true. You said as long as I complied and Buck received the telegrams, nothing would happen to James."

"Oh, I said it, all right." He sneered.

Anger spurted through her. "You lied to me!"

Dillon jabbed the toothpick at her. "I mean business, sis. If you say a word to the police about me, Buck will put a bullet in your precious feller."

She'd known her brother was bitter, but he'd gone beyond that. He was downright vengeful. If she didn't do things his way, James could die.

The very thought sent pain more intense than any she'd ever experienced searing through her. She wouldn't let anything happen to him—no matter what price she had to pay.

The moment Becky's train pulled into Summit Station James's senses went on the alert. Passengers poured out of the cars. Most stepped onto the platform and marveled at the snowshed towering over the train. Massive beams supported a steeply sloped roof. The impressive feat of engineering stood as tall as the three-story Summit Hotel across the platform.

A thickset man with the sides of his face buried beneath fluffy whiskers paid the shed no heed. Instead, he marched past James toward the hotel. He was the man who'd barged out of the Arch Saloon and recognized Becky the week before. Fergus.

James rushed over. The two sheriff's deputies who'd ridden up the mountain with him followed. He tapped Fergus on the shoulder.

"Everything's fine, boss." The burly fellow spun around, and his brow creased with confusion. "Um, I thought you was someone else."

James held open his coat so the man could see the holstered Colt at his side. "Are you working with Donnelly?"

Fergus held up his hands, palms forward. "Easy now. I ain't done nothing wrong. Just kept an eye on the lady is all."

James fought the urge to punch him. "Where is she?" he snarled. "And I'd think twice about lying, considering the company I'm keeping."

Fergus spotted the deputies, and his mouth gaped. He snapped it shut and jabbed a thumb over his shoulder. "In the rear passenger car. With him."

The younger of the two officers led Donnelly's lackey away. James conferred with the other deputy, and they came up with a plan of attack.

"Be careful, O'Brien. This Donnelly character sounds dangerous."

"Will do." James raced to the referenced railcar and climbed aboard the platform at the back end. He stood where he could see through the small window in the door without being seen and waited. Peering inside the car, he noted an older man and woman at the far end of the car, absorbed in one another.

And there was Becky! She sat facing him with that vile brother of hers seated opposite her. The sight of her woebegone expression pierced James to the core. She looked as if she'd lost her last friend.

He longed to call out to her and willed her to hear his thoughts. *I'm here, Becky. You just have to be brave a minute longer, and it'll all be over.*

She turned toward the end of the car where he waited, as though she'd heard him, and smiled. Despite her desperate situation, softhearted Becky could find a reason to smile.

She was just the type of woman he wanted by his side. Kind. Compassionate. Beautiful inside and out. In that moment he knew that if she'd have him, he'd spend the rest of his life showering her with love, a steady stream of the biggest, fanciest words he could come up with—and as many gifts as he could get her to accept.

But first he had to get her out of her brother's clutches.

The deputy entered the car from the front. He leaned over and spoke to the elderly gentleman and his wife. The couple left without a fuss. The lawman continued down the aisle toward James, his hand hovering over his revolver, as planned.

Dillon spied the deputy, pulled his gun and leveled it on Becky.

How dare he! Hiding behind his own sister. It was all James could do not to burst into the car and tackle the beast, but he had to keep his head, for Becky's sake.

The deputy's words, muffled by the door, reached James. "Lower your weapon, Donnelly."

"Stay back, or I'll put a bullet through her."

James bit his fisted hand to keep from shouting.

Dillon stood, grabbed Becky, put the gun to her temple and shoved her in front of him. He slung an arm around her neck and began backing away from the deputy. Every step brought the yellow belly closer to James. Three more, and he could take action.

One.

The deputy advanced.

Two.

Dillon released Becky and reached behind himself to open the railcar's door with his left hand. She sank onto the closest seat and scooted away from him.

Three.

James opened the door and burst into the car. He grabbed Dillon's right hand and jerked it into the air.

The gun went off, shooting a hole in the ceiling.

James smashed Dillon's hand against the doorjamb, and the gun fell to the floor.

He spun Dillon around, dodged his swinging fist and landed a blow to Dillon's chin.

Dillon grunted and hit the floor with a satisfying thud. He rolled over onto his stomach and yelled at Becky. "You stupid girl. Do you see what you've done? I can't get my reward."

She slid to the aisle side of her seat, glared at her brother and let loose. "You don't deserve a reward. You set the fire yourself and had the gall to blame me for it."

"It's what you deserved, stealing Pa's love like you did. I was his son! He was supposed to like me best."

"I feel sorry for you, Dillon. You never could see it. Papa lavished his love on me because you didn't do anything to make him proud. You spent all your time with those troublemaker friends of yours."

"Shut your yap, girl." Donnelly rose to his hands and knees and reached for Becky.

James planted a boot on the bully's backside and pushed until he was flat on his face. "You'd better haul him off, Deputy, before I do something I'll regret."

"You're coming with me." The deputy cuffed Donnelly and shoved him down the length of the car.

Before James realized what was happening, Becky flew at him. "You came!"

Chapter Twenty-Seven

Relief left Becky weak-kneed. She clung to James, unable to stand on her own. He wrapped his arms around her and pulled her close. She burrowed her face in his chest, the suede of his overcoat soft against her cheek.

How long they stood like that, she didn't know. Time had ceased to matter. All that mattered was that James was there. For her.

When she finally tore herself away, Dillon and the deputy were gone. She stepped back, gripped the cushion of the nearest seat and averted her gaze. "I'm sorry I hung on you like that."

"I'm not."

She lifted her head and looked into his eyes. Even in the flickering light from the gas lamps she could see that they were a warm shade of brown. She could lose herself in their depths.

He stared at her for several seconds, broke eye contact and went to close the door.

He returned and stood across the aisle from her. "Are you all right? Did he hurt you?"

"Yes. No. I'm fine. But how are you? He told me what he did to your orchard. Your beautiful orchard." Her eyes misted. She blinked several times, sending a tear coursing down her cheek. She flicked it away.

"I don't care about the orchard. I care about you." He took a step toward her. Just one, as though he were afraid to get too close. "When I got home and found out he'd taken you, I was madder than a bee-stung bull."

"Then you understood the message I had Lizzie relay. That's good. I was afraid you might read my note and think I'd left on my own accord."

"You left a note? I didn't see it." The light left his eyes. "All I knew was that you'd planned to leave without saying goodbye. Why?"

"I thought that if I left and didn't tell you where I was going, we'd both be safer. I'd just gone in to pack when Dillon showed up with Fergus and some man named Buck."

"Buck!" James growled. "I'd seen him around town. A newcomer. I figured he was harmless, but he's the one who set fire to the orchard. They caught him, though. The Strattons."

"They caught him? Does that mean the orchard's safe?"

"It is now. From what Lizzie said in her telegram, I only lost fifty trees. Chung saved the day. He made it rain."

She smiled. "Ah, yes. The irrigation system. He opened it wide, didn't he? I'm so glad to hear that the fire was extinguished so quickly. I do so love the trees."

Silence followed, growing more uncomfortable by the moment. They spoke at the same time.

"How did you—"

"What did you—"

She laughed. "Go ahead."

He held out a hand to her. "You first. Please."

"How did you get here? You couldn't have caught the train to Sacramento City. We were on the last one."

"I rode to Auburn. I'd planned to arrive in plenty of time to meet the earlier train up the mountain in case you were on it, but my horse had trouble. I had to lead him all the way from Cool. Seven miles. Uphill. It was noon when I arrived at the depot. I'd missed you by this much." He held up a thumb and forefinger with half an inch between them. "I was beside myself until I figured out I could take the express and arrive here ten minutes before your train."

"So that's how you did it." His sacrifice on her behalf was to be expected. He was a hero, after all. Her hero. "And the deputy? He came with you?"

"Yes. There were two, actually. The other one hauled Fergus away."

"Then they've all three been captured. I'm very glad to hear that." Dillon had even admitted his guilt in front of witnesses. She was free!

Passengers entered the car, interrupting a conversation that was little more than a recitation of facts. Although she wanted to know what had happened, she was far more interested in what James was thinking.

He went to the seat she'd occupied, got her cloak and handed it to her. "Here. Put this on. There's something I want to show you."

"What is it?"

"You'll see." He grabbed her carpetbag from the overhead rack and helped her out of the car. "First we'll drop this off inside and have the porter take it to your room."

"My room?"

"I booked you one. We'll stay here tonight and head home tomorrow."

Home. The word held such promise. But did he mean

anything by it, or were her emotions getting the best of her? She wasn't exactly thinking straight after her terrifying ordeal.

James had come for her, though. He'd left his orchard knowing it was on fire and set out to rescue her. That had to mean something.

His business in the hotel was quickly concluded. He took her hand and led her back outside. Snow crunched beneath their feet as they left the busy platform behind. The moonlight reflecting off the surface turned a rugged mountaintop into a gleaming spectacle, brilliant white and beautiful beyond words. Although it was well past ten, the night was daylight-bright.

James pointed to a spot in the distance. "Can you see where the snowshed ends and the rugged peak beyond rises to the sky?"

"Yes."

"Tunnel number six runs through it."

A chill that had nothing to do with the low temperature swept over her. She slipped her hand into his. "That's the Summit Tunnel, where the nitro explosion took place, isn't it? You said you'd never come back, but here you are. How are you doing?"

"Fine. All this time I dreaded seeing it again, but I'm glad I have. With the hotel and the snowsheds, the place looks much different than it did then. I realized something, too."

She turned to face him. "What's that?"

"If the accident hadn't happened, I would have chosen a path that wasn't right for me. Instead, I returned home and was there for *Mutti* when she needed me. And I met you." He brushed a hand over her cheek.

Many times she'd imagined what it might be like to

have a man look at her the way James was now, but the reality was far better.

"Tell me. What was in the note you wrote? The one I didn't see."

"I thanked you for all you've done for me, told you I couldn't stay…and said that I'd miss you."

He squeezed her hand and released it. "It's all over now. You don't have to leave. Unless you want to, that is."

"I don't."

"I'm glad to hear that because I didn't want you to. I love you, Becky."

She hadn't realized how much she longed to hear him say those words. "I love you, too, so very much."

"I've bungled things before, but I'd really like to kiss you."

"Please do."

He leaned toward her, setting her heart beating so hard and so fast that she grew lightheaded. Their first kiss had been born of a mutual need for comfort. While she'd enjoyed it, something had been lacking. The certainty of being loved and cherished. Surely that would add a whole new dimension to the experience.

The moment his lips met hers, he moaned. Or was that her? She couldn't be sure. All she knew was that this kiss was everything she'd dreamed it would be—and more. A perfect blend of sweet and spicy.

All too soon James broke away, leaving her wanting more. Much, much more.

"That was nice."

"Nice?" She chuckled. "I thought it was spectacular. If you wouldn't think me too forward for asking, I'd love to have another."

He grinned. "There'll be plenty more, believe me, but

not just yet. There's something I need to ask you…want to ask you."

The lightheadedness she'd experienced before was nothing compared to the giddiness she was feeling now. "I'm listening." Intently. Very intently.

Despite the snow-covered ground, he dropped to one knee. "My dear, sweet Becky, would you do me the honor of becoming my wife?"

"Oh, James, yes, yes, a thousand times yes."

"That's what I wanted to hear." He stood, wrapped his hands around her waist and lifted her off the ground. She rested her hands on his shoulders, and he spun her in a circle. Laughter bubbled from her.

He set her down but kept a hold on her. "What would you say to a Valentine's Day wedding right here, right now? There's still an hour left. I'm sure we could find a minister or a justice of the peace among the hotel's guests. And think about this—I would always be able to remember our anniversary."

She smiled at his eagerness but shook her head slowly. "As much as I look forward to marrying you, I want a church wedding with a beautiful wedding dress, a bouquet of silk geraniums in honor of *Mutti*, my handsome groom in his cutaway jacket and our loved ones there to watch us exchange our vows. It wouldn't be the same without the Lees, Lizzie, Kate and her family, and the rest of our friends."

He ran the back of his hand over her cheek, making it difficult to concentrate on what he was saying. "I don't mean to sound impatient, my bride-to-be, but how long would it take to plan such a grand event? Would two weeks be long enough?"

"How about two weeks and a day?"

"I'm curious. Why the extra day?"

"Because it will be leap day. That ought to be memorable."

He grinned. "Leap day it is. I'll do my best to keep my eagerness under control, but it won't be easy. Not when I'm going to marry the woman I love, adore, cherish, treasure, have deep affection for."

She swatted him playfully. "You're making fun of me."

"No. I'm just telling you how much you mean to me. You could stop me, though. Just give me a kiss."

"Gladly." She wrapped her arms around him, pressed her lips to his and showed him how much he meant to her.

* * * * *

Dear Reader,

I hope you enjoyed your visit to California's Gold Country and had fun meeting Becky, James, *Mutti* and the rest of the characters. This area I'm blessed to call home has a rich history. I could spend days doing research. In fact, I have. I enjoyed learning about the Central Pacific Railroad, the former fruit-growing region around Diamond Springs and the many tasks an apple orchardist performs.

I chose to explore a difficult topic in this story: cancer. I have a hunch there isn't a family that hasn't been touched by this dreadful disease. Mine has. Perhaps yours has, too. If so, my heart goes out to you.

Mutti's character was inspired by my beloved mother-in-law, Mary Lu Gwyn, to whom I dedicated this book. Mother waged a long, hard battle with breast cancer, but the disease eventually won. Since Mother was raised by her German grandparents, it seemed fitting that *Mutti* be German. Having lived in Germany early in my marriage, I was delighted to add the German elements to the story.

I love to hear from my readers. You can visit my Victorian-style cyber home at www.keligwyn.com, where you'll find my email and postal addresses and my social media links.

Warmly,
Keli Gwyn

REQUEST YOUR FREE BOOKS!

2 FREE INSPIRATIONAL NOVELS
PLUS 2 FREE MYSTERY GIFTS

Love Inspired **HISTORICAL**

YES! Please send me 2 FREE Love Inspired® Historical novels and my 2 FREE mystery gifts (gifts are worth about $10). After receiving them, if I don't wish to receive any more books, I can return the shipping statement marked "cancel." If I don't cancel, I will receive 4 brand-new novels every month and be billed just $4.99 per book in the U.S. or $5.49 per book in Canada. That's a saving of at least 17% off the cover price. It's quite a bargain! Shipping and handling is just 50¢ per book in the U.S. and 75¢ per book in Canada.* I understand that accepting the 2 free books and gifts places me under no obligation to buy anything. I can always return a shipment and cancel at any time. Even if I never buy another book, the two free books and gifts are mine to keep forever.

102/302 IDN GH6Z

Name _____ (PLEASE PRINT) _____

Address _____ Apt. # _____

City _____ State/Prov. _____ Zip/Postal Code _____

Signature (if under 18, a parent or guardian must sign)

Mail to the **Reader Service:**
IN U.S.A.: P.O. Box 1867, Buffalo, NY 14240-1867
IN CANADA: P.O. Box 609, Fort Erie, Ontario L2A 5X3

Want to try two free books from another series?
Call 1-800-873-8635 or visit www.ReaderService.com.

* Terms and prices subject to change without notice. Prices do not include applicable taxes. Sales tax applicable in N.Y. Canadian residents will be charged applicable taxes. Offer not valid in Quebec. This offer is limited to one order per household. Not valid for current subscribers to Love Inspired Historical books. All orders subject to credit approval. Credit or debit balances in a customer's account(s) may be offset by any other outstanding balance owed by or to the customer. Please allow 4 to 6 weeks for delivery. Offer available while quantities last.

Your Privacy—The Reader Service is committed to protecting your privacy. Our Privacy Policy is available online at www.ReaderService.com or upon request from the Reader Service.

We make a portion of our mailing list available to reputable third parties that offer products we believe may interest you. If you prefer that we not exchange your name with third parties, or if you wish to clarify or modify your communication preferences, please visit us at www.ReaderService.com/consumerchoice or write to us at Reader Service Preference Service, P.O. Box 9062, Buffalo, NY 14240-9062. Include your complete name and address.

LIHI5